THE
AFTERLIFE
OF STARS

ALSO BY JOSEPH KERTES

Novels
Winter Tulips
Boardwalk
Gratitude

For Children
The Gift
The Red Corduroy Shirt

JOSEPH KERTES

THE
AFTERLIFE
OF STARS

PENGUIN

an imprint of Penguin Canada Books Inc., a Penguin Random House Company

Published by the Penguin Group
Penguin Canada Books Inc.
90 Eglinton Avenue East, Suite 700, Toronto, Ontario, Canada M4P 2Y3

Penguin Group (USA) LLC, 375 Hudson Street, New York, New York 10014, U.S.A.
Penguin Books Ltd, 80 Strand, London WC2R 0RL, England
Penguin Ireland, 25 St Stephen's Green, Dublin 2, Ireland (a division of Penguin Books Ltd)
Penguin Group (Australia), 707 Collins Street, Melbourne, Victoria 3008, Australia
(a division of Pearson Australia Group Pty Ltd)
Penguin Books India Pvt Ltd, 11 Community Centre, Panchsheel Park, New Delhi – 110 017, India
Penguin Group (NZ), 67 Apollo Drive, Rosedale, Auckland 0632, New Zealand
(a division of Pearson New Zealand Ltd)
Penguin Books (South Africa) (Pty) Ltd, 24 Sturdee Avenue, Rosebank,
Johannesburg 2196, South Africa

Penguin Books Ltd, Registered Offices: 80 Strand, London WC2R 0RL, England

First published 2014

1 2 3 4 5 6 7 8 9 10 (RRD)

Copyright © Joseph Kertes, 2014

*Publisher's note: This book is a work of fiction. Names, characters, places, and incidents either
are the product of the author's imagination or are used fictitiously, and any resemblance to actual persons living
or dead, events, or locales is entirely coincidental.*

Manufactured in the U.S.A.

LIBRARY AND ARCHIVES CANADA CATALOGUING IN PUBLICATION

Kertes, Joseph, 1951–, author
The afterlife of stars / Joseph Kertes.

ISBN 978-0-14-319148-3 (pbk.)

I. Title.

PS8571.E766A64 2014   C813'.54   C2014-902415-0

eBook ISBN 978-0-14-319297-8

Visit the Penguin Canada website at **www.penguin.ca**

Special and corporate bulk purchase rates available; please see
www.penguin.ca/corporatesales or call 1-800-810-3104.

Dedicated to the memory of
Raoul Wallenberg and Paul Hegedus,
to Helen, Angela, Natalie, Peter and Bill,
and to the family and friends who have put up with
my literary shenanigans over the years

Beware, oh wanderer, the road is walking too.

—RAINER MARIA RILKE

ONE

ON OCTOBER 24, 1956, the day I turned 9.8, my grandmother came to take me out of school in Budapest's 6th District. We were in the middle of reviewing decimal points because of a mistake a girl in the class named Mary had made. Other parents and grandparents were arriving too with the same aim, although no one had come yet to get my friend Zoll.

My grandmother gripped my hand as we made our way down Andrassy Avenue, but a crowd had formed at the Oktogon, blocking our passage. A tank stood in the street with a bold red star shining on its flank. We saw Russian soldiers, but no one was looking at them. Everyone was gazing up instead at eight Hungarian soldiers, one hanging from each of the lampposts. My grandmother pulled hard on my arm, but not before I was able to join the lookers.

A couple of the Hungarians had stuck out their tongues as they dangled—one seemed to be smiling, four wriggled and bucked, and the one nearest us, straight above my grandmother and me, looked down at us with evergreen eyes, but there was no anger in the eyes, or even light.

Klari, my grandmother, breathed into the crown of my

hair, sending hot tendrils down over me. "Come, please," she whispered. I shuddered.

The crowd was quiet. Even the few people who were sobbing were doing so silently, swallowing the sound. And then we heard from a little way down the street what I thought was an orchestra and a singer, a soprano, singing a sad song. I looked around us as my grandmother turned me toward the sound. "It's a record," she said. "From over there."

We spotted an open window above a lacy café a half block away, the white tongue of a curtain fluttering out from the window. "A record?" I asked.

"Yes, a phonograph record," Klari whispered again, steering me onward. "It's Mozart," she said, "his 'Laudate dominum,' I think. 'Praise the Lord,' it means. I wonder why they would play that now."

"Because they like it," I said.

"Yes, of course. Because they like it. Mozart wrote some moving songs."

"Did you see the man's hair?" I turned back toward the Oktogon, toward the dangling men.

"Whose?" my grandmother asked me.

"The man with the green eyes." She looked with me, but just for a second. The man's auburn hair was parted and brilliantined so that it shone even at this distance. "Do you think he combed it for someone?" I asked.

"I don't know," Klari said. "His sweetheart, I suppose." I thought my grandmother might cry, but instead she said, "Now, please keep moving, my dear. We'll have cake. Let's have cake, at Gerbeaud Café."

"Now?"

"Yes, now. Let's have a treat. You can order anything you want. I know you want poppy-seed strudel."

She took me all the way to Vorosmarty Square. The cobblestones made me think of a great house lying on its side. From the top of the building opposite, two Russian soldiers, both sturdy women, unfurled a canvas sheet so big it covered a side of Kossuth's Department Store from roof to sidewalk. It was a vast portrait.

"Look, it's Papa Stalin," I said. I knew him right away from the picture above the clock in our classroom. He had the same smile and mustache, a mustache that was three times as impressive as Hitler's, which was little more than a black checkerboard square. I found myself smiling back at the giant face, like a circus face.

"Please," my grandmother said, giving my arm another tug. "He came to liberate us, the great father," she said under her breath, "but he forgot himself. He forgot to leave. They forgot to leave. *Come*, Robert, please." She was pulling hard on my arm now.

I was as excited about poppy-seed strudel as I was about Kaiser Laszlo, Gerbeaud's monkey in a golden cage. He squealed as soon as we walked in. I think he recognized me because I'd fed him some apple cake last time. If I were the Kaiser, I'd recognize everyone who fed me cake. He was wearing a bellman's blue cap and vest. He tilted his head in an appealing way and held out his little hairy hand.

As we got comfortable, I felt warm, as if we'd come in out of a storm. The waiter placed our sweets and cocoas in front of us. Klari took out her compact and mother-of-pearl makeup case. I watched, dazzled, as my grandmother, like an artist, applied some lines and clouds, borders and dots. Once done, she fished out her monogrammed silver cigarette case, removed a cigarette from behind the little garter and tapped the end on the case before lighting it. I was just breaking off a corner of my strudel for the Kaiser when the manager walked to the middle of the busy café, clapped her hands sharply and called out to us, saying we all had to go. She was very sorry. The café was closing for the rest of the day, but we could take our cake with us. The waiters brought linen tea cloths in which to wrap up our things. For a moment I thought it might have been the cake—they'd run out of cake—but the glass cases were full of colorful sweets. I spotted a colony of marzipan goblins and other figures. Our waiter brought me one of them, a marzipan monkey with a cap like the Kaiser's.

A woman in a long mink coat brushed by us, trailing the scent of mothballs. For the longest time, I had thought that this was the scent of mink. I knew better now, but I wondered if moths went after *actual* minks or just mink coats.

The woman paused by the door to look back at us but then peered down at her own feet. She wore black patent leather shoes with very high heels and sharpened toes. They were pointing at something. "Look," the shoes seemed to be saying, "right there on the floor. Have a look."

Then, with their fine sense of direction, the shoes turned, pointed the way out the door and took the woman out.

People were leaving quickly and abandoning their cake, most of them.

"What will happen to the Kaiser? They won't hang Laszlo, will they?"

"No, of course not. Not a thing will happen to him," my grandmother said. "He'll be here for us next time."

"When?"

"*Next* time," she said, as if she were saying never.

We hurried home to find my parents rushing around the apartment and making telephone calls. Our mother flitted from one room to the next. She smiled when she saw that I was home. "Sorry you had to leave school, my lambkin," she said, and then went about her business. My brother, Attila, was already home. He was 13.7, and he had our mother's blond hair, while I had black hair, like our father's. Attila was also a head taller than I was, everyone kept pointing out, making me want to plop an extra head on top of mine, a freaky one, possibly.

My brother was sitting on the sofa eating an apple. "We're leaving altogether, my lambkin," he said to me.

I sat down beside him. "Where are we going?"

He was chomping away but said, "West. We're going to the Wild West. You'll need your cowboy hat and spurs."

"Why?"

He was acting as if he knew but wasn't telling, so I said, "I saw the hanging men."

His face fell open. "What do you mean?"

"From the lampposts."

He turned his Arctic blue gaze on me. "Which ones?"

I crossed my arms. "On Andrassy," I said. "At the Oktogon." I pictured the man with the green eyes and nicely combed hair. As if to protect the secret of this man, I said, "Some of the men had their tongues sticking out."

Attila jumped to his feet. "That is *not* what happened.

You did not see hanging men, and they do not stick out their tongues. I know that for a fact."

I shrugged. "Ask Mamu."

Attila ran off to get our grandmother, and I could hear him yelling out questions at her. When he came back to me, he had whitened. His blue eyes looked like marbles dropped in snow. He looked as if he wanted to strangle me. He glared, slapped at the arm of the sofa. "Are they still there?"

"What?"

"Are they still hanging there? *Shit*."

He ran out to the balcony, climbed onto the railing to peer out over the bronze head of Mor Jokai, the old Hungarian writer, whose statue sat at the top of our street, keeping watch over it. Attila turned toward me with his icy look. Then he flew back past me to our bedroom, slamming the door behind him.

That night, as we got ready for bed, my brother looked inside his pajama bottoms—he did quite a study—and then he raised his arms, flexed and turned toward the mirror, admiring the muscles and then the hairs sprouting from his armpits. "We are experiencing the balding of the world, my small brother." He tugged on a couple of the hairs. "These tufts are the last bits of hair left to us. But notice the apes are having none of it. They probably know something we don't."

"What?" I asked.

"I told you, it's something we don't know."

"How do you know it's anything, then?" I said.

Attila sighed heavily but then moved on immediately, which was his way. He peered down again into his pajama pants. "I would have made sperm a brighter color," he said, "if I had been the Lord God, Creator of the Universe."

"What color is it now?"

"You don't know?" he asked, smiling broadly. I shook my head. He said, "Do you want me to bring some forth for you to see?"

"No, I don't."

"It's a drab pearly cream color. It doesn't say how important it is, how exciting, how it makes babies, humans, soldiers, beauties, love, courage, heroism." The image of the hanging men shot through me, this time the ones with their tongues out. Attila was still talking. "The color says nothing, or it says it is nothing. Blood is red. It makes declarations. It says alarm; it says *I am the living stream*. But sperm does not. It is drab and poorly designed, or at least poorly decorated. 'Give it something more,' I would have said to the Lord. 'Color isn't everything. Give the little sperms horns, or feathers.'"

"Feathers?"

"Or full wings. Just fly through air. Right now, the slithery bastards swim upstream. Give them wings. Give them noisemakers, or little voices, so that all together they could sound like a mob storming the gates."

Attila got into bed. I was still sitting on the edge of mine, waiting for more, I guess. I was staring at him, at the back of his golden head, his slender white neck. I was sure that with a noose around his neck my brother would keep his tongue in his mouth, just to prove his point.

By the time I switched off the lights, Attila was asleep. He always fell asleep right away, even when our grandmother told us stories. Now I listened as she and our parents spoke quietly but heatedly in the living room. "We'll go to Nebraska or Utah," my father said. Now he turned on his loudspeaker voice.

"We'll become Mormons. I want to become a Mormon, try on something new." I could hear him creaking back and forth over the floor. He stopped. "We'll go to Canada. Why not Canada?"

I recognized the word *Canada* because my father's cousin Peter lived there.

"What are you talking about?" my mother asked. "And please keep your voice down."

My grandmother said we should go to Paris first to visit her sister Hermina. It would be a good place to start.

"We'll *visit* Paris," said my father too loudly. "We're not *staying* in Paris."

"Why don't we wait to see?" my mother asked.

"Because we've had enough here," he said. "Have you not had enough of Europe?" He was blasting out his thoughts now. "We've had enough of the old bitch. Europe is a failed experiment—it should be paved over and turned into a parking lot."

"Simon, please," Klari whispered. "You would not have said that if your father were still around."

"He's not around. He is resting at last."

"Do you consider that a good thing?" his mother asked.

"It works for me."

"*Simon,*" my mother said. "Why do you always have to go too far?"

"Here's what I know," Klari said. I could hear her huffing. She might have gotten to her feet. "I know that nobody knows anything. And some of us know nothing with greater certainty than others."

No one answered. There was some shuffling of feet and some clinking of glasses, but they went quiet soon after.

In the darkness, I watched the bar of light at the foot of our door. It floated up like a wand into the ceiling. When the living room lights finally went out, I waded through the black milk of the night. I saw the green eyes of the hanging man up ahead in some woods, like the eyes of a woodland creature. I heard music—drumming—from the window and thought of Kaiser Laszlo, deprived all afternoon of his usual morsels. But it wasn't drumming. It was pounding. Our bedroom windows rattled in their casements and lit up as bombs fell in the distance, their sound muffled, as if I were listening to them through my pillow. I counted the seconds between the flashes and the sound, the way Attila and I did with thunder and lightning, to see how far away it was. Then the hanging man's eyes floated up again, greening over my sleep.

As Attila and I got dressed the next morning, it felt strange not to be going to school. It felt like a holiday, but not a festive one. My father's cousin Andras and his wife, Judit, were over, and the whispering continued until Attila and I joined them. They were sitting in the kitchen having tea and walnut cake. Judit was as pregnant as could be and panted as she shifted this way and that. She seemed too small and slight to have all that baby stuffed inside her. Judit had a copper glow about her in the lamplight and a constellation of copper freckles, which shifted with her big smile. She gave me a hug and kiss and smelled of the sweet powdery scent of a baby herself. She said, "I hope I have a child as beautiful and smart as you boys."

"You should be so lucky," Attila said, as he reached for a cup and panted extra hard in imitation of Judit.

Judit wanted me to sit in her lap, but I said I was too big. "You're not," she said.

"He is, my sweetie," my mother said, smiling. But Judit
had already pulled me down into her lap and thrown her arms
around me. Everyone was smiling then as things seemed to
swirl around us.

Judit said, "I just want a good child, a kind one."

"Oh, is *that* all?" my brother said. He had poured himself
some espresso and was adding ten spoons of sugar.

"Yes," was the answer. Judit had a determined look in her
eyes.

"Mamu and I saw people hanging our soldiers," I told her.
"Russians."

Judit loosened her grip on me. "Oh, my dear Lord," she
said. "Oh, dear Lord. My poor young Robert." She held my
face by the temples, looked me in the eyes. "There are good
people and there are bad people, but the worst people are the
ones who think they are good when they are in fact bad, evil.
They would seat themselves right next to the Lord in heaven."

There was a pounding at the door, quite a commanding
one, and we all looked out that way, as if to interpret what it
meant. We followed my father into the vestibule and huddled
behind him, except for my brother, who stood by his side. It
was Attila who opened the door. A man, a soldier the size of
a tree, stood outside. He had such an overgrowth of beard,
he could have supplied a whole room of teenagers with all
the tufts they needed. He barked something at us in Russian.
The red star gleamed from his furry officer's cap. He barked
something again, and Judit squeaked and held her stomach.

The tree man paused, but then he parted us and stepped
up to Judit. He looked at her, gazed down at her belly, then
bent down to listen there. No one knew what to do. He

pointed a long brown finger at her abdomen. Andras looked ready to lunge at the Russian, and so did my brother behind him. Judit whimpered.

The man laughed as he straightened all the way up again. His mouth was like a jewel box, full of gold and glitter. He pushed past us and marched straight to our empire clock on the sideboard in the front room as if he knew where it was. We followed him, and he waited for us to gather. He pointed to the clock, circled his long brown finger a number of times past the twelve and motioned that we were all to leave. Then, to our relief, the officer marched out again and slammed the door.

"We have until three o'clock," our father said to us, "and then we have to be gone."

"For how long?" I asked him.

"We don't know," my grandmother said gently.

"For about two centuries," Attila said, "before we check back in with them."

"What do you mean?"

"They want us to get out," Andras said. "Not out of the country. We're not supposed to leave the country, not *allowed*, actually. We're just supposed to find other lodgings somewhere."

"But we're not doing that," Attila said.

"Be quiet," our father said.

Judit whispered, "We can't leave now." I could hardly hear her.

"We have to," her husband said. "Now is our only chance. The Hungarian rebel army is rising up. There are breaks in the border. It's the only time."

"But Andras ..." our grandmother said, putting her arm around Judit.

My brother looked straight at me. "We're leaving," he insisted. "Forever. I told you—we're going west."

"Why can't we just get the Russians to like us instead?" I asked.

Attila shook his head. "Lambkin, you're not too bright." But my remark made Judit tear up. She embraced me and kissed me on the head before leaving with Andras.

The Russian was back within an hour, and he brought other soldiers with him, two women and one man. But the original one with the beard was obviously overseeing the proceedings. They moved through our home more like movers than invaders. They acted as if we weren't there. From the china cabinet, they gingerly removed Herendi porcelain cups, saucers and platters and a silver sugar box and teapot, wrapping them in cloth before placing them in large canvas sacks. Attila and I watched from the sofa.

They took down the paintings one at a time, leaving rectangular blond ghosts in the gold wallpaper. The largest of these was called "Christmas, 1903." It depicted two old women dressed in dark coats and fur hats, one bent over a walnut secretary desk, writing a letter, the other looking out and down at us from the wall. Between them stood a potted Christmas tree on a table, festooned with bright ribbons and baubles and a star at the top. I always wondered why such a cheerful tree did not manage to spread its joy to the dark women in the parlor, who had most likely decorated it. Now the women were gone, together with their tree.

One solitary picture still hung on the wall among the

ghostly rectangles. It was a drawing done by my brother of a Spitfire fighter plane tearing through the skies, spitting impressive bursts of fire. In the corner of the picture was the sun, and it too fired off spikes instead of rays of light. It was a sketch Attila had done in school, and our mother had had it framed in gold and hung over the gilded double-headed-eagle clock on the sideboard, which stood guard over the room. The fierce-looking bird was the emblem of the Austro-Hungarian Empire.

I had done a picture I knew my mother would like too, a watercolor, but it was still at school. My teacher, Mrs. Molnar, had hung it up where the photographs of Stalin and Khrushchev hung, but on the opposite side of the clock. My painting featured a weeping willow. It was surrounded by impressionable trees, which also wanted to weep, so I gave them their own tears in many colors flying off the leaves. My classmate David thought the other trees might have been sweating after a run, but I explained my intent.

A year before, I had done another picture in crayon of sunflowers. It wasn't a field of sunflowers, exactly, but sunflower after sunflower, quite a few of them. My brother seemed to admire the picture. He said my flowers looked like the handiwork of God as a child, trying out designs for the sun. That wasn't my intent either. I don't know where that picture got to, exactly.

One of the Russian women carrying a canvas bag looked at the Spitfire twice as she passed by us. We watched her closely. She removed her snug army cap to reveal straw-colored hair tied back as tightly as the cap, giving her head the look of an onion. She paused by the drawing but moved on. The eagle watched with its four sharp eyes. On her third trip by, she picked up the eagle clock with a strong arm and wrapped it up like a mummy before bending over to make room for it in her heavy sack.

Attila watched the operation, kept glancing up at his own drawing in its precious frame, waited for her to leave our home with the sacks, and then tore off madly to our room.

I tiptoed to the dining room to see if the Russians had taken our bowl of rose cream chocolates. I cared less about the red crystal bowl than about the chocolates. They were still there. I wondered if it would be all right to sit at the table and steal a chocolate. I took a chance. I peeled the red foil wrapper off the delicacy and put it into my mouth whole, let its creamy sweet essence enjoy its new home. I didn't want to chew, to take a single bite. I put my cheek down on the cool surface of the dining room table. My grandmother had bought this table for my parents for their "wood" anniversary, she told me. She said it was made of walnut by Sebastyan Balaban, the famous furniture maker. He had told her it would last a thousand years. We had had it for eleven years, just 1.1 percent of its lifespan, meaning some nice Russian family could enjoy meals and chocolates off it for 989 more years. I took another chocolate to eat in my room and one for my brother.

But I had a second table to visit first. It was the round-topped pedestal table in the front room. It was the one I hid under when I was in turmoil. Made of heavy black maple and standing on beastly wooden lions' paws, it sat between two dainty ladies' lamps in all its manly glory. I ducked underneath. I wanted to sit in its darkness one last time. When I was much younger, I thought that this unlucky lion had grown a table-top instead of a head, but when my brother taught me the facts of life, I realized that a lion and a table had lain down together to make this child. I hoped it was the table that was the mother. I ran my fingers through the carved fur and the hard claws and said my goodbyes.

I heard something fall in the kitchen, but not a dish, because it didn't shatter. I jumped out and ran back to our room. I found my brother holding his june bug collection up to the light of the window before shelving it again. The collection had won him a science prize a couple of years back.

After that, things moved quickly. Our father told us we could each take what we could carry, no more. I snuck out again to the front room, peered in, making sure there was not a single Russian in the room. Then I ran to the sideboard, no longer watched over by the two-headed eagle, and removed a golden cup and saucer. They looked as if they might have come from a Grecian palace, but they were small, like children's dishes. My parents drank espresso coffee out of them when we had company. I hid them in my shirt and slunk away toward the bedroom. I dashed out again one last time, snatched Attila's Spitfire drawing off the wall, opened my shirt, slipped it past the buttons and slid it all the way to the back above my belt before buttoning up my shirt again.

I ran into the Russian soldier in the hall and thought I'd been caught. My face burned. Instead of stripping me of my booty, he handed me a Russian nesting doll—"*matryoshka*," he called it—and I bowed, feeling the corners of the picture frame claw my skin, before retreating to my room. I slipped the picture under my bed. The brightly painted *matryoshka* doll came apart, and I found that a succession of smaller dolls lived inside, all the way down to a puny one. She was a colorful wooden bean, little more.

As I admired them, Attila said that I was a girl, so I countered with my cowboy hat, spurs, cap gun and holster, all of which I placed in my satchel with the reassembled *matryoshka*. With my back to Attila, I rolled my cup and saucer each into its own sock, pulled his drawing out from under the bed, and finally I added my marzipan monkey, still blanketed in the linen cloth from Gerbeaud. The cloth had a "G" monogram.

"Come with me, my one true love," Attila said behind me.

"Where?"

"Just come. I want to show you something, over by Heroes' Square. I hear something is happening there."

"Where the big Stalin is? The statue?"

He nodded. "Just come."

"Shouldn't we tell somebody we're going?"

"Not if we want to get out of here. We'll be back before anyone notices, don't worry."

Of course we wouldn't be, but I knew better than to argue. From the fierce and determined look on my brother's face, I had a hunch he was taking me to where there were twice as many hanging men as I had seen, and that his hanging men would be Russians, not Hungarians.

We slipped by the commotion in the kitchen, and Attila took me on a trot through the confused streets of our city, streets full of people not going about their business as they might, but looking alarmed, whispering rather than talking to one another. Nobody looked tired or bored, as some did on other days.

Attila had me by the hand. Everyone was pulling hard on my arm these days. We were walking briskly down Andrassy Avenue when a tall woman came out of a white building, a woman with long, straight black hair, wearing a black hat as wide as an umbrella and a black satin cloak which flowed and fluttered with each powerful step she took. She was coming straight toward us. My brother wanted to pick up the pace, but I slowed us down. I was staring.

"What do you want with her?" my brother finally asked.

I stopped altogether. "Want?" The woman had black eyes, black eye shadow.

"Do you want to take her home with you?" Attila said. "She's a black limousine, rearing up on her hind wheels."

She saw us, saw Attila and me looking, and glared at us before crossing the street, though she could easily have run us over.

When we turned a corner, we just about ran down a man ourselves, a beggar holding out his hand. Attila stopped. He seemed to be out of breath for some reason. The man was a Gypsy, propped up against a bakery whose window had been shattered. In the window, a single, dingy lace curtain clung to its rod, shaking its head no in the breeze, "no." I could see a loaf of bread inside on the counter, and a cake that looked blue in the light.

The poor man stood out of the wind on his only leg and held out his only hand. He was like a badly designed tree, with a single branch held out to catch rain.

"What about today?" the man said to us.

"Today?" Attila asked.

"Yes," the Gypsy said.

"I don't know," my brother said.

The man had a crutch lying behind him, together with a battered violin. "Are you back now?" he asked, his hand still held out to us.

My brother looked at me. I expected him to say, "Let's go," but instead he wanted to stay.

I found a single coin in my pocket, put my hand around it. I stepped up and said, "Yes, we've been away, but now we're back. Have you been waiting for us?"

"Oh, a young girl," the man said. Attila grinned broadly. "I have been waiting," the man said. "Lucky girl." My voice hadn't broken yet, and if it didn't soon, I was going to take a rock to it. Compared to me, my brother sounded like a grown man, a man of the world.

I looked into the milk of the man's blue eyes and realized he couldn't see. "How do you play that violin?" I asked. "How do you manage?" I picked it up for him. It still had its shapely *f*-holes, but it was battered—an *I* and an *O* plus some punctuation marks had punched their way through too.

"I haven't played for years," the man said. "The old girl is like a pet I don't have to feed much," he said, laughing. "Are you two musicians?" We didn't answer. "No, of course you're not," he said. "You're someone I stopped on the way to something. That's what I do, stop people on their way to something else."

A young woman flew by us. I could see the whites of her eyes. She turned down an alley between two tall gray stone buildings. She scared me. I thought she was coming right at us. It was impossible to tell whether people were running to something or from something.

My brother said, "Actually, I am a musician." He was grinning again.

The man lowered his begging hand and said, "What do you play?"

"I play piano," he said, "and my sister sings."

"Do you?" the man said, genuinely pleased. I pulled on my brother's arm now. I felt we should give the man a coin and go. The Gypsy said, "What sorts of things do you sing and play?"

"We can do 'Pur ti miro' by Claudio Monteverdi."

"Ah, the duet."

He began to hum, and though I had never heard it myself, I said, "Yes, that's it."

"Can you do anything by Bizet? Can you perform some songs from *Carmen*?"

"Yes, my sister can, some of them."

"Can you sing 'Habanera'?"

I wanted to tear my brother to pieces. I felt my breakfast coming up.

The man started to sing himself, with a sad, raspy voice. If he had not been blind, I'm sure he would have closed his eyes. Now my brother wanted to leave, but I stood firm. I felt suddenly warmed by the song, warmed by the poor man. My grandmother had played the record a hundred times. I started singing along with the man, every word, without knowing what the French words meant.

> *L'amour est un oiseau rebelle*
> *Que nul ne peut apprivoiser,*

Et c'est bien en vain qu'on l'appelle,
S'il lui convient de refuser.

L'amour! L'amour! L'amour! L'amour!

I stared into the man's face. I was sure I could see the thoughts moving behind his eyes like bits of glass. He said, "You have nice tone, young lady."

"She does," my brother said. "That was nice," he said to me, and I think he meant it.

"Now, listen," the man said. I was still holding his violin, and he pushed it up against me. How did he even know I'd been holding it? "It's magic, listen."

I put my ear against one of the extra holes in the instrument's belly, as if it were a seashell.

"Can you hear that?" I heard nothing. "Can you hear the song?"

I could hear a wet wind now and was sure I could hear the river. "What kind of wood is it made of?" I asked.

"Violin wood," he said, "from the violin tree."

I offered it to Attila to try, but he declined. He wanted to go. I set down the violin where it had lain. The torn awning above our heads flapped. I reached for the Gypsy's hand to give him my coin, and his hand closed greedily on mine.

"We have to go," I said.

He brought my hand up close to his lips. "I hope you have a very good reason for coming back, young lady," he said to the hand before letting it go. I glanced at it to see if it had been soiled. I wanted to wipe it on something.

"I do," I said.

"Yes," my brother said.

Another cold breeze blew up, and I shuddered.

The man still aimed his blind gaze at us. "It must be good," he said. "You must have a very good reason. Life and death."

Attila turned away from the man, suddenly panicked. He gave me a painful yank this time, and we took off toward Heroes' Square.

I felt a little strange, but I could hardly wait to see the square again. It had been some time since I'd been there. I had come with my class on a clear day last spring. Stalin had stood like a Titan in the square on a high stone pedestal, a bronze man more impressive than a building. (If you want to make someone look like the Lord himself, my advice would be to make him Big, his right arm raised high, his hand upturned, focusing the blue lens of heaven.)

When Attila and I turned the corner from Andrassy Avenue onto Dozsa Way, at first I thought we'd come to the wrong square. On Stalin's pedestal stood two boots the size of boilers, but no Papa.

"There!" Attila said, clapping his hands and hooting. We ran like mad toward the pedestal. Attila hooted again and jumped.

Stalin lay toppled behind his high stone bastion. He was entangled in ropes and chains, like a colossus hoisted from the sea. But his big bronze boots still stood. Rope ladders hung from them.

There were few other people in the square, surprisingly few, but they covered their open mouths when they saw what we saw and scrambled away, as if the fallen god's dark angels were still hovering, were about to take revenge.

But Attila was fearless. He pulled me along like a dog toward the fallen father.

A shot rang out, dinging something. I checked the windows all around the square, the trees, the moving shadows. A good breeze blew through the trees. Another shot pocked the pedestal.

My brother's tone sharpened. "Come!" he said. "Hurry." He was several rungs up one of the rope ladders. "Come!" he barked again.

I followed him. We scrambled up the sagging ladders. Who could have invented such a thing? I banged my elbow on the stone, scraped the knuckles of my left hand.

Attila was already on top. Several Russian soldiers came running toward their bronze leader from the other side.

Attila helped me reach the top of the pedestal. "We have to get inside."

"Inside *what*?"

"The boots. One each. There's a ladder up the far side of that one. You take that. I can get up this chain."

"We're going inside the *boots*?"

Attila was hoisting himself up the chain, deftly coordinating his hands and feet like a monkey.

I began to clamber up the second ladder. "What are we doing?" I grunted.

"We'll be like Mother Goose. We'll be the Brothers Goose."

Attila waited and watched me. Once I made it to the lip of the boot, I was surprised to see how cavernous it was inside, taller than I was. My brother gestured to me to raise the rope ladder—hoist it up with all my might—and let it fall inside the boot. I watched him do it first with his chain, then I did mine. The ladder was surprisingly bony and heavy. I stupidly avoided the ladder on the inside and instead slithered down into the boot, though I was not the best slitherer, and took quite a fall to the bottom, landing against my shoulder. I'd heard my brother sensibly drop feet first in his.

What now? I was quaking, suddenly taken with a chill, my teeth chattering. I looked up into Stalin's blue heaven. I was overcome with dread that we would soon become the Brothers Corpse, that it would have been a more glorious death to have been strung up in the Oktogon, that if we were to come out of this alive, my father would beat us, as he must.

I wondered suddenly where Stalin's bronze socks might have gotten to before I came to a conclusion I was not proud of: it was that Stalin had no actual feet, at least not this Stalin.

The inside of the boot darkened for a moment, and I distinctly remember thinking what a good idea clouds were, not to mention rain. I wondered if clouds had been an aesthetic choice or a practical one. And what about rain? My brother always questioned whether things had been created or had evolved, but I didn't care quite as much about that. For me, at the time, the difference was only a matter of gradual development versus sudden appearance. Though I struggled with such generalities, I was less concerned about them then and more interested in the mere fact of them. What, I wondered, must it have been like to be the first person to experience rain? *What are these? There's a heavenly river and it is breaking up. These are shattered shards of river. Bits of river. Bits of lake. Lake beads. River beads. What is going on? Am I going to shrink or expand or drink or drown?*

A shot clanged against my boot or Attila's. My teeth clattered like mad, like something loose inside me, a box of buttons.

Then just as suddenly a calm settled over me like a gossamer net. I recall with great clarity that very moment inside the boot. Was this the end? Would they find us in these boots? Would Attila jump out like the warrior rebel he was and take the bullet he was born to take? Would the Hungarians come to finish Stalin and complete their triumph? Would the Russians come first and fill the boots with concrete instead, monuments to Stalin's stalwartness? If they found my brother and me, would they make examples of us, chain us to the boots until the vultures came to peck out our eyes? Was there honor in that? And what was the protocol, the order, of killings? Soldiers first? Then civilians? Men first? Then the elderly? Then women? Finally children? And what was the cutoff mark? Was my brother still considered a child?

The soldier of the Oktogon dangled before my eyes like a clear statement, and I knew that Attila and I would not die like legends but like jokes, the Brothers Grimm without a tale, our family shaking their heads, not allowing our names to be uttered again.

I could not hear Attila in his boot. I wanted to call out to him but felt it best to stay quiet. I edged my way into the dark front of the boot, to where Stalin's toes would have been, and then I heard Attila loudly whisper my name. I crawled out from the toe, and he was there at the top of my boot. He must have pulled himself up. "Let's go, my tender love," he said. "It's all clear."

"How do you know?"

"Look at me. I'm not being shot at." He climbed down into my boot and hoisted me onto the rope ladder, urging me up before climbing out himself.

We flew down Damjanich Street and almost ran into a tank clattering to the right of us. I now saw that these beasts bruising around the streets were not meant to be stealthy or subtle. They were not even vehicles, more like instant buildings plopped down in the middle of the street, daring you to pass.

A squad of young men and a single young woman, a brunette with a determined look on her pretty, red face, turned a corner and came toward us. They were chanting, *"Szabadsag! Szabadsag!"*—Liberty! Liberty!—and waving a Hungarian flag with its familiar bars of red, white and green, but with the Communist insignia at its center cut out of it, leaving a hole.

More shots were fired from somewhere, clipping the stone face of a building. The squad of young people scattered. My brother grabbed me by the shoulder and yanked me into a doorway guarded by two stone lions. They stood on their hind legs, holding up the entrance, seeming to hold up the whole building. Sometimes it was angels who watched over an entrance; sometimes shapely stone maidens. But these were lions. It must have been a very heavy building. Stone lions will do things for you that real ones won't.

We waited several minutes, waited for quiet, before tiptoeing out. Attila and I veered swiftly to the left until we got out to Rakoczi Street. I could not catch my breath—I didn't even want to try. I could breathe later, I told myself. I found myself hoping we might see our parents again, and Klari, and my friend Zoli, possibly. Up ahead, a man stood

calmly outside the Urania Movie Theater. He was dressed in
a brown gabardine suit and wore a matching brown fedora.
He was lighting a cigarette, turning away from the wind that
brought us. The Urania was white and had Moorish windows.
It always beckoned like a foreign land, like an exotic Arabian
bazaar laden with wild and exquisite gifts, gifts with horns and
warm gems.

We caught up to the man just as he exhaled his first full
puff of smoke, just as a shot sounded, taking off his hat. For a
stark and childish moment, the Baby Diviner growing inside
of me traced the path of the bullet through the man's head
as it knocked over everything in its path: his day, his night,
his next puff of smoke, his dinner plate of veal *paprikas*, his
smiling daughter holding up a glass to the light to see if it was
cracked, his wife entering the dining room with the wine,
wiping a damp hand on her apron.

The bullet might as well have struck us too, my brother
and me. "Let's go!" Attila snapped. He pulled me straight
through the doors of the Urania Theater, the white doors
splattered now with blood.

An unsuspecting young woman, no bigger than a fawn, sat
in her ticket booth. She smiled at us.

I was gasping, panting. "A man has been shot," I said.

"A man?" She rose with a creak from her chair to look
out, raised her hand to her heart to protect it. "Oh," she said.
The hand went to her mouth. She started to cry, but silently,
sobbing, hiccupping.

"This way," Attila said.

"What?" she said. She was still looking outside. She could
see blood on the glass.

"Now!" snapped my brother. "Now," he repeated, more gently. He was pointing into the theater, the promised darkness.

My teeth were clattering like a box of nails now, not buttons. The fawn girl's white skin had turned blotchy, suffused with fright, her eyes wide and a crazed white. To escape the hunter, the fawn pattered to the front of the theater near the screen and straight out a side door. I thought we were going to follow, but my brother pulled me down low into the seat beside him.

There, in the darkness, Tarzan unleashed a sound like a jungle aria. The Urania was showing *Tarzan the Ape Man*. The theater was majestic with its tall Arabian arches. A young couple sitting in a private box above us ignored Tarzan and Jane. They were making a meal out of each other's ears and lips. Would their love wither when they found the fallen man outside? Would Tarzan have helped the man in the brown suit?

Attila stared at the screen.

So that was the plan? We were going to sit now and watch a movie? We ran away from home, we hid in Stalin's boots, we saw a man shot, and now we were going to watch *Tarzan the Ape Man*? We saw a real man's head explode, but now we'd watch Johnny Weissmuller swing through the trees? There was an absoluteness to events as Attila experienced them. It is sleep time, and now I will sleep. It is eating time, and now I will eat. It is ducking into a theater time, and now I will duck. Once in the theater, I will watch a movie, which is what we do in a theater.

I could not draw a single satisfying breath. Tarzan fought a lion. Jane was pretty. Tarzan swam with crocodiles. Jane loved Tarzan. Tarzan trumpeted through the jungle. Cheetah cringed. But where was Kaiser Laszlo? Where was the man in the brown hat? Who would carry him away? What time was it? Had the Russians expelled our parents? Did our parents think we were dead?

"I'm going," I said, and got to my feet. Attila couldn't take his eyes off the screen. "I'm *going*," I said again, and began to march to the front of the theater, where the fawn had disappeared.

Attila slapped at the armrest but followed. I took a last look up at the solitary couple in the box, but they had no interest in anyone else, in the world beyond their faces. Attila heaved open the side door with his bum. The sun's yellow smack blinded us, but we ran through it toward home. A cool wind blew up from the Danube flecked with dust and leaves, but soon enough we could make out the familiar landmarks of our neighborhood and let down our guard a little. It was not until then that I finally found the meat of the air and took in a good gulp of it.

I stopped for a moment. "Why did they shoot the man with the brown hat, Attila?"

"I don't know," my brother said. He took my hand.

"What was the man doing?"

"He was lighting a smoke."

"And he got shot for that?"

I stopped, but Attila pulled us along. "Not for that," he said. "For stopping where he did, for being a standing target, for sport."

We got home just ahead of the Russians, who were late. When we slipped through the door, we were met by our father. I'd never seen him in such a fury. He was a snorting bull. He lifted Attila by the collar of his shirt, a mighty act, since my brother was almost full grown.

"You Russian!" Attila shouted at him.

Simon banged Attila up against the wall. But the matadors swooped down on them: my father's cousin Andras, his wife, Judit, our grandmother and mother. My father let Attila down but raised his fist at both of us like a biblical figure.

Our mother slipped between the raised fist and my brother's golden head.

"Don't hit them!" Judit said. She embraced her own swollen abdomen. She gasped and looked ready to faint. "Oh," she said to her belly. She staggered back into the living room with the help of her husband.

Lili, our mother, hugged and kissed my brother and me strenuously, squeezing too hard. "My lambs, my lamblins," she said.

Klari stood behind her. She looked especially disappointed, disappointment to equal my father's fury, as if her faith in life had been shaken, her faith in love.

Just as she hugged me hard too, Attila broke free, bellowed like Tarzan, pounded his chest and flew off to our room. I lost my breath again. My heart took off without a runner. The dead man in brown rose up in front of me, and I started to sob and shake. My grandmother sobbed with me, then my mother too, the three of us swaying together and sobbing.

My father snorted and slapped at his sides. "We have to go."

"Simon," my mother said through her tears, "we have our sons back."

"Great," he said. He slapped at his sides again. "*We have to go*. Now!"

We went to get our few things. Upon returning to the vestibule, we could hear Judit in the living room with Andras. "Are we just going to get on the train, just like that?"

"That's what we're going to do," said Andras. "Don't worry, dear, please."

"And the Russians will let us?"

"They're distracted just now, but not for long. They'll send in reinforcements, and when they do, we'll be stuck here. Our baby will be born here and grow up here."

"Is that so bad?" Judit whispered. "We grew up here."

"It will be bad, worse than we have known."

A short while later, Andras and Judit joined us in the hall. We were all leaving together, Andras and Judit included. They had brought their bags to our apartment, as well as a rolled-up carpet, a very old Persian one featuring a bird of paradise, which they treasured.

Minutes later, the Russians came, not a friendly group like the first one, and they pointed the way outward, out of our home.

TWO

I KNOW NOW that bits of days are all that survive, and some don't survive at all—it is almost no use living them. But some survive almost whole, almost unreduced by memory, 0.9 or 0.95 out of 1.0, versus the usual 0.01 or just plain zero. I remember the day we left home almost in its entirety.

My father had arranged for a small Hungarian army truck to take us to the Keleti Railway Station. The truck was waiting for us at the corner of our street, where the statue of Mor Jokai gazed out at Andrassy. Judit and Andras climbed into the back. Andras asked Attila and me what had taken us so long.

"We went to look at something," Attila said right away. "We had to see something."

"Come, get in," Judit said. "Come, boys." She was patting the bench seat on either side of her. She looked shiny red and bursting. A couple of Hungarian soldiers helped us load our belongings into the back.

It was not far to the station. We could hear riotous cheering and chanting as we pulled up. We got out to find a tank with the familiar red Russian star sitting dead but still fuming in front of the station. Teenagers danced around the steel beast, waving the flags of Hungary with the holes in the center. "Out, tyrants," they were singing, and chanting, "freedom, freedom, freedom."

Behind them rose Keleti Station, as great and grand a palace as any ever made. Here, the train emperors and empresses rolled in and out, in and out, welcomed by the great glass eyes and arms of the building, the high stone angel at its crown, with her attendants and their steeds, blessing their path.

As soon as we stepped inside, though, I saw that the imperial trains were already choked with people. There was such a flurry of excitement in the station, it seemed as if everybody wanted to take flight, revving up with it, but was pinned down by gravity and penned in by the way-high roof and rafters. I looked for some of my friends: Zoli and David and even Mary. It would have been nice to see Mary now, just to know she was heading out too, her notebook on decimal points tucked under her arm. I could see none of my classmates. A man walked by us with a small table inverted on his head. Its legs were smooth and curved like a lady's. We pushed in, and I found someone my age. He was gripping a dog—too tightly, I thought—a terrier, who looked at me with furry eyes. I wanted to pet him, but he was having none of it—nor was his owner, who turned away. For a second, I thought I spotted Zoli and started waving, but it was not even a boy. It was a girl with the same color hair, very dark brown, cut short like Zoli's.

"Sold out," we started to hear. "Sold out for today, and tomorrow. No seats. Sold out."

We turned to the ticket windows to see the last of them

closing. A single uniformed attendant was weaving through the crowd, telling people they could spend the night on the cots around the sides of the building, where the soldiers used to sleep. "Find yourself a cot, " he was telling people, "or please return home. We are sold out."

"What do you mean?" our father said. Beside us, Judit groaned.

"Get her a cot," the man said. "She'll need rest."

"Can you not find two seats on the train?" our mother asked. "Just for them?" She smiled her radiant smile.

"Please," Andras said to the man.

"I have no seats," the man said. "I don't even have standing room." He hurried away from us.

My father had on a look like someone overcooked, set to burst into flame. "We need tickets!" he shouted to no one in particular. The conductor doubled his speed away from us. "Tickets! I'll pay double for tickets!"

"Simon!" our mother said to him.

"We'll be stuck here forever. We've already been stuck in this place forever."

"And yet here we are," Klari said, "still standing, still here."

"There are no Russians," Lili said. "There's no one to stop us or harm us."

"What about tomorrow?" he shouted. "What about the next day?"

"Simon, please," Lili said.

"I have gold," Andras said. "Let's offer a ring, earrings."

Klari put an arm around my brother's shoulders, mine too, but Attila slipped free. "I can get us tickets," he said. "Give me the cash and jewels."

Andras looked at my father, but then a woman approached us. She was wearing an apron embroidered with folk colors, but she also wore a brooch pinned to her sweater just below the shoulder, quite a big brooch, a gold one, a brooch in the shape of Hungary, with jewels where the cities were, and a blue line snaking through, where the Danube ran. She had gold teeth too. The two in the front were gold.

"I have tickets," she said to us. "How many do you need?"

"How is that possible?" our mother said.

"Seven," Simon said. "How much cash do you want? We need seven tickets."

"I want the gold ring and earrings, but I want more."

My father showed the woman the whites of his eyes. I thought he was going to hit her—punch her in the gut, possibly, and rob her. "What else?" he said through the cut of his teeth.

"I want your address and the key to your house."

"No," Lili said.

"One Jokai Street, second floor," Simon said, standing in very close to her, the brooch of Hungary bending between them. He found the key in his pocket and held it up high in the air.

"There are Russians in our house," Lili said.

Simon glared at her.

The woman counted out seven tickets. She appeared to have as many left over. "The ring, the earrings and the key," she said.

Simon snatched the tickets away from her and handed over the key, while Judit removed her ring and earrings.

The train was to leave in two hours, but it was easily three before it did.

Even waiting to depart on board the westbound train, we thought we would be stopped. Attila said we might be, but that he was ready. Everyone looked around expectantly, but no Russians came. Finally, we rolled out into the evening. There weren't enough seats, and hardly enough standing room. My grandmother held my hand as we stood in the corridor and jiggled along. My satchel was clamped between my feet, and Attila helped our grandmother with hers. He asked if she was taking a boulder to Utah or Canada, and a man nearby told us that during the war there was a building called "Kanada" in a camp at Auschwitz. Kanada was where all the valuables, like gold jewelry and gems, were stored. I wondered whether "Christmas, 1903" was headed there.

Attila poked me in the back. He spoke right into my ear so the others wouldn't hear. He made me promise that if I were the first one to be strung up in the Wild West, I would stick out my tongue for him.

I felt someone clasp me around my knees and saw a little girl in a frilly pink dress standing there. Behind her, crawling on all fours, was her baby brother, and behind them both their red-faced mother. I looked down and asked the girl, "How old are you?"

"I'm three."

"And what about your baby brother?"

"Oh, he doesn't have a number yet," she said, and she was very serious, so I tried not to laugh or even smile.

The three of them pushed on toward the toilets.

The train lurched, and Judit gasped and held the side of her stomach. Andras embraced her. He had his dentist's case with him, and some clothing and bedding in another sack. My father was carrying their rolled-up Persian rug.

The countryside outside our window was dark now. Only a single bomb lit up the glass, but I could not hear its pop.

Before long, the train squealed to a halt, but not at a station, just somewhere between stops with fields all around us. The conductor urged us all off, and we helped Judit and my grandmother down before we started walking, the whole mob of us heading off in the same direction. The scent of night was heavy around us.

We left the tracks behind and walked mightily toward the border, hundreds of us, many hundreds, like thieves through the dark. Now and then a bomb fell, and each time it did, Attila and I looked up to see who was dropping them. If they were celestial creatures, they flew without lights. They flew like bats.

Judit groaned and yelped as if she were walking barefoot. My grandmother was beside me on my right, Attila on my left, and our parents were up ahead, keeping pace with Andras and Judit, Lili supporting Judit.

The sun had deputized the moon to give us light. Still, it was very dark—the stars were not much help—until a bomb fell again, again from nowhere, and something struck my brother so that he fell against me. My grandmother and I stopped and crouched beside him on the cool ground. My grandmother fumbled through her bag until she found her lighter. Its flame was as bright as a knife blade. It shone upon a man's shoe. The top of the shoe was red and steaming. My brother had been struck by a man's shoe with the foot still inside it. Some of the blood dripped down Attila's neck. He jumped to his feet. "Where are these damn bombs falling from?" he said. He was rubbing at the side of his face where the boot had struck.

"They're not falling," our grandmother said. "This is a minefield we're crossing."

"Oh," my brother said, and then he took off like a bird.

My grandmother said to me, "I should lift you up. It's not far now."

"You can't. I'm too big. I should be lifting you up."

She took my hand hard and we walked carefully, our feet alive to every step.

"Oh," I said, and I stopped.

"What's the matter?" my grandmother asked. She was looking for her lighter again.

It struck me just then how very keen I was on lamplight, its quiet little yellow show, and I remember thinking how nice it would have been to have some. But I said, "No, it's all right," as my grandmother kept searching. I said, "My teacher, Mrs. Molnar, will be very upset with me. We have to tell her when we're going to be absent. We didn't tell her anything."

"Mrs. Molnar will understand this time."

"My friend Zoli was once strapped when he didn't say."

"This time is an exception, Robert. Mrs. Molnar herself is probably not far behind us." I turned to look into the darkness. My grandmother said, "We'll be finding you a new school up ahead."

"Up ahead?" There was darkness up there too, wide and open. "What about Zoli, and what about David? Are they coming this way too?"

"Everyone who can is coming this way. Maybe you'll see them again."

"What if I don't?"

She paused, put down her things and reached through the dark to get a hold of me. I tried to catch a deeper breath, just to calm my dizzy heart. "Let me say something that I know won't please you today, but it might calm you someday, when you're reflecting on things. You will make new friends. They'll be lucky to be your friends. I have left behind a lifetime of friends. I console myself in knowing that friends are infinitely replaceable, sad to say. There'll be as many up ahead as there are behind us."

I took a last look into the darkness at Hungary. I still found myself hoping that Zoli was coming too. I hoped he was not stuck back there like someone locked within the rules of arithmetic. We were going to a place where three plus three might equal seven, and I hoped Zoli was headed there too. My grandmother took my hand again, lifted her bag and led me forward.

It was just a few more minutes, no more than ten, until we saw a light up ahead, a single bulb, a solitary lamppost. We heard someone say it. My father. "Austria."

As we drew closer to the apron of light—some of us, dozens only, we seemed to have scattered on our march—I saw Judit lying down, her knees up, her head cradled by my mother and Andras between her legs. She was lying on their Persian rug, right on top of the bird of paradise. The rug was darkening under Judit.

I was relieved to see my brother there too. His back was to us, and he was peeing.

My father stood behind us and offered to take my grandmother's bag. "What's in this?" he asked. He opened the bag. "What are these?"

"Phonograph records," she said.

"You brought records with you?" He was rifling through them. They were 78s. He held one up to the light. "You brought *The Barber of Seville*?" He was yelling now. Judit caterwauled. "This is what you brought?" he said. "You brought *The Merry Widow*?" Then he hurled them, smashing one after another against the lamppost and against the concrete at its base.

"Hey, lunatic man," Andras said. "Get away from here."

"She was taking records to Canada. She wanted *music* there."

"And now she's not," Andras said.

My father stopped. I looked at the scattered bits of record, shiny black shards of sound glinting in the Austrian lamplight.

And then we heard a baby cry. Judit was crying, and my grandmother was crying too. "Gisela," Andras said, as he lifted the little thing waist high. She was still tethered to her mother. "She's a girl. Austrian. *Gisela*." Judit continued her crying. She was sweating too. And her fiery red hair fanned out from her head, drawing the rest of the light to itself.

"Why Gisela?" my father asked.

But Gisela overwhelmed him with her crying. Her cry was the shrillest. A small crowd had gathered in the apron of light, mostly Hungarians, but also a single Austrian border guard. The little soprano called out assuredly. She was so new and loud, it felt to me that she would lead us now, wherever she needed to go.

THREE

JUDIT NEVER GOT UP from the foot of that lamppost in Austria. My grandmother and mother cleaned up the baby with cloths and a little warm water some nuns had brought in a hurry from a nearby convent, and they swaddled Gisela in a soft blanket while Andras cleaned up Judit below. My brother and I watched in horror. I thought Attila was going to throw up, but then we were treated to a view of Judit's plump breast as she tried to get her little girl to suckle on it, and we marveled at the size of the nipple, round as a sunflower and alive.

Judit needed a rest and closed her eyes, seemed even to close her ears to the commotion around her, her heaving chest emptying itself of living air, sagging, Gisela suckling now with relish from her dead mother's breast, the rug beneath them awash with their broth.

The whole world frenzied around the mother and child, the two dazzling in their stillness. Just for a moment, the pair of them made more sense in their symmetry than the rest of us: one of them arriving and the other leaving.

But that sense couldn't hold. A flock of nuns swooped down on us as if we were a meal. Their purpose, of course, was different.

Andras let out a wail. At first I thought the sound had come from somewhere else, somewhere deep in the earth, like something molten. Several of the flock went straight to Andras. A couple of the others, along with my mother and grandmother, attended to Gisela. And two more of the nuns, big ones, stood between Attila and me and the scene we were watching. They took us each by the upper arm and steered us toward a building around the corner. My nun had a good strong hold on me.

Attila and I turned to take a last look at the foot of the lamppost, and now a second sound arose, this time out of Gisela, a little trumpet, but with quite a blast, like someone breaking in her instrument. Gisela's face in the lamplight was as red as Mars.

My brother and I were led to an old, gray stone, flat-roofed rectangle of a building, quite an ample one. But heaving up from behind it stood the tower of an even older stone church. A brass sign that said "Convent of St. Elizabeth of Hungary" arced over the entrance.

"I thought this was Austria," I said to my brother.

"It is, but it used to be Hungary. Not long ago. They speak German here, but also Hungarian."

The nuns showed us to a large open room called a *lager*, a dormitory with hundreds of cots covered in clean white sheets and nicely pressed wool blankets. There were some people here already and more arriving. Attila grabbed two cots not far from a window and urged me over. Soon, our grandmother joined us, but I couldn't spot our parents, or Andras or Gisela. I was especially wondering about Gisela. I scanned the room, looking for familiar faces, but saw none I knew. I took a second, extra-long look for Zoli and David and for my teacher, Mrs. Molnar.

There were no tables set out, but we were given linen napkins, packets of biscuits and cheese, as well as milk and wine poured into pewter goblets.

I warmed up quickly, and we were surrounded by Hungarians, so it felt like home, though it didn't look like it. Some nice people, including some more nuns, stopped by to take away the remains of our packets and to give us each a small pouch containing chocolates, a toothbrush, a toy-sized tube of toothpaste (which I wanted to keep and not open) and a bar of soap.

The chocolates were the best I'd ever eaten, sweet and dense. The wrappers had a picture of Mozart on them.

A voice rang out through the hall, a deep, clangy voice, like a bell. It startled me. We all turned to find that a lectern with a microphone had been set up at one end, and standing at the microphone was a priest wearing a black robe and a great sail of a cap that was pinched together at the top. "Today, I am a man without a homeland," he boomed in Hungarian as he raised his arms. "Yesterday, I was Father Tamas, the bishop of Szeged. Today, we Hungarians move as a herd, and our herd has succeeded in eluding the lions to settle peacefully among the lambs. Wherever we have come from, there was our Lord, and wherever we end up, there too will be our Lord. He moves as the stars and the sun and the moon as viewed from the window of a speeding train, as quickly as we move or as slowly.

"Do not grieve today, my friends, my people. Whatever you have left behind, the Lord will restore to you. Whomever you have left behind, He will protect from harm—if not from earthly harm, then from everlasting harm."

A girl my age a few beds away was staring straight at me. Her mother beside her looked stooped and sad and gazed out from under heavy lids pasted with dark blue makeup. Another woman, a brunette of an impressive size, tall and strong, sat facing my brother and me, her nightgown hiked up and her grasshopper legs spread wide. "Look," Attila said to me, "that one is open for business."

The gangling woman had small green eyes like capers. She seemed to know we were talking about her and pulled her ganglios in so she could cover them with her blanket.

The bishop of Szeged clasped his hands in front of him and looked up to the light, searching for the rest of his speech, it seemed. "The time has come to put sin behind us," he said. "We enter a time of consolation, not vengeance. Let us forgive the sons for the sins of the fathers. I refer to those of you among us who were cast out of their homeland some millennia ago and who have wandered from stable to barn all over the lands of Europe and Asia and Africa, seeking solace. The Lord of the prophets once said, 'The land is mine.' It does not belong to the invading Reds. It does not belong to the Turks who lived among us as Cumans, or to the Slavs, the Croats, the Germans, the Romanians, or to the good Austrians who act now as our hosts. Indeed, it does not belong even to the Huns, the Magyars, the Mongolians, the Avars. It does not belong to the Asians. It does not belong to the Africans. It does not belong to us or to them. No one can take away from us that which was not ours to begin with and will one day no longer be theirs. Not the Golden Bull, not Janos Hunyadi, not Matthias with his splendid Beatrice of Aragon by his side, not Gyorgy Dozsa, not Ferenc Rakoczi and not Sandor Petofi. It is our defect, not the Lord's, that we draw lines around things. If the air stood still, we would draw lines around it too. Our lands are those we carry here." The bishop placed a hand flat on his heart. "We too are the diaspora now, we Hungarians. Those among us here tonight more experienced in the ways of wandering must teach us to carry Mother Hungary in our hearts the way you have carried the Promised Land in yours." Father Tamas crossed his hands over his chest and curled them into fists. "I have left behind me a great church built on a rock in the once picturesque city of Szeged on the shores of the River Tisza, bluer than the Danube. I have left behind me a loyal and true flock, some of whom have scattered today and will not return to the shores of the Tisza. But I have also left behind me a synagogue modeled in grandeur upon Rome itself. What I left there of this great temple is not a flock that has scattered so much as a flock that perished, most of it, a dozen years ago, its spiritual leaders ghosts now, talking in the Red darkness to ghostly brethren, the wings of their temple turned to gray and flightless stone. But they walk with us today, those departed, every bit as alive as we are, *more* alive on account of their fate.

"I call upon you of the diaspora, those of you who remain, to teach us that the land of our fathers and the land of our mothers is here with us today where we sit. Show us how its fragrant green mass is without weight as we set out over the four corners of this earth perchance never again to return, never again to cross paths, never again to smell the apricot blossoms and blue waters of our Danube and our Tisza.

"And here is what I would say to you today. *End your crusade.* Yes, that is what I said! End it. Moderate yourselves. *Moderate yourselves*, I urge you." The priest raised his fighting fists into the air and then just as abruptly dropped his open hands to his sides, slapping his robe, causing it to ripple like water. "Find peace," he said, "and spread its word and design out from where you have found it. Teach us to find peace. Travel in safety, all of you, and may these be the last of your wanderings. May God bless each and every one of you. Remember always, I implore you, as the prophet Isaiah urged all of us, 'Seek the Lord while He may be found.'"

The bishop once again raised his fists, this time to cover his eyes. Not a person spoke in the room, nor even whispered. The woman holding her daughter, the one who had been staring at me, had let her go and was weeping black and blue tears. Midnight-blue spots stained her white blouse. Her daughter sat with her legs crossed, her bare feet inverted, the soles turned upward as if to catch rain.

The brunette who'd been open for business still had her ganglies folded up as she faced the priest. I guessed there were no clients for her here, except maybe for Attila, who was game for most things.

But my brother was fast asleep, sitting up. I spotted my father and mother in the room now, a dozen cots away from us. There was no sign of Andras or Gisela, and of course no sign of Judit. I felt terrible dread, felt for the first time how momentous this night was. I shuddered. My father was devouring several packets of food. My mother watched him, then looked back at the lectern, waiting, it looked like, for the great voice to boom forth again. She looked as if she'd been crying, probably remembering Judit and thinking about Andras and his baby. We were all facing front, all of us waiting for more, hoping for it, possibly, even Attila, who woke now again with a jerk amid the murmuring of the place.

The nuns came around with steaming bowls of chicken soup to calm us for the night and with double napkins to shield our laps from the bowls. They waited until we stabilized them before handing each of us a good-sized silver spoon to fit an impressive mouth.

Attila was at his immediately, slurping madly with an ecstasy in his eyes, like someone in love. "Ah," he said. Then he slurped some more, his eyes closed. "Liquefied bird," he said.

He lifted his bowl and drank the soup down, racing to do it, the first to finish, possibly, in the entire room. Then he set it down and shifted on his haunches, still smacking his lips, waiting to see what was next, slapping at something on his collarbone, his eyes casting around the room, searching among the girls. It was as if the liquefied bird had reconstituted itself inside of him.

I wanted to ask my brother about something the bishop had said, but I waited for him to settle. "The father spoke about drawing lines around lands and claiming them. He said we'd even draw lines around the air if it stood still." And now I laughed, but my brother rolled his eyes, so I went back to my question. "Isn't that a natural thing to want to do?" I asked. "Cats mark out their territory too."

"It doesn't make it smart," Attila said. "It makes both cats and humans stupid." And then my brother jumped to his feet. "Look," he said. He was pointing to the front. I stood up to see.

Nuns with musical instruments were arranging themselves at the microphone where the bishop had stood. One had a cello, one a violin, one a recorder, and a fourth one clapped her hands sharply until the room went quiet. The cello and violin players tuned their instruments for just a moment, waited for the leader to nod at them, and then the trio began playing a sad old song. The primary nun closed her eyes serenely, approached the microphone and sang. I was stunned. It was a haunting, mournful song, sung in Italian. It reminded me of some of my grandmother's records.

"What is it?" I whispered to Klari.

"Goodness," she said. "Just a minute." She stood up too. All over the room, others were standing. The crying woman and her young daughter were standing, and the woman's eyes were welling up.

A flock of sounds swarmed over us in the big room.

"Is it a hymn?" I asked, excitedly. "What is it?"

"It's not a hymn," Klari said. "It's an aria, from an opera, *Juditha triumphans*."

"*Juditha?*" Attila said aloud. "For Judit?"

"No, it's the old story of Judith. Listen now. She's singing 'Summa astrorum creator.' It's a sad song, but Judith will prevail. In the end, she prevails, once she cuts off the head of her oppressor."

The singer's voice was deep as a well, as if a young man lived inside her. The nuns were performing an opera, singing their lament. I'd never imagined such a thing possible, and knew I might never see such a thing again.

They sang several more songs, the cello crooning, the violin crying, the recorder fluttering like a bird.

"Her soul is still here," Attila whispered too loudly.

"Whose?"

"Judit's. Her soul is still here, sniffing around."

I considered this proposition for some time. I studied the hushed room. I turned to my grandmother. "Does the soul wait for us to finish what we're doing?"

"I think it does, dear." She held up her finger to her mouth, though, to shush me.

"Does the soul stay still even when we flit around?"

"The soul is as still as eternity and takes up as little room," she whispered. "The soul does not occupy space in the way the body does."

In the darkness of my bedroom back home, over many nights, I'd never thought of eternity staying still and patient the way the soul might.

As the song was winding down, Attila said, "The composer was inspired by God, and the sisters were inspired by God. It's all mysterious to me."

"Why?" I asked.

"Because why does God need to inspire humans to create music just so they can play it back to him? Are we his concert hall, his radio, his gramophone? Can't he imagine the music he wants us to create, save us all the trouble? Did he create us in his image because he didn't have one without us?"

Our grandmother held up her finger, warning us to quiet down.

"Maybe he wants us to enjoy the music too," I whispered, but Attila didn't hear me. "The music's for us too."

Klari said, "My grandsons, the theologians."

The concert finished too soon, and people clapped. Attila and I competed with our clapping, his claps sharp and punishing by the end.

People were still arriving and crowding the door, people who hadn't had the benefit of the bishop's speech or the nuns' concert. It made me think that maybe we'd missed some things too. More bombs erupted, but their sound was faint, like distant thunder. The field with the mines.

Our grandmother took us to a big open bathroom, with more sinks and shower stalls and toilets than I'd ever seen assembled in one place. Attila and I did our business and then washed our hands and faces. He thought we should use up my toothpaste before we started on his. "There'll be less to carry, my ever-precious love," he said.

I gave it some thought before answering. "But we'd have the same result if we used up your toothpaste first."

He snatched away my bag, but our grandmother said, "Use mine first," and we gladly did. Attila brushed more furiously than usual, spat theatrically and stormed back to the dormitory ahead of Klari and me. My grandmother ushered me back before returning to perform her own ablutions.

Before that day, I did not know what a convent was. Attila told me it was a place to get people cleaned up for heaven, if you believed in that sort of thing. I do know that I felt very good here, and I told my brother so.

He patted my head and said, "Well, then, if you are an excellent lad, you could grow up to become a nun yourself."

A few minutes later, our mother came over to kiss Attila and me, but he was already out. He had that magic switch which turned off reality and turned on fantasy with a flick. He was already swinging on vines through the jungle and bellowing, pausing only to pound on his chest. There was never an in-between world, a frontier land. He was gone even before he was down the chute.

My mother was staring at me and smiling. "How are you doing, my darling love?" she asked. She had such boiling gold hair, it made no sense that she was my mother. Except for her smile. I had inherited a slightly subdued and miniature version of her radiant smile. She'd passed all the rest of her looks on to Attila—the golden hair, the blue eyes—but she'd omitted her smile. It was the one trait she reserved for me. Outward traits, that is. Attila had very few of her innards.

I asked my mother about the phonograph records, why our father had broken some of them. On came the smile again, with enough amperage to light a room.

She said, "You know he gets worked up over the smallest things, let alone life and death."

"But we were alive. We'd made it already. We were giving birth to Gisela."

"Yes, but look at what's behind us, and the uncertainty ahead, my beauty." She hugged me. "It will be all right, I promise." And the hug felt strange, possibly because of where we were and when it was, all the excitement. It felt new, as if we were inventing the gesture. We floated up, both of us, on the suds of her hair. And then she kissed me and left, pulling the warm air with her.

When the lights went out, I could still feel the coolness of my mother's kiss on my cheek. It was very dark in the room. The darkness had an absolute quality, like space without stars. People sighed, snuffled, grunted and snored, some nearby, some far across the room, and I found the sounds as comforting as could be.

But then I heard a cry from a distant room, followed by a muffled wail, followed by a release into crying, a surrender to it. A baby was crying. Gisela. Maybe not knowing exactly what she was missing but knowing that it was something. And calling out for it. I could hear Andras's voice *oh-oh-oh*-ing her—*oh-oh-oh*-ing her and jiggling her, jiggling his own voice to comfort her.

Then, deep into the tender darkness, I remember the first strong pull of grief, true grief, the dark loam and grit of it, though I would not have been able to identify it as grief at the time. Yet I recall the moment vividly. I'd always had faith in things—common things, common practices—such as closing my eyes at night and feeling certain that they would open again the next day. I did not want to lose that faith, which I now know is challenged by grief, but I could not help but consider that there were people who closed their eyes with the confidence I'd always had and who would not be opening them again in the morning.

When a nun rolled up a couple of window blinds, the moon entered, illuminating the carnival of sound, silvering over the recumbent figures like old film. And it hit me. The green eyes of Judit, green as the hanging soldier's eyes. They would never again take in the light—the reflected light of the moon, the hot light of the sun—all the switches off now. I was overcome with her passing. I began sobbing again like a baby. I had to pull the covers up over my head before the X-ray moon exposed my unmanly state.

FOUR

THE NEXT MORNING, we were given fresh napkins, and the nuns spread out across the big room to serve us warm rolls and tea with lemon. I could not see the girl and her mother with the midnight eye shadow. Their cots were empty, the blankets neatly folded. Nor could I see Andras and Gisela. Nor the gangly brunette with the caper eyes. Where had they all disappeared to?

My mother and grandmother had left us a little while earlier, and now they came back dressed as nuns, but without the white collar or head covering. They hadn't brought black clothing to wear for a funeral, so the nuns had helped them out. They even said that Lili and Klari could tear the garments at the neck to demonstrate their grief, as long as it wasn't too much and they promised to sew them back up afterward.

Attila and I laughed when we saw them. Our mother told us to keep quiet, but she was smiling herself and trying to hide it behind her hand. She looked as if she were playing at something, impersonating someone.

But then I saw that it wasn't smiling at all but crying. And I thought of where Judit was going, where she would end up—

all those lively colors browned over and dampened down. I thought of how still she would be, the stillness of her in her lonely only grave.

I turned away from my mother and brother.

Our father came in with Andras, who looked bleary-eyed. He was holding Gisela and feeding her a bottle while jiggling her gently. He said, "The mother superior has asked the groundskeepers to make a little fenced-off area in the graveyard especially for Judit."

"Fenced off?" my mother said, looking a little fearful, her cheeks still moist.

Andras said, his voice uneven, "It's a Catholic cemetery. This little section will be her own, a little Jewish section, I guess."

Our grandmother took the baby from Andras and continued to administer the milk. Gisela seemed as content as could be.

"I suppose that's what the holy father was saying yesterday," said our father, as he raised his hands in the air. "The land is mine, sayeth the Lord."

"Please, Simon," our mother said.

"It's in the book of Leviticus," our father said. "I'm sure it's all right to be quoting the Bible here."

"Can we go see?" Attila asked.

"Yes, but don't wander away," Lili said.

Outside and just down the way from the convent walls, a couple of men were driving wooden posts deep into the soil, capturing a corner of the graveyard, while two others were digging a hole for Judit to lie in. The black earth gave off a dark fragrance.

"I guess they couldn't take her back home," I said to Attila.

"We can't go home," my brother said. "There are Russians there. What I don't know is why we can't go up ahead somewhere to bury Judit—take her with us—to Vienna, maybe, where there already is a Jewish section."

"Because she died here," I said, not sure what I was saying, really. "How could we carry her?"

"We won't be walking from here," my brother said. "I'm sure we won't." He closed one blue eye to the sun. He always did that: closed one eye at a time in the bright light.

The men working were strong, like soldiers. One was as big as an army truck. He was already down in the hole he'd made, tunneling away, flinging dirt up to the surface. He looked powerful enough to dig a hole for a dozen people to lie in. The man felt our eyes on him and poked his head up. He was grimy with what looked like old grime—natural grime, if there is such a thing, grime coming from inside him, a spewing black heart and lungs—rather than the dirt of the world.

I soon found myself watching alone. When I turned all around, I spotted my brother halfway across a field beyond the graveyard. He stopped to call to me. "I want to show you something."

"What can you show me?"

"*Something,*" he said. "I know this place."

I started trotting through the grasses toward him. "How can you?" I asked, when I got close.

"I *know* this place," Attila said again. "Trust me."

I didn't know where we were heading—back to Hungary, it looked like. I wouldn't have put it past my brother. The October sky was summer-blue, and the sun was extra yellow and hot. I wondered what it would look like in reverse: a blue sun and yellow sky. I preferred the original choice. And the shape too. Better a sphere than an isosceles triangle, say, pointing its light this way and that, searing into things.

As if it had heard me, the sun reared up in the cool sky now and roared. It was very hot, too hot.

I remember that moment, that exact moment. I had just been getting over that Septembrous feeling—the end of summer, the beginning of school, the new girl in class, the two new boys, one named Karl, the decimal points, the adjectives—blue, nice, sudden, gradual—the sun spread-eagled across the sky, roaring away, and here we were—gone—running toward something, and I couldn't know what.

The field was overgrown but turning to straw and raspy. It felt as if no one else had ever been this way before, no Hungarians, no Russians, no Austrians. But when I caught up with Attila, he said, "There must be as many skulls underneath this land as in the graveyard, if not more. There must be army buttons and spearheads, doubloons and shields, going back to kingdom come."

"Are there girls down there too?" I asked.

"Oh, yes," Attila said. "Think of all that pink love in the ground. Think of it, gone to waste."

There was a little mound up ahead. Attila bent down and scythed at it with a straight stiff hand, chopping the grass off, as if he were scalping it. He studied the clear space to see what might be lying below it.

I stopped in my tracks behind Attila and considered letting my brother continue on his own, but he grabbed my hand. "Don't worry, my ever-present darling," he said. "You're safe with me."

"Oh, I know that," I said. The Baby Psychologist growing inside me already knew that the price of having a Chief Protector in Attila was that he got to be my Chief Jailer and Chief Tormentor.

Sheep *baa-ah*-ed nearby, and we looked over at them. They were standing in a neighboring field, a shadier, greener one, and they were watching us too. They were thick, fluffy creatures, chewing and chewing. Little did they know they were getting themselves primed for sweaters and pots, clumps of them spun into yarn, bits of them lying down with potatoes and carrots.

I wondered what my brother was thinking as he watched the animals with me, his one eye closed. He held up a hand to block out the light. The sun stenciled a perfect black hand onto his face.

"Where do you think Judit is?" I asked.

"Dead," was all he said.

"That's it?"

"She'll be going down deep into the ground, all that milk meant for Gisela wasted. She'll be food for worms and little crawly bastards."

"And?"

Attila opened the extra icy eye and said to me, "Do you see those sheep over there?" I nodded. The creatures were still looking at us, even the ones that had turned away from us. "We are the afterlife of sheep," he said, and then he snatched my hand in his and pulled me forward again.

Attila led me toward a gate in a stone archway greened over with vines. The letters carved into the arch had worn down with the seasons. There was no one else in sight, no parents, no one. We could still hear the pounding-in of the fence posts in the distance behind us.

We stopped before the old gate, but not for long. Attila yanked me along.

"How do you know this place?" I asked.

"I was here with Dad." He was whispering for some reason. "Two years ago. We were here together. Do you remember the trip he had to take to Vienna? He had to get special permission from the authorities. He could take only one person with him."

I did remember, and I remembered wanting to go, wanting to be the one. I remembered the poppy-seed cake I got as compensation for being left behind, filling my mouth with it and the mouth of the Baby Psychologist inside me, stopping us from speaking. We were nothing if not polite and would never have spoken with our mouths full of black seeds. The Baby English Grad Student also growing inside me, fraternal triplet of the Baby Psychologist and the Baby Diviner, might have quoted George Herbert, the metaphysical poet: "You must sit down, sayes Love, and taste my meat: / So I did sit and eat."

Attila was leading me to what looked like stones, heaps and mounds of them, but with human shapes.

"Where are we going?" I asked again, and Attila gripped my hand, which I didn't enjoy and which he normally didn't enjoy either.

The sun was high, and the grass even deader here, tall and rasping.

"Just over there," Attila said. "I want to show you something." And he stepped up the pace. We were almost trotting, making enemies of the spiked grasses with a furious excitement.

Birds erupted out of the grasses in front of us and flew off over our heads. I wanted to pause and take stock, decide, possibly, that it was time to go back, but Attila marched us on.

Now I could see better: there were human forms scattered everywhere and piled up in front of us, but stone humans, marble humans and bronze ones, some outsized, some fierce, some standing and some not, some sweet and charitable, with beckoning arms—all of them frozen in whatever big action they were undertaking.

"This is Statue Graveyard," Attila said, as if he were pulling back a curtain. "This was part of Hungary not long ago, this little corner of Austria. Dad showed it to me." He let go of my hand finally.

As we approached, I could make out the frozen shapes, some huddled as if discussing something, possibly, some toppled, some wearing uniforms, their arms over one another's shoulders, looking as if they were leaving a tavern and singing when they became suddenly encased in metal, one solitary guard holding up a steely flag ruffled by an old wind, one pointing upward, to heaven, probably, once, but lying on his side now so that he was pointing instead at a stand of poplars.

Over to one side was another heap of bronze figures, and Attila guided me toward it. "I'm not feeling that great here," I said.

"It's going to be all right, sweet pumpkin. There's no one

alive here." As we drew up to the mound of metal bodies, I saw the head of a woman statue peering out from the middle of the pile, the eyes blank, the irises hollowed out, the hair in rigid curls, the bangs straight and even.

"Look," I said, "she must have just come from the beauty salon. What is she doing here? What are they all doing here?"

Attila put his arm over my shoulder. The ground was damp here, almost swampy. It oozed beneath our feet. "These statues are the writers and leaders and warriors that the Germans didn't want standing gawking at the people in the squares and parks and outside the museums after they invaded, and now the statues the Russians don't want are thrown in with them too, and it goes on like that—it always happens, whenever invaders come—they knock down the statues, and the Hungarians grabbed these ones all up and piled them here instead of having them blown up. It's in case the Russians leave, and then they can knock down *their* statues—Lenin and his band of Bolsheviks—and put these back up, even though the border moved and it's not even going to be up to the Hungarians."

"Is Stalin coming here too, the big Stalin?" I asked.

"He can't come here, because this is Austria now. The powers shift, the borders move, countries rise and fall." Attila looked philosophical and wise as he said this, or at least he tried to look that way.

"It was the same last century and even before," he said. "Anyway, now there's this place here to save people the trouble of having to cast new hunks of metal every time someone is pushed back out of whatever country."

"Will there be a monument somewhere to the soldiers hanging in the Oktogon?" I asked.

"Not likely. Not while the Russians are in charge, and this isn't even Hungary anymore, as I said, if you were listening, so maybe the Austrians will want to dump other people's heroes here."

We paused to study the monuments. "Sometimes a single bronze soldier stands for millions of other soldiers," Attila said, "and the poets stand for lots and lots of other poets around the world. Look at them," he said. "Imagine. Here's where the glories lie. You can have a triumphant battle one day and win back the crown, become hero of the land, get celebrated, have a day named after you, a brilliant funeral arranged for you with the entire nation turning out, have the number one artist carve a fierce and noble likeness of you, have it erected in a central place and have the square it stands in named after you, for God's sake. Then, just as quickly, that square and the city and the country can be overrun by the Germans or Ottomans or Boogeymen, and suddenly you're dirt. The square is renamed after one of the Boogeys, your chapter is torn out of the history books, the number one sculptor sculpts Lord Boogey, and he gets put up where you once stood. All the heroes who stampeded behind you to victory who were also encased in bronze and stood in smaller squares and churchyards get piled in a wagon, *you* get piled on top, and then you're tossed here."

Attila stepped up to a great sitting figure plonked in the mud, wearing a hood, its arms spread out, a pen of some kind in one hand, a great big book folded in bronze under the other, and he said to me, "Do you know who this is?" He climbed dramatically onto the monument's slippery lap and took the hooded face in his hands, except there was no face, hardly, in the shadows, or at least I couldn't make it out deep inside the opening of the hood. "It's no one." Attila tried to put his own face into the opening of the hood as if to kiss the figure's lips. His voice echoed inside the small cave. He said, "It's Anonymous, that's who. It's a sculpture by Miklos Ligeti of no one, of Anonymous, if you can believe it. Anonymous was the guy who wrote about King Bela III, who lived in the eleven hundreds. But he or she or it was lots of other people who had to hide behind that name to get their work out to the world."

My brother slid off the lap of Anonymous and wiped himself off pointlessly. He squelched gingerly through the mud toward me, then put his wet arm around my shoulders and with the other grandly waved over the looming figures. "Here they are, my beloved boy. Glory be to God and his creatures."

The sight of the noble metal and stone people, all huddled together as they never had before, made me light-headed, as if we had landed on another planet and the air was different, not meant for breathing.

As we turned to leave, I took one last look at the statues all junked together and noticed something I hadn't spotted before. "Look, Attila!" My brother stopped. We saw an arm sticking out of the ooze like a sapling, just an arm, and the hand held a bronze book, smaller than Anonymous's book.

"I have to pee," Attila said. "I have to pee violently. Here, come this way."

He gallantly escorted me behind the heap of bronzes as if we were sauntering through a salon. When we found just the right spot, Attila went straight to work. I became giddy as I unbuttoned myself and joined him. I started cackling, my pee flying in all directions, but my stream was juvenile compared to my brother's. Attila aimed as high up as he could on a badly soiled marble shoulder sticking out of the ground, and I joined him.

As we buttoned up, my brother said, "I have one more thing to show you, my turtle dove." Attila led me all the way around to the other side of the heap of bronzes and marbles, then stopped. "Look," he said. He was sober and serious. "Look!" I *was* looking. "It's Raoul Wallenberg." My brother and I gazed at the man. He was not gesturing, not pointing, not looking at the heavens. The bronze looked black. The figure was simple and thin, but proud, dressed in a long trench coat.

"Who is Raoul Wallenberg?" I asked.

"He saved everyone. He saved Mom and Dad and *me*—I was an adorable babe in arms—you weren't even born yet. He was a Swedish diplomat who saved people—Gypsies, Jews, you name it."

It felt for a second as if we were standing taller, getting set to salute.

My brother said, "He issued fake Swedish papers to people, to Jews, so the Germans wouldn't take us. He saved thousands and thousands of us. And then he disappeared."

"Who did? What do you mean? Do you mean he left?"

"No, he was taken."

"He was *taken*?"

"Yes."

"Who took him? The Germans?"

"No, the Russians."

I stared again at the statue. I wondered what Russian statues might end up here beside him, wondered again about Stalin, without his boots.

"Mr. Wallenberg had helpers, and one of them was Dad's cousin."

"Which cousin?"

"His cousin Paul. Paul Beck."

"Where is Paul now?"

"No one knows. It's like Wallenberg. No one knows what became of Paul. He just went away one day and left no forwarding address, but I don't know why, and no one will tell me."

I looked again at the statue. I wanted to ask more, but it was too quiet here suddenly. I couldn't even hear birds chirping, and there was something fierce in the bronze eyes of this statue. These things prevented me from going ahead with my questions.

FIVE

WE DIDN'T BURY JUDIT until late in the afternoon. My father said we were waiting for a Rabbi Brandt from Stein, a nearby town, but the man never came. A couple of the nuns weren't entirely sure that the rabbi had survived the war, but a third one insisted that he had, that he'd returned from a camp, had a small congregation and was active again.

The bishop of Szeged, naturally, had heard the news of Andras and Gisela's plight and had offered to conduct the service on behalf of the missing rabbi. He even helped to find six more men to add to Andras, my father, Attila and me, to form a minyan. Attila asked whether he and I counted as men. Our father said that we might not, but Andras said it was all right. We counted as men in his book.

Our father looked at his cousin. "They crossed the border on their own feet," Andras said. Simon put a hand on the back of my neck, then the other on Attila's. He gave us a squeeze before smiling at us.

The girl whose mother had been crying the night before appeared at the graveside. The mother, behind her, looked as if she was waiting for the right moment to spring a leak again.

They were joined by a dozen other people, as well as several nuns, and they all huddled around. My father said it was the smallest Jewish graveyard in the world.

Klari and Lili tended to little Gisela, and my father signaled for Andras and me to come and be pallbearers. The four strong men, the fence makers and gravediggers, brought Judit to the door of the convent, and we took over from there. Judit lay on a board but shrouded in a blanket. She seemed to shift underneath it. I wanted to see if she was alive, but I wasn't sure it was my place.

I was near the front as we marched solemnly toward the inevitable grave. I struggled like mad to hold up my end, had to reach up high, though I believe I could have let go altogether without much effect. I kept turning toward our dead cousin and spotted a lock of her copper hair which had fallen out of a gap in the shroud. Then a second lock broke free, the two together flickering like flame.

My class had taken a field trip not a month before to the Museum of Natural History over on Toth Street in Budapest. The museum had an exhibit featuring bog people unearthed from the Great Plain, people who'd lain deep in the earth's bosom for ten thousand years.

A glass case stood at the center of the exhibit. It contained two figures who lay back to back in sweet repose. The small man had ancient sprigs of brown hair still clinging to his bony head. But the woman! The woman had flaming hair, lots of it, molten hair, like Judit's, drawing its heat from deep down in the earth.

And the flame now passed to Gisela, who wailed as we approached with such a redness and fury that, when she paused at the bottom end of the wail to take in a breath, the silence burned.

The grimy man leapt into the grave, followed by his partner, and the rest of us were to hand Judit down to them. But Andras wouldn't let go. We all let go, and the board fell into the grave, but Andras clutched his wife like a big rag doll, seemed to be pleading with her, mouthing words. He turned her upright as if to dance with her, but she was stiffer than I had realized, and he almost lost his footing in the crumbly earth, almost fell into the hole with her. Then the priest and a nun pulled him back, gently, gently urged him away. Several of the men, including my father and brother, rushed to take over so that Judit could be laid to rest. Andras looked painfully into the hole, the earth's black heart, as it waited to receive his wife.

What a sound now rose out of Gisela as her mother was lowered into the ground. It was a Vesuvian sound, like the first wail of the world, the wail of the wild, from the land before birth. The sound was so true and plaintive, she could have been taken from funeral to funeral to set the tone. A nun, the mournful singer from the night before, tenderly pried the baby girl out of my mother's arms and carried her back into the building, where a warm room and warm milk awaited her. I had to look away, look down and away again.

We were all given hats, and a pretty blond nun named Sister Heidi, who looked like a movie star playing a nun, gave me a jaunty Tyrolean hat with a blue feather jutting out of the band. When I didn't take it from her, she placed it on my head, tucking my hair under it, as if she were doing a fitting, giving me extra time to distract me from the proceedings, in fact to admire her face. But these were my pre-jaunty days, and when I reached to remove the hat, my father made me keep it on. My brother said to me, "Yodel something for us." He had on a French beret with one of those wicks at the top, like a candle.

Even the bishop sported his impressive skypiece, the one he'd worn when he first addressed us, the one that seemed to top off his robe. But he did not have on the robe today, just a long dark coat. My mother and grandmother were holding on to Andras. We gazed down at shrouded Judit, and the waterworks began in earnest. How could they not?

The sun, the captain of the skies, blazed away as Father Tamas stepped up, wading right into the crying sounds. In that voice of his, he said, "You want to ask, 'Haven't I believed in you, Lord? Is the message not getting through, coming from my impure mouth? All this mystery. All this tragedy. What can it all mean?'"

Even then—even with the Baby Worshipper growing inside me, trying to take its place among the others—I strained to make spiritual sense of Judit's end, but sometimes things had their own sense. In this place, a priest who had survived and escaped made as much or as little sense as a rabbi who might or might not have survived. But those of us who had gathered could not have had a more common purpose, nor felt a more common feeling.

"Some of us," the priest went on, and he turned to Attila and me, "have our young selves still inside of us, reminding us where we've come from. Some of us," and the priest put his hand on his heart, "have our old selves waiting for us. These selves alone cannot now console or instruct us. A heart has been laid to rest today even before it was too tired to carry on, long before it was used up. Our living hearts beat a tattoo in tribute to this one true heart that has been delivered up to the Lord. May He bless it and may He bless ours."

Father Tamas bent his head in silent prayer and stepped back. Andras broke free from Klari and Lili and approached the gaping hole. I thought he might be hiccupping, but even so he whispered the Kaddish: "*Yit gaddal, ve yit kaddash, she mei rabba.*"

Several people said "Amen," and Andras got to his knees to drop clumps of dirt on his lost wife. Others followed suit with shovels, which the gravediggers now handed us. Attila hurled down muscular loads and for too long. He had to have the shovel taken away from him and passed on to the next person. Sister Heidi dropped in a small bunch of colorful fall flowers.

After my weaker shoveling, I got close to the edge of the grave and didn't want to move. I could make out only the shape of the body by then.

Maybe Judit would be unearthed in a hundred centuries, the hair as red as it was today. Maybe she'd descend with one of the deposed statues—with Raoul Wallenberg—an unlikely couple, searching down in the deep for the earth's pilot light.

SIX

THE NEXT AFTERNOON, the girl whose mother had cried midnight-blue tears told me that Judit was not going to heaven. The girl's soft brown hair was tangly, and she kept sweeping it away from her face on both sides, like drapery. I was hoping she would smile after her assertion, suggesting that she hadn't understood what she'd just said, but she didn't. She just moved her hair away some more. Her gray eyes flickered through the veil of hair.

"Where's your mother?" I asked.

"She went to the bathroom. Where's yours, and where's your brother?"

"My brother went to find the priest to ask him a few questions. My parents and grandmother are making arrangements for us to leave here."

"Oh," she said, her eyes turned down, as if I'd said we were leaving her and her mother behind, as if they were staying.

"We're all going," I added. "No one's staying here with the nuns. They were just being nice."

The hall was all but abandoned. There was a feeling of

movement everywhere but here, a feeling of movement all around us, as if we were the still center of a carousel.

The girl and I were each sitting on our own cots but were quite close to each other. She had a powdery scent. Talcum powder, possibly. But something in addition to the talc: celery, even though we hadn't had celery. Maybe her mother had stashed some away for them. The girl looked at me, her assertion still hanging between us. She looked with a directness that seemed to confer on her some kind of authority. She acted like the Commander of Souls, the way she looked and spoke.

"Where is Judit, then?" I asked.

The dampest and darkest part of the girl's face was her mouth. She had good fleshy lips, too big for her face but delicious looking. It was the first time I remember wanting to taste someone else's lips. I wanted to take out my marzipan Kaiser Laszlo to show her. I wanted to share my *matryoshka* doll with her. I wanted to put on my Tyrolean hat, which Sister Heidi had insisted I keep—put it on at a jaunty angle— tricky though it might have been without benefit of a mirror. I wanted to show the girl Attila's drawing of the fighter plane, possibly pass it off as my own.

But she said, "A priest can't send Judit to heaven. Only a rabbi can. Only a rabbi can send you to heaven. Only a priest can send me."

"But then we'd both end up in heaven," I said, "starting out in the ground."

The girl's eyes were like hair lights shining through the drapery. And now they had turned into luscious mouths too, dark and wet, wanting to say something. But they didn't. Instead she huffed herself onto her feet and went off to look for her mother, taking her moist lips with her.

A moment later Attila appeared at the front of the hall and anxiously summoned me. It looked urgent. I hesitated to join him, but when I finally did, he said, "What? Are you falling for that girl with the banana string hair?"

"I don't know," I said.

Attila said, "If that girl came out of a cake at my party, I'd send her right back into it."

I didn't know what to say. I said, "She has nice lips."

And then the girl reappeared. I was worried she had heard what Attila had said about her, but judging by the warm look on her face, I guessed it was just his voice that had attracted her back.

She sat down on a cot and indicated the one opposite for us to join her. She seemed extra friendly. I saw her smile for the first time. I glimpsed her small, white, even teeth, which seemed to grow out from behind the luscious lips like sentinels.

"Where's your mother?" my brother asked.

"I'm not sure."

"Has she found some quiet corner to shed a tear in?"

The girl shrugged. She was looking down, but soon she looked up and was smiling again. "You don't look like brothers," she said, but she said it in an approving way. "You look so different." She reached her thin arm forward and touched a small lock of my brother's hair. "It's so pretty," she said. "Handsome, I mean. You don't look—"

"What?" Attila pulled back from her admiring fingers and eyes.

"I don't mean ..." but her voice trailed off again. She must have been thinking that when the time came, my brother would get special permission to share her part of heaven, or at least visit it.

Attila saw me staring at the girl still, saw the longing in my foolish eyes. He said, "Give your lips to my brother."

"What?" the girl said, straightening up.

"He's a Beck. He has very distinguished lips. He has better lips than mine. You'd be lucky to kiss those lips." He was pointing at me, at my mouth.

I wanted to dissolve. I wanted to fall upon the thorn of life and bleed. Was it possible to die of humiliation?

The girl saved me the trouble. She stood up and began her retreat. My brother said, "I'll throw in a lock of my beautiful hair in the bargain." She ran away.

My brother got to his feet. "Now, come with me, my alabaster darling. Come."

"I never want to go anywhere with you again," I said. "If I can help it, I never want to speak to you or see you."

Attila actually looked hurt. He turned to leave the hall the way the girl had.

"Where are you going?" I called after him.

"To the chapel," he said, stopping and turning. "I told you already. The priest has agreed to chat with us."

"Chat? I thought you were only asking him some questions."

"Just come with me, my one true love. Just stick with me. You might learn something."

I followed my brother down some dark corridors with many doors, all of them open and, when you looked inside, all of them with their windows open too to let in the fresh autumn air. There was a cot in each room, not much bigger than ours in the big hall, as well as a wardrobe and a small table and chair, as if for a child. There was also a wooden cross on the wall with a bronze Jesus nailed to it. "These are the sisters' rooms," Attila whispered. I knew how hard it was for him to whisper. "This is where they sleep."

We followed a corridor that ended in a great stone chapel. It seemed that all the glorious fervor in this community had been saved up for this building. It was grand, like our temple on Dohany Street in Budapest, but grayer, flutier in shape and tone, flutey like Matthias Church, up in Buda.

The former bishop of Szeged was waiting for us, sitting in what could only be described as a throne. He looked especially unsuited for the golden seat, as he had on just a charcoal suit and black shirt with a white collar, but no robe, no rings, no skypiece.

He beckoned us with his hands. "Approach, approach." He pointed to a couple of plush footstools, and Attila and I pulled them up and sat before the father.

Attila said, "Thank you, Your Honor, for the service you gave for our cousin yesterday." He was still almost whispering, but his voice rang out here. "It was special, unforgettable."

I gazed up and all around at the brilliant windows. What a festive place this was. It was raining droplets of light and color—not just over us but over the many paintings featuring glowheads.

Attila said, "My brother and I are here to 'Seek the Lord while He may be found.'"

The priest nodded. He said, "Your people have been

through a terrible time. We all have, but your people especially." The father always spoke in an inflated, wondrous way, as if he were trying out new verses for the Bible, as if he knew that God was monitoring everything he said. "We can comfort ourselves with the thought that many who passed will nevertheless become forebears to a new generation. Some, though, I'm sad to say—families whose children perished with them—their lines never got to transect the other lines of humanity. Their tributaries will not join the river of humanity. May the Lord our God look after them especially."

"Judit's lines transected," I said. I was asking more to confirm that I had understood what he was saying. "Isn't that right?"

"It is," Father Tamas said, and he looked up at her in the rafters. I felt reassured.

He said, "Still, you've taken a blow." He smoothed the hair at the back of my head. His hand was warm and dry. "You've had to leave your home behind."

"I got to say goodbye to Kaiser Laszlo, the monkey, at Gerbeaud," I said. I didn't want to mention the hanging men, or the man in the brown suit who'd stood in front of the Urania. I felt another chill come over me, thinking of the brown hat exploding, the man with the nicely combed hair and very green eyes, the foot that had struck Attila in the dark.

The priest smiled. "I'm glad you got to see the Kaiser."

Attila piped up. "We were at the zoo a few years ago, with my school." He got to his feet. "It was not that long after the big war. People had been going to the zoo to eat the animals because there was no meat." The priest nodded. He looked somber. "We saw a tamarin monkey," Attila said. His voice was shrill. It rang out like a bell. "Tamarin monkeys are very protective of their families, the way humans are, but even more, very protective. But there was a mother tamarin there with a baby monkey, as well as a pregnant daughter, who was lying off to the side looking hungry. That tamarin mother suddenly snapped the head off the smallest one, her own baby—just like that, with a twist—killed the daughter's baby brother, I guess, so that the pregnant daughter could eat the rest of the baby, have some nourishment for the one coming along. We waited to see the girl monkey bite into her baby brother's shoulder. Some of us were sick as we watched, not just the girls but the boys too."

"Good Lord," the priest said. "Good Heavenly Lord." He looked down, clasped his hands in his lap. Attila took his seat again. Father Tamas said, "At what point, I sometimes wonder, did we cross over from being inhabitants of this planet to being trespassers?"

The father looked extra solemn now. Attila wanted to cheer him up, I think, so he got to his feet again and said, "Your Honor, may I ask you some design questions?"

"Design?" the priest said. He looked ready to smile. "I don't know if I can answer them, but I'll try."

Attila rubbed his chin. "The Lord created us in very ingenious ways, but why did he give each of our parts multiple functions?"

"Just what do you mean?" Father Tamas asked. He sat back a bit in his throne. He looked us both over.

"What I mean is, when the Creator was designing us, at what point did he decide the various parts would have more than one function, that he would *group* functions together in one part?" Attila raised a hand to the side of his mouth, as if he were confiding in the holy father. "If you think of the parts down below, for instance, they have multiple functions — transecting, as you were just saying, being one."

"Yes?"

"And then they are also used for peeing. And they are our alarm clocks. If you didn't have to pee, you could sleep for a week. And it's the other kind of alarm too." He raised his conspiratorial hand to his mouth again. "If you didn't get aroused now and again, there would be very little transecting. If you're a girl, a whole baby has to live and grow in those parts. It's really quite ingenious."

The priest gazed upward toward Judit and the Lord, up into the sprinkling light and color, then down again at Attila, glaring at him now, but with a holy look still.

"Take the mouth," Attila went on. He was pacing back and forth in front of us. "You use it to eat. You use it to breathe. You use it to speak. You use it to smile. You use it to kiss on the cheek, and kiss on the lips and kiss wherever ..." He paused.

"And?" the priest said.

"And all I mean is that when God was cataloging the various functions of things, I wonder how he came up with these groupings, that's all. The nose smells and sniffles and holds up glasses. I mean, the mouth could just as easily have been used to smell and the feet to reproduce. The brain could have been placed inside the throat, so that each time you swallowed you'd have a thought. How did these functions get grouped in the ways that they did? Then there are the ingenious groupings having to do with color. Take brown, for instance. You get brown hair, the brown ground, the brown trunks of trees, yellow bananas browning, brown—you know—brown excrement. How did the color get chosen for it? Except that I guess it had to have *a* color—why not brown? But was it a random choice? Conversely, what an ingenious idea to have the *same* thing come in different colors: brown eyes, green eyes, blue eyes, white carnations, red carnations, and such. And what about blue skies? What a nice choice. Boy blue. What was the plan there? Blue skies, boy? Pink skies, girl?" Attila shrugged his shoulders. "I even wonder if the Lord broke things up into color groups, and if so, how did he do it? Did he start out by breaking them up in other ways? What I mean is, at what point did the Lord decide that grass would be green rather than Mondays being green?"

"Did you say Mondays?"

"I mean, having come upon the concept of colors, did he start out making everything green on Monday, say, then everything red on Tuesday, everything yellow on Wednesday, but I mean *everything*, like a baby God coloring over the lines?"

"A baby God?" the priest said.

"Or maybe it was God's brother." This time the priest did not repeat my brother's speculation. Attila said, "What about that? A brother maybe. Maybe the less creative one in the family."

The bishop's face was flushed. I thought, possibly, that he was going to leave us. He huffed and was about to say something, but Attila wasn't finished. My brother was like that. His many thoughts lined up at the gate, jostling to get out. He said, "I love the common design of things, like wings, arms and fins. They all propel creatures, but they also flutter—they enable things to flutter—do you know what I mean?—hummingbirds, black molly fish, ballerinas?" The priest sat back and nodded faintly. "And," my brother went on, "I'm interested in the order of things. For example, did the Heavenly Father think up feet before deciding they needed to patter over something, or did he think up the earth before deciding it needed patterers upon it? Or did he think up everything at once because he is omniscient? I guess I'm saying, how does that work, being omniscient, I mean? Did he start out, as a baby God, being *somewhat* omniscient? Did he start out as God of the Milky Way, only later to become God of the whole universe?" The priest looked at me. "I guess," Attila went on, "what I'm struggling with is this concept of *always* as opposed to *gradual*. Was it *always* thus and so?" My brother paused to breathe. "Also," he said, "why do you suppose there are pairs of some things, like nostrils and kidneys and hands and arms, and only *one* of other things, like brains and hearts— in humans anyway? How did the Lord decide on two ears and one nose, rather than two noses and one ear in the center? That way, you'd have stereo smells, lavender on one side, toilet on the other. There are two eyebrows, but some people have one long one. I mean, I just wonder how that decision was made: two nostrils and such. Why not one titty in the middle, a bruiser?" Attila demonstrated by outlining the shape of one in the middle of his own chest. "Imagine it," he said.

The priest didn't answer, not even with an opening word like "Well ..." even though Attila had a fierce, determined look on his face, a look that said, *Help me with these riddles or I shall surely die.*

"The senses are the most ingenious of all: touch, taste,

hear, smell, see. Imagine designing those—imagine designing
eyes," Attila said. "They will take in the light—they will be the
receptors of the light I have spread over the world. They will
identify objects, shapes, colors, gestures—interpret them—
love, hate." Attila clapped his hands together and brought
them to his face to look at and smell. "Sorry if I haven't been
clear, sir," my brother said.

"You've been clear enough."

"Or do you suppose, possibly, that the Lord had a workshop
of designers—except he would call them a *host* of designers
rather than a workshop—with each designer responsible for
one thing, the angel or the elf who made the mouth, say, and
his or her assistant who designed the yawn, so that all yawners
yawn in the same way—the fox, the rat, the human and the
cat? Do butterflies yawn? I haven't seen one yawning. And also
I wonder about the placement of things. How did the parts
down below get placed down below, you know, as opposed to up
above, and so on?" Attila hardly broke stride. "I commend the
Lord," he said, "for his choice of color for blood, an impressive
crimson. It says, 'Alarm!' It says, 'Stanch my flow. I cannot be
a river flowing out into the round red sea.' And how clever to
make the human rivers flow underground—under the skin—
rather than over the surface the way real rivers do. Imagine
how the red rivers would look flowing over our bodies, the
little valleys they would have to carve out in order to conduct
them." Attila shuddered. He turned on his heel. He said, "And
what about poppy red? What about poppies? How could it be
that poppies toss upon a green field like ladies' hankies, yet up
through their stalks flows a powerful dream serum, to make us
rest, to make us leave the field and the earth, while the flower's

seeds—its very *seeds*, meant to give us more poppy babies—can be added to sugar and baked into the holiest of cakes, like black earth, between layers of pastry?" Attila pointed to his own chin. "And then there's the centipede—the millipede! Surely, this is someone's idea of a joke. All right, eight legs, like a spider, or eight tentacles, like an octopus, or *none*, like a snake, but a hundred, a *thousand*? They were created with holy tongue in cheek, were they not? As was the giraffe. Hmm, let's give an animal a three-story neck and decorative little body—and the ostrich and the warthog—more in the humor column. And then how did the Lord work out the concept that *little* would be cute? That you would be drawn to the littleness, hold the tyke, give it love and food?" My brother raised his inquiring arms to Judit and the Lord. "If heaven is so fascinating, why do God and his angels spend all their time staring down at us? What would they do without us? What did they do *before* us? Is there such a thing as *before*?" He dropped his hands to his sides the way the priest had done during his sermon. And then Attila raised a Eureka finger in the air. It was his finest performance. "Before all of *this* got under way," he said, "if there is a before, whatever *this* is, God must have been looking out at nothing, and he must have thought, 'Why not have *something*? And what a thing to dream up, too. Life! Life's the most clever currency of all, isn't it?"

"Clever?" the priest repeated.

"Oh, yes. It's because everyone who has it—*every thing*—wants to keep it, if they have any sense left. So it's powerful to make life, powerful to risk it and powerful to destroy it. Yes, it is," Attila said, "as you yourself were saying, sir," and now he paced back and forth in front of us again. "Very powerful, very

tempting, very delicious in a way. If you can't put things right—
if you can't make your own life work—then taking someone
else's life makes a lot of sense. And it gives you the same kind
of thrill, the same kind of power—*almost*—that someone has
who can make life, make babies, make countries. How great it
is to knock them down." His voice quieted down. "Gellert,"
he said. "The hill in Buda is named after him. Gellert Hill. The
bishop in Budapest. He was like you, sir, a bishop. He brought
Christianity to Hungary, but they put him in a spiked barrel
and rolled him down his hill, filling him full of holes. Think
of how clever it was even to invent the spiked barrel. Think
of how pleased his tormentors were to have come up with the
idea. You have to be smart and inventive to devise evil deeds,
just about as inventive as when you devise good ones. That's
all I can say."

The priest said, "All *I* can say is that it's a good thing we're
the only planet in the galaxy with life on it. There'd be plenty
of trouble if we weren't. There's plenty of trouble as it is."

I looked up and all around me again, as the good father
had done earlier when he was searching for inspiration. I was
admiring the celestial community of seraphim, cherubim and
glowheads. I had a question too, which I'd been holding, and
since there was a lull in the proceedings, I thought I might
go ahead with it. I said, "I'm wondering what seraphim and
cherubim do." I asked only because, in my search for a future
in those days, I was intensely curious about the roles creatures
played.

Father Tamas looked relieved. "The seraphim and
cherubim," he began, "are agents of the Lord. They carry

messages to us and from us. They ..." He looked up into the rafters with me but didn't finish. Attila looked up as well.

It seemed to me that if you could take wisdom from the air in this way and send faith up into it, you could take offence from the air too, or on other days delight. Being especially good at this surely was what made you a glowhead. The seraphim, cherubim and glowheads floating up into the air—these must be added to the things that fluttered.

"I was just wondering," I began again. "I mean, I was wondering—" but I stopped myself, because it was at this point that the Baby Worshipper growing inside of me cried out, saying unto me, "The good father is growing tired of you and your brother."

Father Tamas rubbed his eyes and head in the headachy fashion of adults. "Excuse me," he said, as he rose from the golden chair. I rose too. Attila was already standing. I could see that my brother was getting ready to start another line of questioning, probably the one about how Abraham chose one God—how he landed on that number. Why not two or even possibly three, assuming the Greeks and Romans were wrong and there wasn't a whole heaven full of gods, a host of gods. But the priest held up his hand in anticipation. "I know you boys have been traumatized. You've lost your homeland and friends; you've left behind so much that you love."

"Oh," Attila said.

What the holy father didn't understand was that, for my brother, everything was a game. He could have asked these same questions a month or a year before. This was the board game of Creation he was grappling with. Our escape was the ancient game of marathon running, one in which the players always hoped they were running loveward but couldn't be sure. The best thing was that all the players got to ask as many questions as they wanted.

My brother said, "Thank you so much, sir," and, strangely, he bowed, so I bowed too, understanding it to be the only safe gesture.

As we headed back, we didn't discuss Attila's questions or my one question. I didn't know if they were stupid or smart, but I sensed we could have parted from the holy father on better terms.

My brother muttered a little along the way. He stopped to tell me, "It's a good thing God was a Realist. You could have been designed by Picasso and had your ear nailed to a wall and your dick hung up on a fluffy cloud."

We walked some more, and just for clarification, I asked Attila, "Has someone checked to make sure the millipede actually has a thousand legs? I mean, has someone counted?"

"Yes, my angel."

"What about a millipede with, say, nine hundred and fifty-seven legs? Would he be disabled, like a one-legged man?"

"He would," Attila said. "He'd be a mistake, and he wouldn't make it, like the one-legged man. Nature doesn't like her own mistakes. She's very vain that way. She'll do away with them if she can."

We walked, then, for a moment in silence, but the lack of answers from the priest crazed my brother. "Let's face it," he said, "God was the *Creator*, and he created *something*, but the rest was a mess." He was whispering too loudly. We were passing the nuns' rooms, glancing into each one. "He was the Creator. He was not the Maintainer. Why do we expect him to maintain and destroy and judge and wash away and rebuild? The fun must have gone out of it, once he was done with creation. It's a tricky thing, creating the universe, watching it turn into a mess and then feeling you have to start again, just about, by flooding it over, with the exception of an ark with two of everything on board to make sure you don't have to do the *whole* thing over, except for the light and the darkness, the water and the land. It couldn't have been fun to drown the rest, or to turn people into pillars of salt—some into pillars of pepper—or smite their firstborn.

"You have to wonder sometimes why the Lord got started in the first place," Attila said. "Why bother? Especially since you can *foresee* everything. I guess he had to. It would be sad if you were Creator of the Universe but decided not to go ahead with any creations."

"Try to be quiet," I said, as we stepped up our pace. I was peeking into each room to look for a slightly more glamorous one, maybe with gold curtains or festive lighting, or even just a pair of red gloves left on the little table. I was guessing it would be the cell where Sister Heidi resided, but I saw nothing out of the ordinary, just a single gray umbrella in one room standing in the corner.

"What happens at the Second Coming," Attila went on, "when the Messiah is executed again? Is everyone going to string a golden noose around their necks, or seat a bronze Jesus in a holy electric chair to hang on the wall beside the crucifix?"

"Attila, be quiet."

"What about the new Virgin at the Second Coming? Won't *she* be surprised when she finds out she's pregnant, after not sleeping with anyone?"

And then Attila stopped in the corridor. "Do you know what?" he said. "The Lord must have foreseen the Boogeymen, as I said. He must have foreseen Statue Graveyard. He must have foreseen Hitler and Stalin. He could have hurried along the process before the lion and the lamb got to lie down with each other, saved people so much unnecessary suffering. He could have made some white mothers give birth to black babies, but not *always*. It would be random. If some white mothers *routinely* gave birth to black babies, they'd be burned at the stake. So let's say we don't know what's coming. One time the white woman can give birth to a black baby; the second time to a white baby, but maybe a homosexual; the third time to a giraffe. Do you see what I mean?" I shook my head no. "Why don't dogs give birth to cats?" he said, and he slapped me on the chest with the back of his hand—quite hard, actually. "Do you see what I'm saying? Help us out a little, oh Lord. You already had a good idea by making people have to mate to have a child. A very good idea, actually, possibly your finest one. But why not go one step further?"

I tried to continue walking, but my brother wasn't having any of it. I said, "And what happens once the lion and the lamb lie down together?"

"Exactly," Attila said, and slapped my chest again.

"What?" I said. "Exactly what?"

"Then you wouldn't need to mate with anyone anymore. It would all be quiet and serene."

"And would that be the end of all species? Would that be paradise or death or whatever—the *end*?"

My brother considered my proposition. We walked five more steps, but he stopped us again. "Good one, my tiny brother. No, we wouldn't need to mate. We'd be perfect by then. We could be self-pollinators, like some plants, I believe. You could just make yourself pregnant, lie around all day and feel up your own special places."

"That would be paradise for you. But then there would be no one to impress."

"Don't be rude, my tender and small brother. It's just another plan, a suggestion, that's all. We'd be in a place that would not require a redeemer. We would never need another flood to wash away the filth and degradation." Attila was still thinking very hard.

"Then why would we need more babies?"

"Oh, dear Lord, we *wouldn't*," he said. "We have babies to steer us toward perfection. We wouldn't. No cross-pollination, no self-pollination. I have taught you well, my ever-present darling." He gripped my face like a vise and kissed the top of my head.

And I looked at my brother in a new light—how could I not? He had a Baby Creator of the Universe growing inside of him.

I blurted out, "Maybe God is *still* a baby."

My brother froze. He gripped me even tighter. "What did you say?"

"I said"—my voice was distorted as I squeezed another thought out of the vise—"maybe there's a ratio of years

between Creator and human, a million to one, say." We had
just completed ratios in school. "Possibly the Lord is a little
older. Kindergarten Lord. It would explain some things."

My brother further tightened his lock on my face, if that
was possible. I couldn't say another word. Then he kissed
me on the forehead this time. "What thoughts you have, my
raven-haired beauty." And he kissed me again on each cheek.

We continued on our way, and as the blood returned to my
face, I saw, suddenly and vividly, that we had been diverted,
that life was a floating between these two poles, diversion
and version, that one minute you were running away from
things and the next toward them, that one minute you were
talking about two nostrils and one titty and the next you were
facing the fact that you had lost your home, lost Judit, lost
your friends Zoli and David, possibly, and probably you would
never again see the grim ladies with their bright tree in the
painting called "Christmas, 1903," that you might never again
see the girl with the delicious mouth or the tall woman with
the caper eyes, that a man with combed hair might swing
through your dreams for quite some time to come.

When we got back to the big hall, many people, including
our family, had returned and seemed to be packing their few
belongings. I noticed that the cot adjacent to mine, where the
girl had sat that morning, was stripped of its linens and the girl's
little sack of belongings was gone. Her mother's cot, naturally,
was also bare. I was quite sad about it. I wanted to tell the girl
how much I liked her two eyes, two lips and one nose, that my
brother was just being silly. I wish he hadn't said anything to her.
I never did see the gangling woman again. A balding man with
hair on the back of his neck was in the cot she had occupied. It

was as if the hair had all shifted backward and downward and might shift some more. He felt me staring and turned. I saw that he had hairy eyes too, wild eyebrows and lashes. What a seedbed he must have had under his skin.

Our parents told us that we were making an early start tomorrow. Our mother said we should make sure we ate our entire dinner before getting ready for bed. Lili said that Andras wouldn't be traveling with us. He would be going somewhere else. We saw them, Andras and his daughter, with our grandmother at the far end of the hall. He was bouncing the little redhead too hard, I thought. Klari took over the baby.

"Where are they going?"

"Somewhere else," our mother said again.

"What does that mean?" Attila asked, huffing. The question was powered by his annoyance with Jesus and Father Tamas.

"We won't be traveling together," she said.

"Where are we going, and where are *they* going?" he said again.

"We are going to Paris first," she said. Our father glared at her. "But just for a visit," she quickly added. She was fixing Attila's collar.

"What about them?" I asked this time.

"They are going to Israel, my love." She turned to fix my collar, though I thought mine was fine.

Our father said, "They're starting in Vienna, but they're heading out tonight. They're meeting someone from an agency to help them."

Attila and I went over to our cousins to say goodbye, and for the first time I was stabbed by the blade of this departure, was wounded more deeply than by our initial escape from our home. Maybe then all the excitement of it—the minefield, the hot darkness—had distracted me.

I couldn't even look at Gisela. Andras gave me a snapshot of Judit, who looked rosy, even in black and white. I hugged Andras around the waist and he clasped the back of my neck with both of his hands. I made my way directly to the bathroom, where I lingered until I could be absolutely certain that Gisela and Andras had left. I kept staring at the photo of Judit. I longed for the three-dimensional version of her.

Later, in the big room, I waited stupidly for the girl with the delicious-looking mouth and her tearful mother to return, but of course they didn't. They'd fled into the interior of Europe somewhere, after taking the trouble to banish Judit from heaven.

Attila asked our grandmother why anyone would go to Israel. He was quite insistent, but when his head met the pillow, the question got switched off.

What a freak of nature my brother was. He was awake or he was asleep, a Hungarian one second and Tarzan the next, winter one day, summer the next, no spring, no fall. These were not his seasons. There was nothing gradual in his nature, the gradual seasons, the gradual times of day, dawn and sunset. Big things seemed to me to be gradual in their movement. Winter didn't just switch off. The sun didn't just switch off, switching on the moon in its place. It handed over the light during a whole evening. I don't know how we could have been brothers, Attila and I. We were the Adjective Brothers: Sudden and Gradual.

When the lights went out, I waited, as awake as I could

be, among the diminished number of breathers and snorers. I got up and snuck to the window. I looked up at the clear, star-flecked sky, following its dots and joining them into dippers and the Butterfly of Hercules and the Braid of Ally. Just then my grandmother put her hand on my shoulder, making me jump. She was like a stealthy assassin. She whispered for me to be quiet, crossed out her mouth with her finger. She gazed out the window with me, seemed to be studying the stars as I'd been doing. She said, barely audibly, "Some of those stars out there are gone now."

"What did you say, Mamu?" I turned toward her to see if she was possibly mocking me. But she had a tender look in her eyes. "Just how do you mean?" I asked.

"I mean they're so far away that they sent out their light many, many years ago, and the light is only just arriving, even though the star has extinguished itself since. All the light you see is old at the very least, but more likely ancient."

"Ancient light," I said.

"And other light, new starlight, is being sent out right now, which you *can't* see, which, by the time it gets here, we won't be around to see, not I, not even you."

"Other light? What does that mean? Does it mean that Ursa Major—the Great Bear—does it mean that some of its leg is older than other parts, that some of it formed earlier, *before* it was a bear? Is there another bear or a fish up there still waiting to be born?"

"Yes," Klari whispered into the crown of my head. "Yes, possibly, yes. Now why don't we go to sleep? Why don't you go to bed?"

"I will," I said, gazing up at the thorny darkness. "But what about the North Star? What if it goes? How will mariners find their way across the sea?"

"I don't know," my grandmother said.

"What about people in love—*lovers*—walking along as they do, holding hands as they look up at the stars? Do they know it's old light they're seeing, that the source of the light is expired, in some cases? It's not the light they think it is?"

"I don't think they know that or imagine it," she said, "or *worry* about it."

"What about the sun? What about *our* star?" I said. "Will people in some distant place be seeing its light long after we can't see it anymore?"

"Maybe, yes, maybe."

I wanted in the worst way to wake Attila to tell him what I had just learned from our grandmother. But I knew I couldn't wake him, wouldn't, that it wouldn't be wise—I wouldn't tell him, not even the next day, that this discovery fell into the category of the hanging men, or at least the one hanging man.

SEVEN

I WOKE UP to piano music. My grandmother was sitting on my cot, holding my hand, her eyes closed, swaying to the lilting sound. I sat up to find beautiful Sister Heidi, her back to us, playing the upright piano at the front of the hall. Attila was still asleep.

"It's Beethoven," Klari whispered. "His *Waldstein* Sonata."

Sister Heidi was coming to the end of the soft middle movement and about to bang out the finale.

My grandmother squeezed my hand. "Listen to it," she said.

"I'm listening."

"Wait for it."

I stared at Sister Heidi's shapely form moving inside the bag of her habit, her body stirring the rough cloth from within. The habit made no sense to me. The sister was a soft cream cake inside a coarse sack.

But the playing was as nice as the player. Klari was still squeezing my hand—too hard, I thought, which is what people seemed to be doing to me lately. "Listen to it," she whispered.

"You can hear the whole of the composer's bursting heart through his fingers."

"*Her* fingers," I said.

"Yes, of course, hers, but Beethoven is saying, 'Behold the mountain, delight in the rose, rise out of yourself.'" My grandmother closed her eyes again as the sister turned the keys into thunder-makers. "Listen to it," Klari said with closed eyes. "Listen to the man."

"The woman."

She opened her eyes. "The man and the woman both. The truth of it. The truth of the composer. Beethoven. I can only think his education began inside his mother." I looked at my grandmother. "Yes, inside his mother," she said. "His mother running, his mother afraid, his mother at rest. Listen to the beat of it, the truth of it." I gazed at Sister Heidi's back. "The trouble," Klari said, "the deep trouble"—her eyes were wide open now—"the trouble is that the listener is as important as the player, the trouble and the blessing both. The player is an interpreter, but the listener is an interpreter too. 'Crush your enemies,' it is saying to some people. 'Rise up,' it is saying to others. 'Believe in yourself,' it is saying to still others. You can see why he sometimes sent these fists of music flying at you. And not just fists—his lips, his eyes, his heart, as I was saying. Great sounds are like that. They have their own language. 'Behold the mountain' sometimes sounds like 'Be the mountain.'"

I kept staring at Sister Heidi. She played with such authority she made me believe she could set the world right. None of it made sense—the drab habit she wore, the square hall we sat in, the cots we slept on—the music lifting us out to distant lands that nevertheless looked familiar. And then the music roared to an end, stomping through its own flowerbed. The few of us who were listening clapped extra hard. I wondered why Heidi hadn't sung with the other sisters the night we arrived. I thought, possibly, she didn't know the words.

Heidi rose from her bench, timid as a fawn. She didn't turn to face us for a moment, but then she did. She smiled, bowed her head and withdrew too suddenly. The heat rose to my face. Attila had slept through it all.

My grandmother went to get me a roll with cheese and jam, together with a cup of warm milk. Then she took her seat beside me again while I spread apricot preserve on my roll. "Can I help you?" Klari asked.

I shook my head. It felt very warm in the room. The anvil of grief fell down on me. I could feel myself salting up again and stuffed some of the warm roll into my mouth. Finally, I said, "Mamu, that man we saw hanging at the Oktogon—"

"Please try not to remember him, my darling." My grandmother's eyes were caramel and soft.

"He was the eighth dead person I've ever seen," I said. "The first seven were hanging men too. And then there was the ninth, the smoking man. The tenth was Judit—maybe the eleventh, if you count the foot that hit Attila. The person it would have been attached to probably didn't survive." I looked down into my lap, took another bite of my sweet roll.

"No, that person didn't live, and that is far too many—one is too many—for such a young man to see."

"How many dead people have you seen?" I said with a full mouth.

"I've seen too many too."

"How many? Who?" I took another bite out of my crusty roll, stuffed my mouth.

"My dear parents," she said, "my dear husband—your grandfather Robert, the man whose name you have. How he would have loved you, especially. You look just like him. But let's stop. Please, I'm begging you, try to forget the dead people, especially that sad last man hanging, especially Judit. I know it's hard, but try, my darling."

"That man that was hanging—did people know him?"

"Yes, of course people knew him, and someone in particular loved him, the way Andras loved Judit, the way we loved Judit."

"How about the people who killed him? Did they know who he was?"

"Please eat your breakfast."

"Did they?"

"How could they? They killed him because of what he stood for, the colors he was wearing. Who he was might even be beside the point. In war, you don't know the people you are killing. You can shoot a man because of the flag he flies, just as he can shoot you because of the flag you fly. Those landmines in the field we crossed were intended for anyone crossing the field, for the very fact of it—not because someone is saying, 'I don't like you, Robert Beck,' but because you are one of the others. Child though you are, you are other."

"What if you are a dog crossing?"

"No, not if you are a dog crossing. If you are a dog crossing and you get blown up, it's just your dumb luck, even if you are a Russian dog stepping on a Russian landmine, even if you are a Russian person who didn't know. These people—the hangmen and the hanged both—might hear the powerful piece of music we just heard and misread it, misapply it. A Russian might misapply Tchaikovsky and a German misapply Beethoven, or vice versa. I'm not criticizing, actually. When you hear the power of the music, there is something delicious in the absoluteness of it, just as there is something delicious in the absoluteness of destruction— no sense, it's beyond sense—like the feeling in the song, the rightness of it, the rightness of the fury—pound, pound, it says to whoever wants to hear—pound through the frustration, free yourself, blast through the barrier, the inhibition, the civilization, the *sense*. It's very powerful. It makes you bigger. It makes you mountainous. 'Behold the mountain,' Beethoven is saying. '*Be* the mountain, if you must.' Look, he's wearing those colors. He's flying those colors, the blue and the white. It's the colors we're hanging, the blue and the white strung up on the pole, strung up by the neck."

"The sky and the clouds."

"Yes, today we're hanging the sky and the clouds. Tomorrow we'll hang the sun and the moon."

I looked outside the window at the bright sky and clouds. What if clouds reflected things, carried pictures of things, pictures of souls entering into them, one at a time, each adding a drop of color—red Judit, red combed hanging man, brown smoker—carrying the message abroad, looking down on other peoples, until they were ready to rain down their essence, letting the foreign lookers know that these newly colored clouds could nourish the land with the best of them?

A diesel bus soon pulled up in front of the convent. It was

to take the rest of us to Vienna, and then another bus was to get us to Paris, where my great-aunt Hermina, my grandmother's sister, was waiting. I was feeling queasy. I was feeling as if I could have stayed a little longer among the nuns. I thought I could have continued with school here, possibly, found the right skypiece and learned how to make speeches. I thought some of my friends might eventually join us to fill out the class.

Sister Heidi appeared again. Her presence cheered me up. Her eyes were cornflower blue in this light. When Heidi saw me staring, she stepped over to hug me, and I took extra long over it. She seemed smaller and as soft as I'd imagined under the habit, and she had a clean fragrance. I wanted to know about her. I wanted to know if she had red shoes stashed away somewhere, or red gloves. I wanted to ask her if she thought Judit had made it to heaven, but I didn't have the nerve and didn't want the answer to be a troubling one, if that was what it was going to be.

Heidi was wearing her coif but not her white neckband, and for the first time I got a good look at her neck. It was the whitest, most supple neck I had ever seen. It was what marble was trying to be when it was trying to be flesh. My eyes traveled up and down the soft white column. What messages could it be carrying from her heart to her head and back to her heart again? What messages flew in through the blue windows? What messages about God and Jesus and Beethoven, the passion for them all—all colliding in this passageway? Were there other passions too, unspoken ones? And if this was just a passage, why was so much art and charm put into the making of it?

My own heart danced wildly and artlessly in my chest.

"Where are you going to go?" Heidi asked.

It took me a moment to find my bearings. "I don't know," I said. "Paris first, but then Canada, I think. I wish I could stay here and have my family send for me eventually."

Sister Heidi must have found this to be the funniest remark she'd ever heard, because she laughed up a storm, laughed until she hiccupped. I watched her magical neck convulse with it.

The sister straightened herself out and said to me in earnest, "The meek shall inherit the earth." And then she smiled, turned and strolled away. Is that what I was, then? Meek? Should I cling to meek, console myself with it?

My head was hot under the Tyrolean hat. I took it off to smooth back my hair. Attila came up behind me. "What's that one's name?" he asked.

"Sister Heidi,"

"That's the one from before, right?"

"Yes. Before."

"Wow, she would be the Virgin I'd select for the Second Coming. And she's a nun! Certainly, she wouldn't ask any questions about the mystery of it all. What did she tell you?"

"She told me the meek shall inherit the earth."

"Great," Attila said. "Very wonderful and very great. Is that what she is? Is she meek? If that's meek, then take me to your leader."

Attila and I got on the bus, and I turned right away to look out the window for Sister Heidi. I knew now that she was out of reach, even as a friend. She and I couldn't stay friends any more than I could have stayed friends with the girl with the stringy hair and exceptional lips.

We were not at a place where we could stay or even visit again. We were at a place from which we had to move on, and the sister with the neck and the girl with the lips seemed suitable only in this place. Back home, bombs were dropping or rising out of the ground, asserting who was to sit on the throne, who was to lie in the cemetery, who was to be moved to Statue Graveyard and who the meek would be. And there was no going forward in the direction of something that was only a word. *Canada*. It was just a sound. It had no shape or weight. You could not take its temperature. It was just a sound, an unpopulated sound. It was hard to imagine Canada as a place where people were sitting and eating eggs or taking a walk or hugging nuns or playing cards. It was hard to imagine that full simultaneous worlds were being lived over there, as we sat here on diesel buses and admired certain songs and sisters and cousins lost in childbirth. If God switched off gravity, maybe we wouldn't be bound to Canada or Paris or Utah or here, and we could fly where we pleased, or just tread the air, become fluttering things. I thought I might suggest it later to Attila, as he sorted out the various designs of creation.

I kept straining to see Heidi by the convent door. Several other sisters stood around the bus as we sorted ourselves out inside. I was overcome with sadness. I knew that Sister Heidi was trying to make me look forward to things, but I couldn't help but feel the finality of it all, that I was seeing things for the last time. In those days, that feeling came over me in waves, like the memory of Judit.

I don't think my brother ever felt the finality of things in the same way. When he was confronted with finality in any of its forms, he would prevail over it. "Death to Finality!" he would say to it. Only the meek can understand finality in this way. My brother would listen to Beethoven and know he was on the side of the right and the just. He would live forever, and who was going to stop him?

As we settled onto the bus, I carefully placed my satchel in the rack overhead and checked it a second time before taking my seat.

I said to my brother, "What about gravity?"

"Ah, gravity, my impish boy," he said. "Yes, gravity. Well, you see, the Lord had created all these creatures, and now he needed for them to stay put, keep them where they were, roughly, so he laid down a carpet of gravity. It's quite ingenious, because it's really a great invisible sucking mechanism, but its force needed to be adjusted to make it just right. You can't have everything sucked down into it—the sun and the universe, all slamming into it—and you can't have it be too strong even for the creatures. You don't want them pinned to the earth such that they wouldn't be able to move, wouldn't even be able to hunt or mate. You couldn't have them be stuck to it and wriggling themselves to death."

"And you couldn't have it be too weak," I said, "such that we would all float up and become fluttering things. I guess, once you have fluttering things, you need things that fall too."

"Precisely," my brother said. "Precisely. Fluttering things make sense only in the presence of gravity." He gently slapped my face a couple of times and sat back. "I have yet to figure out, though, if gravity is a force for good or evil."

A woman was getting on the bus just then, all decked out, her shiny long brown hair hanging and bouncing, her pearl earrings dangling and a pearl necklace curving down from her neck to her black dress. This was gravity at work. I had once watched a designer of curtains, quite a prissy man, come to our house along with two assistants, a young couple who kept praising the work of the designer as they hung his curtains in our dining room, long, thick, green curtains tumbling down, a rich new evening gown, the room all got up for a fine dinner. I had seen a man with thick glasses hang a portrait of my great-grandfather, framed in gold garlanding, over my grandmother's bed so she could admire her late father in the solitude of the night. I had watched my brother, the gymnast, hang from a bar by his own hands, hang, grunt, twirl and hang. I had seen meat hanging from hooks in a butcher's window, pale chickens and ducks, the large red parts of a pig and the long red parts of a cow, the butcher admiring his handiwork, smiling out at me from behind his bright window. I had also seen people hanging from lampposts in a public square. These are some of the ways in which we have put gravity to work.

I stared at my brother, extra hard. I asked him, "What will you do in the Wild West?"

He tapped his chin with his index finger. He was taking my question very seriously. "I'll become a cowboy rabbi," he said. "And a fur trader as well. Beaver and otter and silver fox, I think." He patted me on the head. "And you can pursue your dreams of becoming a singing nun." I shoved his patting hand away.

"Will Dad be a tool-and-die maker again?" I asked.

"Not if he can help it," Attila said.

Our father had been a tool-and-die maker during the war because he couldn't become a lawyer. By the time he was ready to go to university, Jews could not be admitted.

Sunlight beamed into the bus now. My brother shut his one eye against it. "What about the sun?" I said. I thought Attila might say it would burn itself out, stop sending out its light.

But that's not what he was thinking. He said, "Yes, of course, the sun." He took a deep breath. He opened the cool eye. He had the serious look of a professor or a judge. "What an orb it is, what a bright creation. Sweet orb, giver of light and warmth and life. Sweet invention, far superior to the tufts of hair in our armpits. It could have been worse. The Lord could have tried out other things. He could have made *us* revolve instead of the planets. He could have made us spin about and spin about rather than make the heavenly bodies move. It would have made more sense, in a way. We could have roved and spun, day and night, over the surface of the earth. But it is all arbitrary. Instead of the sun hung out there to give us life, in order to stay alive we could have been made to pass daily through stringy curtains. Who knows? The Lord could have made us be the only creatures who could sire things—*all* things—beasts and plants. We would have had to screw all day long to keep life going. He could have made us carry our balls in a glass case only to be taken out for the issuance of life. Or we could have shared the one set of balls for whole counties, the rest of us geldings, the one set stored in a diamond-studded box, to be brought out only on special occasions."

"What are you talking about?"

"I'm talking about creation. There are many ways it could have gone. It's all arbitrary, as I said. Your head could have been made out of rock, and your heart out of green grass, to be watered by your veins. It's arbitrary. 'Let me just make a hot orb, the sun, see how many functions it can serve, like a mouth or a hand. Let me aim the sun: too close and you roast, too far and you freeze. It's all sleight of hand. The earth is round, but I'll make it *seem* flat.' It's round, and we're all stuck to the side of it, thinking we're upright, on account of gravity. Well, there *is no upright*. It's obvious, now that we know it. Once we figure out everything, everything will seem obvious. We'll say we've been silly—haven't we?—fumbling around with this and that—bloodletting, flappy flying machines—look how stupid it all is, look how obvious now. Once we figure out *everything*, we'll be back in paradise, sitting with a smile on our faces and not a word in our mouths. When you know everything, it cancels out the need to know anything. It'll be like knowing nothing. We'll be in the land of Eternal Delights, not a care in our hearts, not a hair out of place. What would you need words for? No need, my effervescent little Gypsy."

"Ah, the Brothers Karamazov," our father said. He startled me. He was checking our things above our heads too and was standing over us.

"I don't know what that means," I said, and I looked at my brother.

Our father patted me on the back of the head. I had an excellent head for patting. Simon made himself comfortable opposite his mother and ours. They were smiling warmly, Lili especially.

A minute later, my brother was asleep again in the seat beside me, his grasshopper legs like the gangling woman's, up and folded back beneath him. I wondered if the Lord had considered retractable limbs for when they were not in use.

My mother said to my father, "Are you not worried?"

"Of course I'm worried. But I'm happy to be on my way to something. Something new."

My mother stepped across to sit with my father. She took his hand in hers. "You *are* worried. Please don't be so anxious," she said. "When you're anxious, everybody is anxious."

"People are quite adept at being anxious on their own," he said.

"They get *more* anxious," said Klari, "when you go mad."

"I'll replace your records," he said.

"It's not my records. A child was being born right before our eyes."

"And Judit was dying," he said, and my father covered his face with his hands.

It was the first time I'd seen him cry. My mother cradled my father's head and told him it was all right. It was not his fault. A few minutes later, he was asleep.

I stared again at Attila. He was eager to go forward—he and I, the two musketeers. We'd left plenty behind, but whatever lay ahead, we would overcome. First, though, we needed our rest.

EIGHT

THE BUS STOPPED for a short time at a place called Eisenstadt, jolting my brother and me awake. I saw from the window that the town had an impressive church and railway station but not much more. It looked like a country town in every other way. Carts and wagons rolled in, bringing chickens and milk and cheese. A single fountain stood in the center of the main street. A bronze chubby naked boy peed out water to anyone who wanted some. Today, only the pigeons seemed interested.

We'd had our feet up on the empty bench seat opposite us, but a young gentleman got on and chose to sit opposite us, so my brother and I straightened up. A handful of other passengers got on who looked as if they might have been farmers and who carried bulging sacks. Klari and our parents shared benches facing one another directly across the aisle from us. Our father was asleep, but not the ladies, though they looked hypnotized by the ride.

The gentleman said something to us in German, but when we looked puzzled he switched quickly to Hungarian. He said, "Are you going very far?"

I told him our destination, and he cheered up immensely.

"I'm going to Paris too, finally!" He sounded for a second like one of us, younger than he actually was.

"Have you always wanted to go?" Attila asked.

"I've been there twice, but it has been difficult these past couple of years."

We nodded that we understood, and he looked us over, as we did him. Where had he crossed the border? Had he crossed a minefield, or did he know a better way? The young gentleman had an elegant old-world look about him. He was dressed in a gray three-piece suit with a herringbone pattern, a starched white shirt with French cuffs and a black ascot cap, which he'd removed with a flourish when he greeted us. His hair was thick and as black as the cap. He carried only a black leather briefcase, which he tucked under his arm and kept secure on the seat.

"My name is Peter Halasz." The gentleman offered us his hand.

My brother took it firmly. "We're the Beck brothers," he said, eyeing our companion suspiciously. "Attila and Robert. Robert was named after our grandfather. I was named after the warrior, the ruler."

"Of course."

"The Hun," Attila added, and the man smiled.

The bus bounced along the road. The countryside looked like Hungary's countryside. I would not have guessed we were in another country, except for the odd sign in German, sometimes with Gothic lettering to give it an elevated feel.

The bus slowed slightly for a man riding a white horse on the road. He passed right by our window. "Nice horse," my brother said with authority. "Fine leather saddle."

I wondered if this was our future as cowboys, or were Austrian cowboys different, this not being the Wild West? It also dawned on me that the piece separating the man from his horse was cowhide. The man sat on the crumpled-up hide of a cow. He also wore a deerskin vest and a lambswool hat. What a piling up of animals was here, some living, some dead: horse, cow, cowboy, deer, sheep.

Suddenly I wished I had worn my brown loafers instead of the black lace-ups I was wearing. They were not as nice, but they were roomier. I wondered if I'd left my brown shoes by the front door at home, or underneath my bed, and what the Russians would do with them—throw them out or give them to someone who could enjoy their roomy comfort.

For a short time, Peter Halasz looked out the window, as we were doing. Our mother kept an eye on us and flashed her characteristic smile. It was hard not to smile back at her many times a day.

"What do you do?" Attila asked.

"Guess," Peter Halasz said. The man didn't know what he was getting into.

"You're a lawyer," Attila answered.

"No."

"A professor?"

"No."

"A government official." Peter shook his head no. "A doctor." No. "A chemist." No. "A manager of a department store—the manager of Kossuth's." Peter shook his head. "An army officer, a milliner, a sommelier, a volcanologist, a diplomat, a landlord, a crystal physicist, an engineer, a researcher in fabrics." No, no, no.

"I'm—" Peter Halasz was about to say, but my brother wouldn't let him.

"A haberdasher," Attila said, "an archaeologist, a philatelist, a conductor, a fabulist, a playwright, an opera singer." Attila was red-faced. I dared not guess in case I got it right, nor did our mother, who was listening. "A botanist, a zookeeper, a Communist spy, a film director, an architect, a tool-and-die maker, a millwright, a linguist—"

"I'm a master perfumer," Peter cut in.

"What?" Attila said. He seemed ready to jump out of his seat.

"I am an expert in scents." He pointed to his nose. "I am a master perfumer."

"You are?" Attila and I were impressed and curious. "Of course," Attila said, slapping his own head. He looked at me, then back at our companion. "You're going to Paris!" He slapped himself again. My brother was very hard on himself, and me, and everyone. "A master perfumer," he said. "I've never heard of such a thing."

"You have heard of more professions than I was expecting, but, yes, that is who I am," the gentleman said. "I'm glad we got that out of the way." He pointed to his nose. "I smell heather from a field coming up ahead. I smell paprika. Hay for horses and flax for linen. I smell coffee from a thermos up near the front of the bus. You must smell it too." We both nodded. We studied the strange man's cheerful face. Our mother was doing the same. "I smell some herring, a single serving most likely, not much more. I smell its onions and salt. You might smell it as well." Attila stood up to see if anyone was eating. I did too. There was an old woman hunched over something, an open jar, but it was not easy to tell what was in her jar, which she guarded in her lap. "But the difference," Peter said, "is that two days from now, I will smell the fish oil flowing under her skin, settling there." Our mother shook her head, but she smiled some more. "I smell earth on board," he went on, "black earth, not much, earth drying on boots, farmer's boots almost certainly."

"Yes, but you got on with farmers," Attila said.

Peter closed his eyes. His nose became his eyes. "I can smell the powder of moths' wings."

"What do you mean?" Attila asked. "What does it smell like?" My brother was sitting right up in his seat, all set to hunt for moths.

"Well, it's actually not powder," Peter said. He was not smiling. "It's very fine. It looks like powder. Butterflies have it too, but it's more prominent in moths. The powder consists of tiny scales, cells like your own skin cells. But in moths the scales protect it from water and abrasion, and they are slippery, allowing moths to escape a spider web. I can smell male moths and butterflies better than females, because they can turn on a scent with their scales, to attract a mate. I can smell the scent of sex in insects. You can imagine it in humans."

Attila looked alarmed. He sat back in his seat.

"I can gauge the humidity of the air within a single percentage point," the man said, "the ratio of water particles to air. I smell microbes, spores, pollen, the feces of mites, all the way up the ecosystem to the large mammals—whales. I can tell if water particles have passed through the spout of a whale or fallen unimpeded to the earth. I can tell if droplets of rain have picked up wood smoke, coal smoke, the exhaust of an airplane, whether a bird's wing has changed the droplets' course and sometimes even what kind of bird. And, of course, I know the essence of flowers, their youth, their descent into sweetness before death, the wisdom of their nose.

"When I go to the theater, I smell the bones of bygone sounds in the room, concealed behind that evening's naphthalene, the cedar of fur closets, citrus aftershave, the rose note of Chanel No5—the five-petal *Cistus* rose—which conjures up the boyish flappers of the 1920s, clean and simple. I smell the filaments of wool, whether from upper-highland sheep or the Merino lamb of Vermont's rolling hills and the green valleys between."

"What are you?" said Attila. "You're a freak. You're like a fox or a bloodhound."

"Something like that," Peter Halasz said, "except a fox or a bloodhound can't name what they're smelling, even if they have an instinct for what it might be."

"No, they can't name Chanel No5. But we're cheating," Attila said. "*We* named it Chanel No5. Foxes don't speak human. But then we don't speak fox."

"It's a gift," I said, only because I thought my brother might be insulting Mr. Halasz.

"It's a curse and a gift," Peter said.

"You have a sixth sense," our mother said.

"Not a sixth one, just an outsized version of one of them, outrageously outsized. I'm like a blind man, a deaf mute."

We all stared at the man's nose as if it were an instrument, an artefact—the Magic Nose. He raised his fingers to cover it.

"You're like a superhero," Attila said. "I wish I had that. You're like Superboy. Do you know Superboy?" Peter Halasz nodded. "Do you know Batman? Flash?" Peter nodded. "But you're Noseboy. You could be Noseboy."

"That's why I'm a perfumer. You can see why."

I nodded, but Attila said, "You could do so much more, fight crime, or save people."

"Yes, possibly."

Our mother said, "My sons love Superboy—and Superman—the same boy grown up. Attila especially can't get enough of him. Batman too."

The bus rolled toward Vienna. We were on a bigger road, a highway, not rocking quite as much in our seats.

Attila said, "Can you smell your own heart beating, Mr. Halasz? Can you smell the red flow of it, the iron of it?"

"I don't need to smell it, Attila. I still have other senses." He was blushing now. I'm not sure why. Peter cupped an ear, put a flat hand on his heart.

"You're amazing," Attila said. He was admiring our companion as if we were actually sitting with Superman.

Peter said, "I smell honesty. I smell eagerness, anticipation. I smell charisma, the musk of it. I smell fear. I smell fertility." Attila's eyes widened. "You might smell the coming of rain the way I do," Peter said, "but I smell more. I smell the earth opening itself up to receive it. You might even smell the coming of snow, the crystal cleanness of it, but I smell light. I smell the sun coming up, the coming of blue air and its going, the light reflected from the moon's rocks."

I wanted to ask whether Peter could smell old light, the ancient light arriving from the stars. How old did light have to be before Peter lost its scent? Did the scent of old things blend in with new, young things, so that they might be concealed in that way to preserve them in the earth, or did all things somehow lose their fragrance someday along with their essence? In other words, was it possible to destroy something absolutely the way it was possible to create it, to eradicate a thing by natural or unnatural or supernatural means, by fire or by Hitler or by the Devil? It was too much of a question, I knew, and I was not confident enough to ask it.

NINE

IN VIENNA, WE WERE once again ushered into a great hall, which held hundreds of other Hungarians and hundreds of sleeping cots. The hall was immense. It could have been in a school or a hospital, but it seemed so suited to the purpose of receiving people that I imagined that was what it was for. Vienna must receive many people all the time, was what I imagined. The hall had a vaulted ceiling hulking over it, and its wooden ribs made me think of a fairy tale, though I wasn't sure which one. Certainly, there were no glowheads of any kind up there.

I was impressed with how many of us had made it out. I noticed right away that, after an official looked at some of Peter Halasz's papers, he was allowed to leave. He waved at us from a far door. I'd imagined we would be traveling to Paris together and was crestfallen when I saw that we wouldn't be. I'm sure Attila was too, but he didn't say. It was a new trend: people coming into our lives and leaving just as quickly.

I felt a twinge when I thought about Judit. She seemed even farther away, gone for months, even a year.

Attila told our father all about Noseboy, and Simon asked

if we were sure. "Of course we're sure," Attila said. Lili was nodding too.

"What if he was a fake?" our father asked. "A good one, a smart one, but a fake?"

"What do you mean?" I said.

"What if he was an actor?" said Simon. "Or what if he was insane?"

"I hope not," Attila said.

"You *hope* not. Why?"

"Enough, Simon," our mother said, and she glared at him. He glared back. Her glare was always less effective than Simon's because you could tell she had a smile waiting behind it.

"What if he was a *genius*?" Attila said. "A freak, a genius, like Mozart?"

He looked ready to hit our father, so Simon said, "Well, it's possible, not likely, but possible."

"How likely was Mozart?" Attila asked, and he slapped at the air. My brother was a real slapper and puncher.

This new building was not as welcoming and warm as the convent had been. We were given nice food, rounded off by more nice chocolates, in fact the same Mozart chocolates, but the place felt more regimented. These Austrians seemed to have a job to do, a processing job, not just helping us on our way.

There was a single standout, a boy no older than Attila who wheeled a cart around the room and stopped at every child, giving each of us a package. When he got to us, he said, "PEZ," and then in labored Hungarian told us that PEZ candy was invented in Vienna. He handed Attila and me one each. They were quite wonderful. They were figures from *The*

Wizard of Oz. I got the Tin Man. I held it tightly in case the figure Attila got was an inferior one, like Glinda or Toto. But he got a good one too, luckily: the Scarecrow. Within seconds, we were lifting the heads of the dispensers and pulling the delicious rectangular candies out of their necks. Attila wanted to bang the heads of our figures together, but I put mine away before we could get under way.

Then a girl came by our cots. She was as blond as Attila and dressed in a green-checked gingham dress. The outfit was very tight to accentuate the figure eight of her form, except she was much smaller on top than on the bottom, so the eight configuration was more two plus six than four plus four. She seemed attracted to my brother, floated by too slowly, I thought, wanted to linger extra long, but my brother gave off his blue glare. Some girls didn't know when they were flying too close to the sun. My brother half turned away from her, paying more attention to me, actually. I was worried he would offer her to me, but he didn't. He ignored her outright, and she floated away.

Before we settled in for the day, each of us, including Attila and me, including our parents and grandmother, was ushered into a curtained-off booth and examined by a doctor and nurse—our noses, throats, ears and armpits most thoroughly, and even our nether parts, the parts made for an ingenious combination of functions, as my brother had pointed out. When the doctor was down there, I told him at some length about Peter Halasz, what a chance the doctor had missed not giving the man's nose a good going over, but the doctor didn't even speak Hungarian, and the nurse spoke only a little.

Even worse, these medicals took my blood, had me pee

into a bottle and gave me a shot of vaccine, which, for all they knew (because they didn't ask in any language) I'd already received back in Budapest. I was then taken off for an X-ray of my chest, for which I had to hold in my breath, and which a technician demonstrated rather than told me while they got ready. One of them even turned to take a gulp of coffee to fortify himself.

My brother and I met in the communal bathroom. I saw my brother enter one toilet stall and I ran to get the one beside him. We sounded like the percussion section of an orchestra warming up. It was some time before Attila asked, "How fast does crap travel out of your ass before it lands?"

"How *fast*?" I asked.

"Yes, does it travel as fast as a car backing up to park, or an airplane taking off?" His voice echoed, had quite a clang to it.

"It depends," I said. "Sometimes it exits like a snake on the prowl, and sometimes it's volcanic."

"Right," he said, "so two kilometers per hour versus— bang, an explosion—five hundred kilometers per hour?"

"I would say so, yes," I said.

"How about piss?"

"How fast?"

"Yes, how fast?"

"It's generally faster: sixty or seventy, I'm guessing, sometimes much faster and more violent, but sometimes slower, like people going through a gate, a few at a time. In fact, that goes for the crap too."

"I guess," Attila said, as if he was calculating something. "I guess that's right." Then he said, too quietly, "What a strange thing."

"What is?"

"It's strange," he said again.

"*What* is?"

"This inward movement and outward movement, food in, food out, water in, water out, air in, air out. Turning all this fine food into crap. Turning enticing, fragrant things into stink. You have to wonder why it's necessary. You have to think there must be a lesson in it somehow."

As Attila was talking, I was thinking of Judit in the ground and of the sheep my brother and I had seen, how he said we were their afterlife, but possibly just the afterlife of things— of material things—not of the light from dead stars. I wasn't sure. "It's a cycle," I said. "Everything's a cycle."

"Yes, and the cycle is always the same," my brother said. "We just don't always see it. Different food, same crap; different lives, same ground; different lives—holy lives, poor lives, long lives, short lives, glorious lives and inglorious, farmers, adventurers, homebodies—same bed, same ground. Then you and the crap grow new weeds, new carrots, new food to take in and crap out. Sometimes this cycle is easy to see," he said, "and sometimes it's not. Sometimes it's as subtle as the curvature of the earth. People think they're moving straight, moving straight, moving forward, moving forward, but they're not. The Garden of Eden was flat. No one died. No one crapped. The Garden of Eden was flat. Everything outside of it is round."

We sat, then, in silence. The radiator ticked in the bathroom. It was quite warm. There was a snapping sound like a towel being snapped and then some pattery footsteps.

"It's the same cycle," my brother said, "the same circle, except a little different each time, not a perfect circle, a shade

different each time, an eyelash different, just a little different."
And then he said quietly—I could hardly hear him, as if he was
just working it out—"It's that simple. We are all part of this
cycle: the arc before we are born, the arc after we die and—the
one that looks like the flat bit—the arc that is life."

By the time we were finished, washed, fed and sitting
out front on our new cots, dressed in gowns we'd been given,
which now doubled as nightshirts, my brother and I looked
like swashbucklers who'd been stripped of our capes, swords
and three-cornered hats.

Our father was having words with an official as he held out
our papers, but a larger official (in size and station) stopped by
us, and my father shrank into a meek and sheepish look. With
this look, he would surely inherit the earth.

Across the room, I was sure I spotted the tall woman with
the caper eyes and I jumped up. I searched frantically for
others: the girl with the mouth and the mother, Zoli, David,
Mary, Mrs. Molnar, Andras and Gisela in case they were still
en route, and Father Tamas—where was he going?—on what
rock was he going to build his new church? I was always
expecting something, looking for someone familiar. I did see
the blond girl with the green-checked dress—she was peering
back our way from the distance—but that was all. I wasn't
sure if I should wave but decided not to.

I was on the verge of salting up when Attila noticed
someone, a boy, taller, bigger and darker than Attila was, pass
by our row of cots. "Look!" Attila said, jumping up. "He was
on the swim team that beat us in the relays, from St. Hilda's
School, over in the 8th District, and they beat us in water polo
too, and in both they cheated their heads off. They pulled

little tricks under the surface and brought in a ringer. What's his name?" Attila was punching his own side.

"I don't know," I said.

"What's his goddamn name?" Attila punched the air and even jumped once. The boy was some distance away now. "Hey," Attila yelled, and the boy turned. "Hey!" The boy came over and looked down at my agitated brother's sunny hair. Clearly, he could not make out who my brother was, let alone name him. "You!" my brother barked.

"What?" the boy said, except he was really a man in every respect but age.

"You don't know my name," my idiot brother said, as he poked the man-boy in the chest. "You don't know who I am."

"Do you know my name?" the boy said, poking Attila all the way back down into a sitting position on his cot.

Attila leapt up again into the boy's face. "Do you know what?" He poked him again. "You don't forget my name. I forget *yours*. You got that?"

The boy tried to push my brother back down, but Attila stood firm and glared up furiously into his opponent's face. Our father was now standing too, but the boy moved off.

Within ninety seconds of this incident, my brother was asleep.

Lili, Klari and Simon filed by to kiss us, and the lights soon went out. I didn't want to disturb anyone or trip over anything searching for a window, so I stayed put in the darkness.

I don't know how long I waited, but I heard someone whispering in a cot not far away, and then I heard the unmistakable sound of kissing and cooing. I lifted my head off my pillow, strained in the darkness to see the sloshy, gaspy couple, but to no avail. I tried to imagine what the pair looked like, how old they were, how they managed on these little cots, but in the end I didn't want to know, not even in the morning. It was better to make it up, paint my own picture. I wanted to add it to my bank of secrets. The warm sounds flowed for some time, made me tingle too, until the flow stopped. Not long after, I must have drifted off.

TEN

AS WE WERE BOARDING the bus marked "Paris," an Austrian police officer with a man dressed in a black trench coat and holding a notebook detained our father. Simon urged us to get on in and take our seats, but Attila wouldn't hear of it. He leered at the men and looked ready to lunge, and Klari and Lili had to stand in his way.

Luckily, our father was soon released. He was shaking his head and had a furious look on his face when he joined us.

"What did they want?" Attila said.

"Not now," our mother said.

"They wanted to know about Paul."

"*Our* Paul? Paul *Beck?*" Lili said.

"Yes, Paul Beck."

"Our cousin?" my brother said.

"What did you tell them?" Klari asked.

"I told them what I know—nothing."

"We do know nothing," Lili said.

"That's what I told them."

"Were they both Austrian?" Klari asked.

"No, only the policeman."

Our grandmother looked stricken. I knew right away that the conversation was over.

The bus driver urged us to take our seats. He spoke to us in French. My mother shot him numerous unanswered smiles, and I shot him several less-pronounced ones, but the man was all grim business. He glanced at our papers. These, naturally, didn't excite him either. He was keen to get going.

"What about Paul?" Attila said again, as we worked our way to the back.

"Nothing," Simon said.

"What *about* him?" my brother insisted.

"You know as much about him as I do. Now be quiet." My father looked fierce, which only sometimes made my brother back down. This time it did.

It was my turn. "Was Paul your first cousin?" I asked our father.

"Yes," he said more kindly. "His father, Heinrich, and my father were brothers."

The bus was full, and here the seats did not face one another. We were all arranged in pairs facing forward, the usual way. Attila and I had quite a wrestling match over the window seat, but our mother intervened and sat with Attila so he could have a window. Klari sat with me across the aisle so I could too. Our father sat with a man with an impressive mustache, its ends sharpened, giving it the look of a propeller blade. The man had been a lawyer and judge, and was meeting his nephew in Paris to plan his flight.

Our father told him we were visiting our aunt Hermina, and he told the man who Hermina was, the famous opera singer.

The man knew about her. "She's quite a singer," he said, "but she has not been back in Hungary for some time."

"No," Simon said. "She's been living in Paris for years now."

"Naturally," the man said, strangely. I didn't know what he meant.

I got out my PEZ Tin Man and pulled a candy from its neck. My grandmother didn't want one. I was worried suddenly about the marzipan monkey in my bag. I hoped he had made the long journey without getting deformed.

We drove quite a long way before Attila leaned across the seats and said that we were meeting the Crow Woman.

"Who is that?" I asked back across the women.

"Our aunt Hermina," Attila answered.

Both women jumped in. Lili said, "Don't speak about your grandmother's sister in that way."

"But it's true," my brother said. He held up his fingers like claws. "Her hands are like a crow's talons. She can't straighten her fingers." He was still making his claws, raking the air and, for some reason, hissing like a tiger.

"Is that true, Mamu?" I asked.

My grandmother said her sister had suffered a trauma in the war and was not to be mocked. "Why would you add to her misfortune by making fun of her?" she asked us both.

"What happened to her?" I asked.

"Ask *them*," my brother said.

"Attila, please," said Lili.

My brother lunged at her. "I feel we have a right to know, now that we are men, or at least I am. You said you'd tell me what happened once I was ready to hear about it."

Our father, in his seat in front of us, turned his head. "You'll never be ready," he said.

"Simon, why must you say such things about your bright sons?"

"They're not that bright."

"They're very bright."

"Brightness is not the point, in any case," he said. "You know what I'm saying."

"I don't know what you're saying," I said. I turned to our grandmother. "Why can't we know?"

"News like that can wait. Trust me, my angel."

"But I can't wait," Attila said.

"You will wait," Klari said. "Don't make fun of your great-aunt, especially since you know she suffered. Hermina doesn't like people to know about her degradation. She has a right to keep these matters to herself."

"Mother," my brother said, "I need your help."

"Not this time," she said. She was not smiling, and because Lili's smile was so true and natural, its disappearance was like the cancellation of happiness.

Attila huffed and turned toward his window but was back looking at us a second later. "What if I turned into a mute?" he said. "There he was. It happened on the bus to France. He was never heard from after that."

He made the claw again, raking the air and hissing like a tiger. Then he turned back to his window. There was a lot to be said for being Attila. I was sick now, sick and sorry. What had happened to our cousin Paul? What had happened to our aunt Hermina? Why had so many members of our family been marked in this way, made to suffer? And those were the lucky ones, the ones who'd survived. At that moment, I could not look out my window at my half of the world the way Attila was looking at his half. If my window had served up the Eiffel Tower or plopped down a pyramid, if it had dangled Nefertiti's bust out in front of it and said, "Look what I can do—I can soften the face of the pharaoh's wife and bring her back to life right before your eyes," I could not have cared, not when yet another person was being inducted into my Hall of Horrors.

My brother had met Hermina just once, and I had known her only through glamorous photographs, especially one of her dressed as Nero's bride, Poppea, gracing the cover of a Hungarian National Opera program. Attila had seen that opera with our grandmother, but I hadn't. Klari was worried that I was too young. How well did she know each of us?

I said to my grandmother, "Does Aunt Hermina still sing?"

"Oh, yes, she sings," Klari said. "She might even sing for you. She loves baroque. She might sing some Handel or Bach. Do you remember the songs the nuns were singing, from *Juditha triumphans*?" I nodded yes. "Those were baroque too. Vivaldi."

I told our grandmother about the statue graveyard Attila had taken me to. She had never seen it.

"We saw the Swedish man there, at the graveyard. We saw Raoul Wallenberg."

"What?" she asked. Our mother had heard me too, even our father and the man with the propeller mustache.

"I don't mean the man. I mean the monument."

"Oh." Klari put a hand on her heart. Lili smiled.

I wanted to know, specifically, what Raoul Wallenberg had done for us.

"Quite a bit," Klari said. "We wouldn't be on this bus if not for him."

"And my cousin Paul," our father said.

"Not now," said Klari.

"Tell us about Paul," Attila said right away.

"He's—" Simon began.

"Not now!" our grandmother insisted and stamped her foot.

Even Attila backed off. "Then when?" he asked.

"Your poor grandfather would not have wanted you ever to know."

"Robert?" I said.

"Yes, my Robert. Dear Robert, your namesake, or you are his namesake." She sighed. "Another time," she said. "I promise."

A while later, Lili took my brother and me to the back, to the water closet, and when we returned Attila put his head down on our mother's lap and went straight to sleep. I wondered, suddenly, if the statue of Mor Jokai would still be allowed to watch over our street back home, how long he would last. Would he outlast the street? I strained to hear love sounds as I had back in the dormitory in Vienna, but the bus's motor was too loud, even if there were any.

Except for our driver and me, everyone on the bus was having quite a snooze, sitting straight up or lying on someone's lap or leaning against the side, their head rattling against the window. The driver himself must have been fighting off sleep.

The moon was full and outlined the shape of things, like a night artist. I wondered why the moon had to be round. What if it were square to line up with windows? It would be like a Picasso I'd seen at the National Gallery—a painting of lovers, all their features raked to the front, sitting under the bright glowing square. The only risk I could see was that if the moon were square it might mock the sun rather than doing the important job of reflecting its light.

ELEVEN

WE WERE ALL ROUSED by a jolt. A shoe and a sack fell off the rack above our heads. A bottle rolled toward the front and shattered on something. My tired eyes struggled to interpret the vinegary French dawn. My father and the man with the propeller mustache were looking coldly at each other, like strangers who'd suddenly found themselves together. My mother had ripe pears in her bag, and she offered each of us one, including the propeller man, but the man declined. The bus kept rolling into the thin light.

France.

The countryside seemed too bashful to be France, to be the land of Napoleon and Louis XIV and the Three Musketeers. There wasn't much to it: some rocks and fields, a bridge over a creek, some wooden houses with small vineyards out the back, a weak sun.

My pear was juicy and sweet. I finished mine first, before Attila, and he knew it, but he acted as though he didn't notice. Attila hung his hands over the seat in front, our father's seat, and said to him, "Can I hear now about Raoul Wallenberg and Paul Beck?"

Our father didn't answer him. Our mother and grandmother looked straight ahead.

"The war was over in Hungary," Attila said. "Can you at least tell me why the Russians took Raoul Wallenberg?"

The man with the propeller mustache, the former judge, half turned in his seat and said, "The Russians removed Wallenberg because he was a menace."

"What did you say?" our father asked.

"The Swede was an interloper. He had no business in Hungary."

"Are you saying you did not agree with what he was doing?"

"I believe in law and order," the man said.

"You mean the law of the Germans, the deportations, the killings."

"The Germans were the allies of the Hungarians, or have you forgotten? We were never officially the enemy of Germany. The war did not come to Hungary for that reason until 1944. It was the price we had to pay for five years of peace."

Attila was standing now, hovering over the men from behind.

"Wallenberg tried to impede the Germans' removal of people of impure blood," the judge said. "Cosmopolitans. Gypsies. Jews. Swedes, or *manufactured* Swedes, I should say."

"The Germans were removing Hungarian nationals," our father said. "I am a Hungarian national, an ex-patriot, a refugee. As are you. As are we all on this bus."

The man said, "That's a matter of opinion," and he turned to the window.

My brother was huffing right into the man's hair. Our mother had a pleading look on her face. She reached over to put a hand on our father's shoulder. Her look said, "Enough. Please, leave it alone."

But Simon said to the man's back, "I really am sorry we're exporting these feelings to foreign lands. I guess we weren't satisfied poisoning our own nation."

The man turned back toward him. Others on the bus could hear the two men now. "Just as I thought," the judge said. "By not finishing their work, the Germans have unleashed a species twice as noxious as the original. Survivors who have been wronged. Righteous whiners. Seekers of justice all over the planet. Hounding the rest of us to an early grave. Wanting—nay, *needing*—to make us repent. I knew it would happen. I knew it instantly."

The man got to his feet.

"By 'the rest of us,' do you mean those of pure blood?" Simon asked. Both men were standing in the aisle now.

"That's exactly what I mean. It is what *you're* now exporting to foreign lands. Your impure selves. Your righteousness. Your victimhood. It's what we'll hear until the end of time. Prattle, prattle, prattle, until we're ready to do anything, give you anything, to make you stop." The man made a prattling mouth out of his hand, flapping it in our father's face. "Everyone will go on hating Jews. You might succeed in driving the hatred underground. People will appear to like you. People will want to side with what is right and just. But even the people who appear to like you won't. And they'll look for the first excuse to let you know it."

Attila lunged at the propeller man's neck, nearly knocking over our mother in the process, but our father stood in his way, shoved Attila back down.

"Do you see what I mean?" the judge said. "Cage your hellcat."

Simon lifted the judge by the collar until the man's feet left the floor of the bus. A woman called out—screamed, actually. It was the woman with the dangly pearl earrings and matching necklace. The driver slowed down the vehicle and shouted something over his shoulder at our father. He even blasted his horn twice.

Simon let the judge down. The man had a smirk on his face. His propeller mustache was as crisp as ever, its blades turned up. "Just as I predicted," the man said. "Ha!"

Then out of nowhere, as if it had been a concealed weapon, my father's fist shot up, a Superman fist, straight up into the man's chin.

There was a terrible clacking sound, and then the jaw unhinged and the man fell back to the floor with a thud. The woman in pearls called out again. I could see blood at the side of the judge's mouth. The bus swerved over to the side of the road.

Another woman tended to the man. "Is he dead?" my brother asked. The woman shook her head. She bent down to feel the man's breath, hear his chest.

"What did you do?" Lili said to Simon.

"I shut him up," Simon said.

The driver came back toward us. "Drive!" our father said in Hungarian. "Drive!" He held up his iron fist. *"Paris!"*

he added with a French accent. The word, the way he said it, didn't seem to go with the fist.

The driver stopped, turned and timidly resumed his place at the front.

Our father was still standing over the fallen man when he said to Attila, "Now, what was it you wanted to know?"

"Simon!" Lili shouted. "Sit down. We're in enough trouble."

Our father was still huffy. I could see his heart pounding through his shirt.

"We're not in any kind of trouble," he said, half out of breath. "We're all equals now. We're refugees. If the man complains, I'll say he attacked me."

"He won't complain for some time," the woman with the pearls said. She was tying up the judge's jaw with a scarf. The man moaned but stayed put.

We were all agitated. The mood of the whole bus had changed. My brother and I were both sitting in the aisle seats now, beside each other. My grandmother gripped my hand. Attila looked hot and pink.

Our father was sitting again, saying nothing, staring out into the gray-complected French morning.

"Aren't we Hungarian?" I asked my brother.

"We're not anything."

"Aren't we Hungarian until we become something else? What did the man mean?"

"Dad should have finished the bastard off. I would have stepped on his neck once he was down, crushed it into guts and powder."

"Why did we need special protection from Raoul Wallenberg and Paul Beck?" I asked. "Why didn't other Hungarians need special protection?"

"You need to leave it alone now," our mother said, "both of you, I beg you."

I joined my father, and he took my hand and moved over to where the judge had sat. We both spent a long while staring at the silver sun, the imposter sun.

In Paris, Simon and Attila helped carry the man out. They laid him down on a bench. Our father stared the driver down and the man loped away, busying himself with whatever luggage the passengers had stored.

Our father checked on the judge again, still lying on the bench, his eyes open. One of his propeller blades was turned downward now, giving the man half a frown. He looked alarmed when our father asked him how he felt. The judge reached up to feel his jaw. Then he waved our father away. When Klari tried, he waved her away too. "Go," he was telling all of us with a violent wave. "Go."

TWELVE

WE TOOK A TAXI from the bus station to the 16th arrondissement, as Klari called it. The driver wanted to be paid in advance and would not accept Hungarian currency, no matter how much we offered, so our grandmother gave him the pinky ring with the turquoise stone she'd been wearing. She said she didn't like it much anyway, though I'd never seen her without it on.

When we pulled up in front of Hermina's home, the whole street rumbled beneath our wheels. It was as if an entire opera house had been squeezed into our aunt's white townhouse. We had to ring the doorbell repeatedly. No one answered until there was a lull in the aria.

Then the door opened, and there stood Hermina, every bit as glamorous as Nero's Poppea about to receive the crown. Hermina was a thinner, younger, taller version of her sister, our grandmother, but she had the same caramel eyes, the same auburn hair, if highlighted with strands of gold and whipped up onto her head in weaves and folds.

But the music here was gigantic, big as a canyon.

Simon pushed past his aunt, shouting, "You're disturbing the peace."

Hermina spoke back but didn't shout. "Darling, Handel is incapable of disturbing the peace."

Our father went searching for the phonograph and switched it off. As we stood in the ripe quiet, Aunt Hermina hummed the last notes of the aria.

"Did you like what you heard, my darling?" she asked my brother.

He shrugged. "If you like a lightning bolt to the ear," he said.

Of all the people I had met in my 9.8 years, Attila was the only one who had a single self, no more. He didn't have a self that was kind and polite in the company of some people such that they could remark, "What a kind and polite fellow," and a self that was wicked in the company of other people. He was kind and polite and wicked as the circumstances dictated.

"Where is Andras?" Hermina asked. "Where's Judit?"

Klari took her sister's face in her hands and told her what had become of Judit, and Andras and little Gisela. The sisters put their foreheads together and began to sob. Lili joined them, and the three swayed together and cried but said nothing more.

I was going to join the huddle with the women but wanted to see what the men would do first. They stayed where they stood and both hung their heads, so I hung my head too. I gulped repeatedly in an effort to hold back my own tears.

It seemed like a very long time before my brother said, "Our father beat up a man on the bus."

"He did what?" Hermina asked, pulling away from Klari and Lili.

"Please, darling, let's not talk about it just yet," Klari said, as she kissed her sister again.

We left our bags and stepped into Hermina's salon, which was like stepping into a French pastry, all billowy with creams and pallors, marzipan and peach. There was nothing crisp about the place. It was all soft lines and colors. An ivory grand piano sat poised in a tall bay window like an albino alligator with its jaw open wide. A portrait in oil of Hermina in her young years, her warm eyes gazing out over the room, hung above a plush blond sofa. On the opposite wall hung a painting of a summerhouse with two children standing on the grass out front. The children had no faces. "It's called *Garden with Trees*," Hermina told me as I gazed at the picture. "Do you like it?"

I nodded yes. I did like it, though I didn't know how I would fill in the faces.

Hermina herself was dressed in a cream floral gown that went with the room, as well as blush-pink gloves. She smoothed my hair at the back with the warm cup of her hand. "My little dark beauty," she said with a honeyed voice. Now she cupped my face in the bowl of her gloved hands. "So this is the one," she said, looking at Klari. What about the golden beauty, I wanted to know? What about Attila? "My dark beauty," she said again, as she raised my face to the light and kissed me straight on the lips, sending a charge down my spine to my tail. She kissed my brother in the same way, but she was moving on, directing all movement in the room, inviting everyone to sit, get comfortable. Her housekeeper, Babette, brought in a tray laden with croissants, petits fours and apricot preserve, tea, coffee, as well as cocoa specially made for my brother and me. Our parents and grandmother asked for a few minutes to sort out our things and left the room.

Babette was young and blond and brown-eyed. She smiled radiantly. I could easily see a smiling duel lining up between Babette and our mother. She reminded me a bit of Sister Heidi, but Babette did not conceal her beauty in the way of nuns. She lingered an extra moment, fluffing up a cushion as my brother and I gawked at her.

Attila and I shared a large ottoman and were eating and drinking heartily as our great-aunt watched us. She was childless and a widow now. I found out later that Uncle Ede had retired to this house after teaching medicine at the university, but then died quietly one morning behind his newspaper.

"You never had children," my brother said.

"No," said Hermina.

"You couldn't?"

"We could, I think."

"So why didn't you?" Attila asked.

Hermina sighed. "I'd have been a bad mother," she said. "I'd have been a bad mother even if I'd given birth to myself."

She chuckled, but we both stared at her in horror. She looked away. My brother took a bite of pastry, nudged me with his elbow, pointed with his face at Hermina's hands, wanting me to take note of the claws.

"Aunt Hermina," my brother said, "what happened to your hands?"

She said gently, "Can we save our dark tales for a dark afternoon, when we're locked up in here?"

Attila finished what was in his mouth before saying to our aunt, "I saw you in the opera in Budapest."

"I know, darling. I knew you were there. I was very glad. Did you like the opera? It was Monteverdi's masterpiece *L'incoronazione di Poppea. The Coronation of Poppea.*"

"I liked one song," Attila said. He licked jam from the corner of his mouth.

"Just one?" she asked, chuckling.

"Yes, and I've been meaning to ask you a series of questions ever since."

"A *series?*" she said, and laughed again. "Let's see if we have answers this time." She sat up in her white chair and clasped her gloved hands together in her lap.

Attila said, "I read the program carefully, Aunt Hermina. I read it straight through at home. You played Poppea, with Mr. Bruno Holtz playing Nero." She nodded and smiled. "Anyway," he said, "I thought I was going to die a slow, writhing death." Aunt Hermina sat as still as her painted self. "The opera was endless," my brother said. "Until that last song. When stupid Nero is crowning his Poppea, his second wife, I guess."

She nodded. Her warm eyes widened. I looked at her lips, with which she had kissed mine.

Attila said, "For me, it was the first true moment, the first one, that didn't feel fake."

"Fake?"

"Yes. It was hard to believe a pretty girl like you could love that big fat Nero, but then suddenly I did believe it. I believed

Nero loved you and was giving you a crown to prove it. Until then, he thought too much, and he sang out every boring thought, really talk-singing rather than just talking. Maybe Monteverdi should just have written a play, I kept thinking, a boring one, to be sure, but adding musical notes didn't make it more interesting."

"And then there was the song," Aunt Hermina repeated eagerly.

"Yes, then came that song. For me, it was the one single real moment, as I said. The two of you sang 'Pur ti miro.' My grandmother helped me later with the words. 'I gaze at you. I delight in you.' The lovebirds finally talk to each other sincerely: *'Pur ti miro, pur ti godo, pur ti stringo, pur t'annodo.'*"

Attila closed his eyes dramatically. He put his hand on his heart. "'I adore you,' Poppea is saying, and he is saying it back, 'I hold you. I want you. I *enchain* you.'"

"But, darling," Hermina said. "Remember, he is crowning her. There is irony there."

Attila opened his eyes. "Irony?"

"Yes, he's—"

"Not in the song," my brother interrupted. "The song is about real love."

"Yes, real love. Real love and real power."

Attila looked startled.

Hermina said, "The opera is called *The Coronation of Poppea*. You were perhaps too young to appreciate what went before it."

"But you were the one who sang it for me," Attila said, "you and Bruno. I'm not Bruno or Nero. I won't ever be Nero, I'm thinking, I'm hoping. I was Romeo that day, maybe, after all that thinking out loud of the opera. For me, it was Romeo and Juliet who'd walked out into the wrong opera, and you made it that way. Your voice. Yours and Bruno's."

Hermina raised a gloved hand to her throat.

"The style and feeling of that final song," my brother said, "didn't even match the songs that went before it. It was like someone else had dreamt it up and written it."

"Maybe it was another composer," our great-aunt said good-naturedly.

"Yes," Attila said. He jumped up off the ottoman. "What if it was?"

She didn't seem to think the question needed an answer, but my brother was waiting for one. He looked ready to lunge.

"What if it was what?" Hermina said.

"Another composer. It was a long time ago."

"The seventeenth century."

"Yes, the seventeenth century."

"You've done some research," our aunt said.

"Claudio Monteverdi had students," Attila said. "It was someone young, a young man, probably, and he was studying with the master, and maybe one day the student presented the master with a little tune he had composed, a song inspired, maybe, by the master himself. He wanted the master to approve of his work. Can you see it? Can you see what I'm saying?"

Hermina nodded.

"The boy, maybe my age, or maybe a little older, not much older, might have said to the composer, 'It's called "Pur ti miro."' Claudio looks over the pages of music—it's maybe written out a couple of times by the boy to make sure it's extra neat—the master glances at the sheets and falls into the music—he reads music very well, naturally—as the student stands in front of him, the younger man standing while the older man is sitting. He looks up at the boy, who is not wearing a wig the way the master is. Claudio Monteverdi knows what he is holding, what a good thing it is for his opera, one of the first operas ever made, after all. He says to his pupil, 'Let me think about it. I'll look it over again. Let me just give it a second look.' And he rubs his chin, most likely, almost certainly, and pulls on his sharp beard for effect. Can you see it?"

"Yes, I can," Hermina said warmly.

"The pupil grins and bows and raises his hands as if in prayer to his own god, the composer, the father of opera, and backs out of the room, tiptoes out, and never comes back. Somehow, he disappears. He never comes back to find out what's happened to his song. Just like that." Attila snapped his fingers. "But not his song. Not his lovely song. His song moves to the top of the opera. And it stays there at the finale. Until now. Waiting for you to sing it with Bruno and for me to hear it."

"Sometimes these things drop from heaven, quite by accident," Hermina said. "Sometimes an angel comes through the window and sits by the composer until he has his song."

"Yes, a beautiful song could come from heaven," my brother said. "Maybe an angel carries it to Earth, comes in through the composer's window, as you're saying. My only question is, which composer did the angel visit? And did the angel visit one composer while the Devil visited the other?"

I shuddered. I felt the heat rising in my neck. If I could have, I would have flipped open my Tin Man to eat a PEZ. I reached instead for a plump chocolate. It was very, very good, molten sweet. It flowed brownly down my throat.

This was also who my brother was: one day he was singing an aria by Tarzan, the next he was questioning an aria by Claudio Monteverdi. He was a tricky customer. No one could tell him he could not be a cowboy one day and an opera critic the next, so he tried his hand at everything. He must have got this quality from our father, who could have been a lawyer one day and a tool-and-die maker the next, depending on what his circumstances allowed, and his circumstances allowed much less in the big war just past.

Our aunt was staring at my brother. "What an imagination you have, you dear boy," she said. "But let me ask you. What if Monteverdi did compose 'Pur ti miro'? Why would you take it away from him?"

"It doesn't seem to fit—for me, I mean. That's all. It doesn't fit. So I'm just saying."

"Does that matter?" she asked. "It doesn't matter, dear. What matters is that we have the song. Can't we just be happy for the song?"

Attila moved close to our aunt. She looked a little alarmed. She was pinned to her seat. "But it bothers me," he said.

"What does?"

"Truth. Doesn't truth matter?"

"It does," Hermina said, "but the kind of truth you're looking for relies more on a feeling, a hunch, rather than on proof."

My brother was leaning over our aunt like a police inspector. "Don't most investigations begin with a hunch?" he asked. He was rubbing his chin the way Claudio must have.

"A hunch lives in the world of instinct and belief, not proof," Hermina said. "You said the song that touched you suited *Romeo and Juliet*. That beautiful play has its own creator, not Monteverdi and not his student, and possibly not even Shakespeare. Yet we have the expression of love for all the ages. You loved the song, my darling. Love is its own truth. Isn't it?"

Attila considered the point. He looked at Hermina without responding. She said, "In the end, my dear, the person hardly matters. The person lies down in the earth. No one knows where Mozart is buried, but it doesn't really matter. He has left his music above ground to frolic among us. The labels don't matter. They never do. It's what you do in the name of the labels that matters. Sometimes that is good and sometimes it is not." She looked down at her gloved hands.

My brother sat back down again beside me. He was glowing like a glowhead.

Hermina stroked the column of her neck again with her gloved, blush-colored hand. I thought she might have been blushing herself. "What an imagination you have, my dear. Do angels visit you?"

"Angels and devils," my brother said, very satisfied with himself.

I ate another chocolate.

Our aunt reached for a mother-of-pearl box beside her on the table. An ivory swan perched on its lid. She opened the box and released the music trapped inside. "It's *Swan Lake*," she said. It was a snuffbox. Using a snuff spoon, she lifted some to her nose and breathed in. "Snuff?" she said to us.

"Sure," said my brother. He took a wad in his fingers and snorted it hard, all the way up into his brain.

And the inquiry didn't end there. Over a glittering dinner that evening in a dining room with windows as tall as masts, our father asked Hermina why she was staying in Paris still. We were having veal goulash with dumplings, to remind us of home. Babette had served it from a porcelain tureen. She'd smiled at each of us as she did so. My brother and I followed her every move. Babette knew we were admiring her but didn't break her stride. When she set down the tureen between us and stepped back, my brother whispered to me, "If only I had the gift of that Noseboy on the bus, just to interpret these joyous scents."

Babette was blushing as if she knew what we were saying. The pink suited her blond face. My brother and I kept staring, but she withdrew, aiming her warm blush away from us.

"Why don't you come with us across the ocean, move away with us," Simon said again to his aunt. "It seems like the best plan, considering."

Hermina chewed and chewed and chewed while we watched and waited for her mouth to come to a stop. The Baby Etiquette Advisor sitting straight up inside of me realized, long after the Creator of the Universe would have realized, that when tripling and quadrupling the tasks of a single body part, in this case the mouth, it would have been unseemly for that body part to perform several of its assigned tasks simultaneously. The Creator would have foreseen an additional function for each part: that it taught patience and forbearance. Yes, you could chew and speak at the same time—yes, you could speak and kiss at the same time—or speak and kiss and chew—but it was better to wait through one function before starting another, the better to enjoy the full value of each before enjoying the value of the next.

Finally, Hermina said, "I can't start again somewhere else. My Ede and I started again here. I can't go back to Hungary or ahead across the ocean. This, for me, is as good as it gets. My Ede is buried here, in Passy. I visit him and chat with him. Sometimes, if I have more to say to him than usual, I set a place for him at this table. I go to concerts and galleries and museums. I sing here and watch others sing and dance. I love the culture that has taken all these centuries to plant and grow here. It has a special quality."

"Yes, culture," Simon said. He said it as if it were a bad thing.

"Yes, culture," Hermina repeated, turning up the heat in her voice.

"You are like my mother. You believe culture is restricted to a few special places."

"No, not restricted, but it doesn't spring up just anywhere like a mushroom. It takes centuries to cultivate, as I have said. You are going where—the New World, New York, *Canada*? I sang in Canada once. I sang in Montreal. What is the formula there in Canada—draw everyone together into a huddle and then refrigerate? It's a place to start only. A nice, clean, fresh place, to be sure, but a place to start. I still have hope for Europe, for France."

Klari blew out a breath and sat back.

Simon took quite a scoop of dumplings into his mouth. He was a fast eater at the best of times, but now he wanted to add drama, so he chewed and chewed and chewed the way Hermina had.

Finally, he said, "So we are the cultivated ones on this side of the planet—the supremely cultivated."

Hermina set down her mighty fork and knife. She was at the head of the table, looking regal in a powder-green evening gown with her hair up. "In a word, yes, some of us are," she said. "It's never all of us. But it takes centuries to grow a Handel or Beethoven. Millennia. Think of the achievements of Europeans, of Europe."

"I do," Simon said, "but I think achievement is overrated. We're on the rebound from achievement—on the run from it. One day you're living in a golden tower, the next it topples. One day you're in your fragrant garden, the next you're covering your disfigured hands."

"Simon!" Klari shouted.

"It's all right, Klari," Hermina said, taking a breath but looking hard at my father. "Do you think Handel and Beethoven and Goethe are overrated?" she asked.

My father did not put down his cutlery. That would have been going too far. He said, "No, but only because they achieved without ever considering that that was what they were doing. Yes, Handel and Beethoven, and Goethe and Schiller. The Germans were the most cultivated people on earth, weren't they, the highest achievers."

No one spoke. Now our mother sat back. Attila's cheek was bulging with food, but his eyes were alive with questions, glittering in the lights of the room. He was bobbing back and forth in his chair.

Our father said, "The most cultivated culture we have ever

known, the Germans. Tell us what happened to you there, in the land of Handel?"

Klari said, "Simon, why are you tormenting my sister? Why do the Beck boys always torment my sister?" My face burned.

"Please," Hermina said. She held up her gloved hand, forest green on this occasion. "I haven't had such lively conversation around this table since my Ede took his leave. I'm glad to have the dazzling Beck boys with me, and, of course, the Beck girls." She turned back to her nephew. "I'm not moving to Germany either, my dear," she said. "But the Germans have now to go through their cycle of self-hatred after loving themselves too much, needing to hate others to sustain their delusion. Hubris. It will do us all in. It does in whole nations, whole empires."

"Hubris. Is that what it was? Is that all it was?"

Hermina shrugged.

"Yet Germany remains with us," Simon said. "You love your Handel, do you not?"

Our mother rolled her eyes.

"I love him more than I care to admit," said Hermina. "But Handel belongs to all of humanity, not just Germany."

"Certainly," my father said, "but the same culture that produced Handel also produced Hitler. You can't have one without the other. You can't have Handel without Hitler."

"No, you can't have Handel without Hitler. That is my point. You are making my point for me. You need that darkness to brighten the light. Handel's beauty has a darkness at its core, a sweet, incurable sadness." We were all staring at our aunt. "That was his secret," she said. "We all have secrets, don't we?" She looked first at our father, then at the two other women, stopping at her sister.

"Please, Hermi," our grandmother said.

"What's wrong with that? I once had white, supple hands, and now they are forever clothed." She held up her hands to the chandelier. "What is your secret, boys?" She looked good-naturedly at each of us. I was blushing hotly, though I was not sure what secret I had been concealing. "What about it, Simon?" Now our father blushed. "Lili? Klari?"

"Why are you tormenting *us* now?" Klari said. "What is the matter with this family?"

"What?" Attila said. "What is Aunt Hermina saying?"

"We all have our dingy badges of shame we hide away somewhere. We all have our shameful deeds to forget."

"And what shameful deed might that be in our case?" Simon said. "Surviving? Surviving one war only to welcome the next one? Is that our evil deed? Fleeing our hostile country? Is that it?"

"I didn't say *evil*."

"Shameful, then."

"Have you heard from Paul lately?" she asked.

"Hermina!" Klari said, getting up from the table.

Our father said, "I'm not sure what this has to do with us, Aunt Hermina."

"What about him?" Attila asked. "Paul Beck? What about him? What happened with him? The last time I asked, my father ended up breaking a man's jaw."

"The man on the bus?" Hermina asked.

"We are a family of many cousins," our grandmother said. "Happy cousins—some less happy than others. It's like culture, isn't it?" she said to her sister. "Some have it, but most don't. Even Hitler had taste in music. He had his Wagner and his Beethoven. He loved Beethoven. He loved the Ninth, the 'Ode to Joy.'"

"Why are you changing the subject, Mother?" Simon asked.

Klari looked directly at me. "We're a family of cousins, close cousins. I married my cousin, your grandfather Robert, my dear Robert. So I didn't have to change my name. Ha!"

Simon said, "My cousin Paul—"

"*Don't*, Simon," our mother said.

Our father said, "We have nothing to be ashamed of. We did nothing wrong. My father—"

"You could have stopped it, all of you," Hermina said. She looked at my parents, my grandmother. "Everyone stood by. You should have stopped it."

"Stopped *what*?" Attila asked.

"Enough," Klari said. "Thank you, Hermi, truly."

Everyone was getting up, ready to abandon dinner before dessert.

"What could we have stopped?"

Hermina had a smirk on her face I hadn't seen earlier, as dark as Handel's, possibly, maybe darker.

I stayed for a dessert of chestnut puree with whipped cream but was alone at the table when Babette brought me cocoa too. She smiled as if there was nothing amiss in the festive dining room. She seemed to be admiring me, and I admired her back. Everything smelled of cream—warm cream. And also chestnuts.

THIRTEEN

ATTILA AND I WERE to sleep in the library. We each had a day-bed situated beneath bulging bookcases mounted on the wall.

"What were they talking about?" I asked my brother.

"I'm not sure, but we're going to find out. Give me a day, my ever-curious darling."

Hermina came in to see that we were settled. She said, "I have something for each of you." She was holding a leather-covered slipcase with two books tucked into it. "I picked them out especially for you. They're your first books in English. We can start to read them together, if you want to try. I don't speak English the way Paul did, but I do speak some, and read some."

She pulled the first book out. "They're both by Mark Twain, a prescient writer who lived in the New World, where you're headed." She gave it to my brother. It was *The Adventures of Tom Sawyer*.

She then gave me mine, and I tried to sound out the title: "*Udventoors of Hoockleberry Feenn.*"

Our great-aunt smiled at me and kissed me on the forehead.

She was followed by Klari, who did the same, but on this night our mother didn't come in. Klari said she might later. I could hear her talking heatedly with our father.

I wondered who would get to keep the nice leather case for the two books. Wouldn't the books have to stay together when they weren't being read?

Once we switched off the lights I could think of nothing but the wall of books above me, the voices entombed in the pages, the bulge of them. Were they wondering if I could hear them all? Were they listening to one another? What would happen if each book were given its own room, like the room it was written in? What a palace you'd need to house them all!

I strained to listen to my brother's breathing, but he was as quiet as could be. Given what a warrior he was, I was surprised that Attila could surrender himself to anything so abruptly.

I thought I heard the sound of running water and someone humming, a woman, certainly, but very faint. I crept out of my room into the corridor and saw a light at the far end to guide me, but just a crack of light, standing on the wall. I continued toward it as quietly as I could on bare feet over the prickly warmth of the carpet. I got close enough to the creamy beam of light to hear it, the soft siren sound of it. My childish heart could not keep its beat, thought it was in a marching band. The floor creaked once, but the water and the siren sound continued, so I did too. When I got there, I held my breath as I peered in. What I saw could have cured blindness.

Babette was inside. She was drawing a bath. She barely looked real to me. Her form was soft and white. She could have been a sylph living in a myth or a fairy tale. Her robe slipped off her shoulders, even the shadows softened by her skin. I was not sure I was breathing, but my timpani heart took all the hungry air it needed, making me want to flee, making me want to faint.

And then she saw me. She looked over her white shoulder and saw me. She didn't gasp, didn't hide herself, or even turn away, but smiled her creamy smile. I was the one who gasped, who ducked into the shadows and dashed back to my room with a terrible clamor.

I found my bed below the bulging bookcase, tucked myself into it, tried to catch a single deep breath, but my heart kept pounding for several minutes still, anticipating something, hoping Babette might visit, but possibly not, better not.

And then it started to rain, quietly at first, but then harder, louder. It rained tables and chairs, but strangely no thunder or lightning. It felt warm and dry in this bed in our aunt's townhouse in Paris. I found myself hoping the man we'd left on the bench at the bus station had made it inside.

That first night in Paris, I dreamt about Gerbeaud. I was alone and walking through rain, but I could see Gerbeaud clearly ahead through the wet light. I rushed toward it, skidding sometimes on the cobblestones of Vorosmarty Square.

But then a single skid winged me all the way to the banks of the Danube, where all five bridges were down, even the Liberty, even the Chain Bridge! Only its central pillar punched itself out of the water. What had the Russians done? Or was it the Germans, the Ottomans, the Avars, the hordes? The destruction looked bigger even than war. It looked biblical. It looked like a decree: I will smite you down. I will divide Buda from Pest, ever to remain so.

Small boats chugged between Buda and Pest. On the other

side, wings of buildings were down, if the building remained standing at all. The Gellert Hotel's grand entrance had sagged into its thermal baths below. The mighty flagpole that stood upon its promontory in front of the National Gallery flew no flag, though I could still see the great bronze eagle perched on its stone mount, getting set to take flight, always poised in this same way but never managing to lift itself up. A row of elegant white townhouses lay on its back down the slope of the green hill, the vertebrae disconnected from the caps and spines.

I stood in the drizzle and thought I spotted my friend Zoli on the other side. I tried to call out to him, but I had lost my voice to the dampness. Where was he headed? He lived on this side, in Pest. Who was he running from?

A single motorboat sat throbbing in its slip below me. The riverbank under my feet trembled. I turned toward Gresham Palace, one of its shoulders damaged by a bomb. Russian soldiers floated in and out of its grand doors and even above them—in and out of its windows—but not fluttering, strictly floating. These were not fluttering things. I had to get back to Gerbeaud Café. I went the long way around Gresham Palace.

My heart flapped in its cage. I took off at full speed as if I were being chased.

I could not see the banner of Papa Stalin draped down over Kossuth's Department Store. The store was gone, the building, the corner it stood on. But up ahead, the beacon still stood, waiting for my return, and it was guarded, yes, guarded, by—what?—a Russian soldier, the *same* Russian soldier with the bushel of beard who'd given me the *matryoshka* doll. He glanced at me as if he'd been expecting me and waved me on, not knowing what to say, I guess, not knowing how. But there was no one entering Gerbeaud or leaving it, no one in sight, and it was dark inside—in the middle of the afternoon.

I moved close to the window, lifted my hand to shelter my eyes from the rain. The monkey's golden cage still gleamed in the center of the café, even with the lights out, but its occupant was missing. The generous glass cases which had contained the cakes and chocolates and marzipan figures were empty. Not a crumb remained.

The kitchen door opened and a rectangle of light imprinted itself on the room. There was a man back there, a baker, and he was talking to someone. He spotted me. I could smell baking. The aroma reached me like a warm hand. I checked the Russian soldier and scooted around to the side of the building.

The door opened, and at first I saw no one, until the monkey tapped me on the knee. He was not wearing his bellman's cap and vest but acted now like a doorman, showing me the way in. I was thrilled.

The baker beckoned. "Please," he said, and offered me a wooden kitchen chair.

He was baking, had taken out a few loaves of golden braided egg bread from the oven. He was dressed all in white.

"You're still here," I said, "and the Kaiser."

"We were lucky to get him back."

"Why? Where was he?" I felt steam rising from my back in this warm kitchen.

The baker whispered. "He was taken by Tarzan to his home in the woods. Tarzan wailed out and the Kaiser wailed out, and the man called him Cheetah, but Cheetah could not swing through the trees like the man. He strained himself, hurt his hand on the jagged vines."

The Kaiser took the baker's hand. He'd heard this story before. Maybe it was the whisper that gave it away. The baker's mustache was the exact same oak brown as the Kaiser's fur, and he and the monkey both had the same brown, downturned eyes, like clowns' eyes. The monkey was patting the baker's hand and urging him on.

"It was then, after Cheetah fell to the forest floor, that a golden-haired beauty called Babette came out of the warm water, kissed his fingers and made them well." As if on cue, the monkey held up the healed fingers. I took them and looked them over. "The Kaiser then found his way back here, though it took some stealth on his part."

"Like a cat," I said, patting the monkey on the head.

The Kaiser stood up, squealed and leapt with ease onto the baker's board, took the liberty of selecting one of the loaves of egg bread and broke off a piece to offer to me.

"Please take it," the baker said. "The Kaiser will be offended if you don't."

"Yes, I'll take it. Thank you."

The Kaiser took a good piece for himself, bowed and sat back down. I marveled at his opposable thumbs. Attila was big on opposable thumbs, frequently commending the Lord and Nature for coming up with them.

"I gave him cake," I said, "and now he's returning the favor. He must be very pleased to be able to do it."

I tasted the morsel, the warm goodness of it, the egg, the flour, the milk, fresh from the farms in the countryside around Budapest.

The baker held out another piece for me. "Would you like some marmalade?" he asked. His sad eyes were smiling.

"I like it the way it is."

"It's the only thing we can bake for the time being. No sweets, no cakes, no gateaux, no pastries, no marzipan goblins." Here, the baker gestured toward the Kaiser, and the monkey nodded. He showed his grinning teeth.

"Why can't you?" I asked.

The Kaiser crept closer and seemed to be insisting I put the bread I was holding into my mouth. He shoved my hand with both of his, causing me to stuff the whole hunk into my mouth. I coughed and chuckled and chewed.

"Necessities, not luxuries," the baker said. "Bread is food. Dessert is a luxury. And I must say, young man—how old are you—eleven, twelve?" I nodded yes. "I must say, I am mad with baking. I imagine filling out the ceiling of the Sistine Chapel and then they give you the inside of a hat to paint. They're going to change the name of the place too. I heard them talking about it. *Gerbeaud* is too pretty, too frivolous— decadence once more."

"What are they going to call it: Kaiser Laszlo?" I was still chewing.

"I don't think so," the man said. "There's to be no Kaiser here, no heads of state." He smiled at the monkey. "The Russians do love this Kaiser as much as anything, and he obliges. They pet him, and he pets them. It is the end of the Kingdom of Sugar, the Palace of Chocolates, the Royal Grove of Nut Trees—almonds, walnuts, hazelnuts, chestnuts—the fall of the Palace of Excess."

"Oh," I said, finally finishing what was in my mouth.

Maybe the next time the Kaiser returned to the woods, he could open his own place, treat his former friends to a little café life? He could bake tarts and breads for them, enlist them to gather berries and nuts for his creations. After all, how many monkeys in the world had thought to have desserts? It would easily make him Kaiser to monkeys large and small, as he had been to women and men, boys and girls. What I mean is, was there ever any going back to the woods for Laszlo?

What I mean, number two, is that it is desserts that set us apart. How many other species eat dessert? The eating of desserts, living indoors, the wearing of alluring underclothing and the thinning out of populations with the use of explosive devices — these are just a few of the things that set us apart.

The Kaiser stretched himself out on the baker's board. I patted his shoulder, but he moved my hand to his chest, his heart. The place was soft with fur, but most of all it was warm. Something happened to me, a current running up through my arm like a rising sound, emanating from a distant place, the notes of an extinguished composer, calling from a cave out into the light.

I felt myself lifting out of the chair, floating up, gazing back down at the flagrantly brown eyes, at my hand on the furry heart, beating under my palm like an unborn child.

My hand burned. My own heart yammered. I yanked my hand back and stood up out of the lean chair. The Kaiser stood too on the baking board, threw his arms around my neck. "I have to go," I said over his arm to the baker.

With some difficulty, the baker took down the clinging monkey.

"I'll come back, though," I said. "I'll be back."

I looked up through the Paris darkness into the bookcases bulging above me with the narrow tombs of books. I felt a sound-shadow pass over my ear, stirring the hairs on the back of my neck.

I sat up in the library and shuddered. I could hear someone faintly down the hall, a woman speaking and another singing. Was it Babette again? I was hoping it was. I got out of bed and made my way out of the room and saw right away that the sound was coming from the opposite end of the corridor, to my left. It was a twangling sound. I made my way out like a floating thing and glided along the corridor in the direction of the sound.

But the lights of the creamy salon were on. I stopped to peer in, and the room seemed narrower. In place of the grand piano stood a slender white harpsichord. My aunt's portrait had narrowed too, stretching her out. In fact, it was a room of slender things *for* slender things, for the spines of things rather than the things themselves, for sylphs and swans and splintered things, things to move among, not settle on.

I did not enter the room but moved on, resuming my glide. At the end of the hall, a door was ajar. It was the solarium, but it was mooned over at this hour—making it a lunarium instead, I guess. My aunt was inside, dressed in a primrose nightgown, her hair still up but her face shiny with cream. A single lamp, a tulip looking down, cast the room in an amber light. My aunt stood and swayed to the pretty music, a soft aria, her eyes closed, her expression swoony, her shiny face glowing, arms hugged across her and warped hands open, each cupping a shoulder. She had become a glowhead. She spoke to the record as she swayed. She said, "Lie down in your own green meadow, your *verdi prati*, my Handel, my everlasting George. Let's spread out that woolen wig of yours on the long grass, the green grass stirred by blue breezes. How do you even lay that bouncing, swaying head down on a pillow, down anywhere? Can you, my George F.H.? How can you? Look at you, lamb, still asserting yourself after all these years. Lie down and let me sing your own sad songs to you. I'll sing about the mournful meadow. I'll sing 'Con rauco mormorio.' Has someone disappointed you, lambkin? Is that it? Who is your *scherza infida*, your unfaithful woman? Did she know, lamb? Did she know she had failed you? Oh, if I could have been there that one day—if I could have been there to console you. Did your *scherza infida* know she was condemning you to a life alone, that she was pulling a shadow over your meadow? What young woman sat for you in what London church's echo corner, or what cut boy, cut like crystal, the would-be testosterone rising up in his throat"— Hermina put her curved hand to her own throat—"singing your *Messiah*, intoning your 'He Shall Feed His Flock'? And to what far meadow did that flock wander? Take off the wool, my lamb. Let me feel your pale warm head. What was out there in the green of that meadow that gave you a chill? Rest here now with me on the hair pillow warmed by your pate. Let us make us an English child, leave ourselves behind, take our green sad selves to the Promised Land, the German and the Jew dissolved in the union of that ancient meadow."

At the end of the song, Hermina turned toward the door and noticed me. I expected her to yelp or jump with embarrassment, but she didn't do either, not at all. She beckoned instead. "Come in, my dear."

I hesitated at first—in fact, I was once again the one who felt embarrassed—but Hermina came to get me, cupped me against her warm breasts with her hands. She said into my head, "Handel gave regret a sound." She smoothed my hair at the back, which she must have sensed was standing on end. People spoke a lot into the top of my head. "Do you know what I'm saying?" she asked, holding my face now. "Handel gave regret a sound. Do you understand?"

"I am very young," I said in response.

"Ha!" she said, releasing me. "You were never young. You were born old."

"How do you know?"

"I know these things," she said. "Please, let's listen to a song together." She approached the phonograph, found a record already out of its sleeve and put it on top of the one that had been playing. "My Ede would have been appalled," she said. "His records were pristine, virginal, but I'm much too hungry to keep them that way." She chuckled. I hoped she might replace some of the records my grandmother had lost. I hoped she wouldn't mind.

I sat and listened. It was cool in the lunarium, but the amber lamp warmed the room like a glowing hearth. I sank into a soft, ample chair.

"This record is Handel's *Teseo*," my aunt said. "Dame Martha Bolingbroke plays the part of Medea." Hermina was already swaying to it, though she had not yet found the song she wanted. But she stopped herself, came over to ask me something. She took my face in her bird hands again. The whites of my aunt's eyes were big and glowing silver. I was uncertain of what was to come. "Do you know who Medea was?" she asked.

I shook my head, which served the added purpose of freeing my face from her clutches.

"Medea was married to Jason, the leader of the ancient Argonauts. Medea had two children with him, but he betrayed her." Hermina was shaking her head. "Oh, yes, he betrayed her. He left Medea for another woman, and when he betrayed her, Medea murdered her own children so that he could not enjoy them either. It was the ultimate revenge."

I sat up in my chair, wondering if I should leave, feeling I might. My aunt turned her glowing face away from me and found the song. "This is the only recording of this sublime opera, made in 1915 in London, in the middle of the Great War, some two centuries after Mr. Handel himself premiered it in the same city. Listen," she said to me, her face glowing. "Medea is addressing her children, after she has slashed their throats."

I sat up straight in my chair. "What are their names?"

"They are called Mermeros and Pheres."

I repeated the names. They sounded musical.

My aunt said, "She wants them to have a sweet sleep—a *dolce riposa*. Listen to Dame Martha. Her voice is as dark as a well."

> *Dolce Riposo, ed innocente pace*
> *Ben felice, è quel sen*
> *Che vi possiede*
> *Sempre fu a me tirano*
> *Il pargolette Amore.*

And then the dark voice sang the words again. Hermina's humming voice rode aboard the recorded voice. It was a beautiful song, sad but beautiful. I was riveted. The Baby Actor rose up in me alongside the Baby Diviner. I felt transported to a time before letters and reading when, like the ancients, I could remember every word that was sung or spoken, in whatever language—just the sound of the words, if not their meaning—just by hearing the song.

"Oh, yes, Medea," my aunt began to say to the record. "Yes, yes, the one and only Medea." She was swaying and swooning again. "Oh, yes, revenge." My aunt turned to me, the whites of her eyes showing large. "Sweet revenge. How can I ever repay you for your acts of cruelty?" My aunt held up her curved hands to the moonlight. "Look at me," Hermina said. "Look what you have done." She was gazing up in the lunarium. "How glorious it would be to exact revenge equal to the cruelty you have inflicted." I didn't know who she meant, who she was talking to. "Single-minded Medea," she said to the record. "Can there ever be a cost more dear than the lives of your children, a vengeance more absolute, a triumph more complete over self and husband? How far could you go?" Hermina asked, and then paused as the song played on. Then she said, "Did you gorge yourself with the absoluteness of it, that moment of delicious power, the satanic purity of it? Did you taste their blood, the iron in it, all the lamb they'd been eating, the sweetness of the red grapes, the serum of serenity?" Hermina was alone now with the song, alone in the room. "It is the best drink in the world," she said. "Better than Hitler could drink, better than Stalin and Mussolini and Genghis Khan and Vlad the Impaler put together. Did any one of them dare gas himself, starve himself, freeze himself, cut off his own head, impale himself? Not one. But you dared, Medea. You drank your own blood's blood. You humbled them all. You dared."

I wanted to bolt. I considered for a moment whether my aunt had always been without children or if she'd made a meal of them.

And then someone coughed, someone in the middle of the crackling recording, made in 1915, in the middle of the First World War, someone in that London concert hall, someone listening to Dame Martha sing tenderly about sweet sleep to her murdered children, coughed. Then he coughed again, a cough as loud as the song. Did the man have a cold, back there in 1915? Was he a smoker? Where did he take his smoke? Did he take it in a café like Gerbeaud, over a hand of cards, or in a tavern over a beer and a conversation about the world coming apart, or was it in a room like this, a salon after dinner, with brandy, with his guests, with men who wanted to talk about the Terrible War? Did he pass out Sobranie Black Russian cigarettes with the gold foil filter, the kind Hermina smoked, and sometimes Klari too? Did they lie behind a garter in a monogrammed silver cigarette case? And then did the gentleman travel with his darling by carriage to the opera in London to hear Dame Martha sing the song of horror, the song of Medea, the dark voice soothing itself more than it was soothing the dead children, the children who were beyond soothing? And on this night in 1915, in the middle of the Great War, with another war looming when this one was done, another one yet to come, did the coughing man and his darling hear for the first time that even a murderer could be tender, if only for a moment, and if only for her own sake?

The song was just finishing. "What happened to you, Aunt Hermina?"

She turned. She looked at me calmly. I was a little scared. "What happened?" she repeated.

"Please tell me what happened to you, to your fingers. Why do you wear all those gloves?"

"The gloves? I suppose you've heard things now, *seen* some things in your tender little life. No wonder you are old, my angel." She smiled at me, took my face into her hands again. "You know," she said, "it's not a story for the ages."

"I don't know what you mean," I said. "I'm not asking for a story for the ages. I'm asking what happened to you."

She let my face go and looked down at her hands, held them up to the amber light for both of us to look at, as if they were someone else's, a stranger's. I took a glance at my own hands and wanted suddenly to hide them, sit on them.

"Before you or your brother was born, back in 1941, we had it just so, back in Budapest, my Ede and I. We had lost some things—Hungary was allied with Germany, as you probably know." I nodded. "So there were deprivations, but we had it just so. We had our circle of friends; we had my sisters and brothers—your grandmother—and their families; we had our walks in the park and our coffees, our celebrations, if a little quieter than before, our weddings, births, our holidays. We had it just so." She looked down again into her lap, at her hands. "And my Ede was invaluable as a surgeon. He wrote the book on it—*books*. They are used to this day in German and French and English teaching hospitals. So we, especially, had it just so. And then one day in the winter of 1941—December 16, to be exact—they came to get us."

"They came to *get* you? Who did?"

My aunt put my hands in the warm claws of hers. "Germans,

German soldiers. They burst into our home near the river—you know, near the Erzsebet Bridge." I nodded. "They came in the middle of the night, turned on the lights, tore us out of bed. They would not let us get our things, would not let us *dress*. I was still in my nightgown. They took us down, out into the freezing wet wind, to a black Mercedes waiting in front of our building. Then they injected us with something. I barely had time to see where my Ede was sitting before I dropped into a deep, deep black hole. When we woke—it had to have been seven or eight or nine hours later—we were in Germany, in Munich, at a military hospital. It was colder here than in Hungary, as cold a day as I can remember, but they hustled us inside. They put a surgeon's gown over my Ede's pajamas and told him he had to operate on a wounded officer, who turned out to be Josef Dortmund, Colonel Josef Dortmund, of the Alsace region. I stood there in the cold corridor in my nightdress, trembling and humiliated. I thought that we were finished, that we had no hope. So I'm afraid I was the one who told my husband, in Hungarian, of course, 'You don't have to operate on German officers. You don't have to make them well so they can go back to their killing, starting with us.' And I said this without even knowing the full extent of their killing. We had no idea. We had an inkling but really not much more."

My great-aunt was looking down again at her lap, her hands. She was trying not to show me that she had begun to cry. I wasn't sure what to do. She said, "They took us to a window overlooking a courtyard with an iron cable strung across it. The sky above it was steel gray. They said they were going to hang me out there in the yard by my fingertips while Ede performed the surgery and would not let me down until he was finished. 'No, please,' he begged them. 'I'll do it,' he said. The officer in charge said, 'Yes, you will do it, and you will do it while your wife waits for you out there.' And so they made Ede watch as they pushed me out onto a platform, fastened my fingertips to the cable with steel clamps, pulled me out to dangle above the winter courtyard and even ran water along the cable to freeze my fingers. It was so methodical, it seemed to come to them naturally, as if they were hanging out laundry: *Oh, here we are—laundry day again*. At first I was in shrieking pain. I kept looking up at them, imploring them. I trembled so violently I felt it was my own fingers that had become my captors. I begged my fingers to release me, let me fall, let me shatter on the cobblestones below me. I felt like a frozen, captured, fastened angel.

"And then something happened. I don't know if it was minutes or an hour or two hours later. I'd been trembling, everything about me clattering, my bones, my body turning to bone, when I felt myself calm down. The noise and violence, the ringing in my ears, it all stopped, and I actually felt calm, serene—warm, if that was possible."

Hermina looked at me, the amber light of the lunarium glowing on her face, scaring me slightly. "I got a glimpse of the other side," she said.

I could hardly get a sound out of my throat. "The other side?" I asked.

"Yes, the other side. The place beyond life. It was really quite peaceful, insensate. I floated up out of the courtyard. I went to a place beyond things, beyond the brutalities of men and nature. Beyond the sound, beyond the howling wind and lacerating storm. Quiet. It was quiet and painless. Even the sky seemed to soften. It seemed to take on a faint blush, to pink over the icy courtyard, and I believe I smiled, cracking open my freezing face. Can you imagine how I must have horrified my tormentors, turning the nightmare back on them! Ha!"

My great-aunt stopped talking. She was breathing evenly. She took my hands in hers again, but warmly, calmly. I gazed down at the red shiny hands, searching for the evidence, imagining the scene of the crime.

"Please go on," I said.

"That was not a story for a young man," she said.

"No, it was a story for the ages. Please tell me the rest."

She looked me straight in the eyes, a tender look, one I recognized. My grandmother had that look. "When I woke," she went on, "I was in a hospital bed myself, quite a nice one, a clean one. My Ede was beside me, kissing me over and over, speaking softly to me. I could hear his voice even before I could wake. I thought I might have been elsewhere. When I did wake, his eyes welled up immediately. My hands were in bandages, and for whatever reason my forehead and cheeks were too. It was days later—several days. A few minutes later, in came the German colonel in a wheelchair, pushed by a nurse. 'How is the patient?' he asked. 'She's back,' Ede said. 'She's alive.' 'I'm an admirer,' Colonel Dortmund said to me. 'You have a strange way of showing it,' I told him. The colonel clasped his hands together. Of course, he couldn't answer me. What he did say was, 'When you are a little better, will you honor us with a song?'

"It was my turn not to answer, but by Christmas Day I was a bit better. I was sitting up, taking meals, with help, of course. I was asked by a nurse, who spoke a little Hungarian, if

I was well enough to move a little, to leave my room perhaps. I answered in German that I was. She wheeled me down to a small chapel attached to the hospital. Colonel Josef Dortmund was there in full regalia with his wife and his beautiful boy, half your age, and several officers. A piano accompanist, a young woman not much bigger than a sparrow, awaited me. And of course Ede was there, and he stood to assist me. He whispered to me that the colonel had asked for a song from me." Hermina was shaking her head. "Imagine. I was to sing now. One day, I was to be hung out by my fingertips to be frozen and dried, and now I was to sing. Even odder, there were no Christian emblems in the church. Jesus on his cross behind me was covered over with a bedsheet. Even the altar was draped over."

"Did they do that for you?" I asked.

"No, of course not. Of course not for me. In the kingdom of Hitler, Christ and Christianity didn't fare well. There was a single throne in Germany at the time, a single throne and a single king sitting on it. The kingdom of Hitler was a one-man show.

"So the young pianist came up to me and gently asked what I might like to sing. I studied the faces of my little audience and told her that 'for Christmas' I wanted to sing an English carol. Did she know 'Once in Royal David's City'? She said she did. And so, with my Ede by my side, I sang, my voice small, like a small boy's, but ringing around nicely in the chapel."

Hermina closed her eyes, placed her hands on her heart and sang the song for me with the same small voice.

Once in royal David's city
Stood a lowly cattle shed,
Where a mother laid her baby
In a manger for his bed;
Mary was that mother mild,
Jesus Christ her little child.

And our eyes at last shall see him,
Through his own redeeming love;
For that child so dear and gentle
Is our Lord in heaven above;
And he leads his children on,
To the place where he is gone.

Not in that poor, lowly stable,
With the oxen standing by,
Shall we see him, but in heaven,
Set at God's right hand on high;
Then like stars his children, crowned,
All in white, his praise will sound!

"And then, do you know what I did, my darling boy?" She
opened her eyes wide now. There was extra sound coming
from her eyes. She was beaming. "I was looking straight at
the young blond boy, who seemed very pleased with my song.
My Ede bent down so I could whisper a request to him, and
then he marched over to the Jesus on the cross and pulled the
drapery off him with a flourish, like a magician."

FOURTEEN

I WOKE WITH THE WEIGHT of the world on my chest. I couldn't breathe. We have a heavy planet. I opened my eyes. Attila was sitting on my chest. "Wake up, *mon petit chou.*"

"Get off me." I tried to push him off.

His head was right up against the bulging bookcase. He was fully dressed.

"Wake up, my little plum dumpling. I want to show you something."

He gave me a PEZ for breakfast, one from his Scarecrow, very generous.

"Are we going to see Paris?" I asked.

"Not yet, my pumpkin loaf. Just come with me."

I put on yesterday's clothes while Attila told me I had an important mission ahead of me. "You were born ten thousand years after the last ice age, ten thousand years since the end of the Pleistocene era."

"*Exactly?*" I asked. "So were you born nine thousand, nine hundred and ninety-six years after the last ice age? What date did it end?"

"What?" he said.

"What date? You'd think we'd mark such an important event."

"Come, my little imbecile, my birdling."

My brother led me quietly downstairs. We stole toward the back of the house, past the bright solarium and out. It was still damp outside after the night's heavy rain, but the sun was shining.

"Isn't it strange?" my brother asked.

"What?" He didn't answer me. "*What?* Everything is strange lately."

"That part of you is always attached to something outside of yourself, thanks to gravity," he said, "your feet, say, on the floor, just the bottoms of them, but never *all* of you at once, not even when you're lying down. Fish and birds don't share this problem, but birds do land sometimes, and some don't fly at all. Of course, we can jump in the air or swim underwater, but the escape for us from this principle is temporary."

Attila led me toward a small white house, its gables ornamented with gingerbread trim. It looked like a fairy-tale house, but it turned out to be a shed. My brother pushed open the door. The lock had been jimmied. I examined it for a moment and looked at my brother.

"When did you find this place?" I asked.

"While you were sleeping," he said. "Wait until you see what's in here."

"What?"

"I just said *wait*, my frolicsome puppy."

The shed was full of household effects, a tarnished silver tray, several vases, lampshades, shelves of things, bulging like the bookcases in our room, as well as old lamps, a chaise longue, a small writing desk, like a student's slope-top desk, its lid unhinged on one side and, sprawled out on the floor, a grand crystal chandelier, waiting to rise again.

A doctor's bag stood by the door. We opened it to find it loaded with good things: a stethoscope, a thermometer, syringes, medical hammers, a blood pressure cuff, a nifty flashlight, which Attila beamed straight into my eye, a brilliant assortment of scissors, one of which my brother clacked menacingly near my ear, and a small silver saw.

"These are great," I said. "I wonder what Uncle Ede used this for?" I was holding up the gleaming saw.

"To saw through bone, probably." I looked in horror at the instrument in my hand, tried to spot traces of blood on it. My brother said, "I wonder how many bones Uncle Ede sawed through, whether he kept a record."

"Of the number of *bones*?"

Attila didn't answer me. "This is not why we're here, though," he said. "Not for this stuff. Not now. I'll do a full examination later, with your cooperation, naturally." He pocketed the flashlight. "This could come in handy."

Attila led me to the room's primary treasure: a great black leather chest sitting in the far corner. He aimed the medical flashlight at it. It too had a lock, and it too had been jimmied.

The surface of the chest was incised with the images of colonials riding camels on safari. Lions, zebras and gazelles watched as the parade of humans went by, one with spectacles, one smoking a pipe, one with his arm raised, expounding on the world, it looked like.

I ran my hand over the figures cut into the soft black leather. My brother lifted the lid. Inside were packets of

things, and several thick sheaves of papers and photographs
bundled with ribbon.

"Are we supposed to be looking at this stuff?" I asked.

"I don't know—*you* decide."

He handed me some official-looking papers, like
passports, but they were yellow and blue. They were written
in a strange language and each had the word *Schutz-Pass* on it,
and below that *Schweden* with three crowns.

"What are these?" I asked, as I looked at a photograph
of an unfamiliar face on one of them. It was a man, looking
slightly bewildered. The next one had a photo of a woman,
again unfamiliar. I didn't know what to make of the documents,
though it did feel exciting just to be holding them, especially
here in the secrecy of the shed.

"Are you ready for these?" Attila said. He handed me four
other documents, blue and yellow like the others.

At first I didn't know what he expected me to notice.
I felt I was being tested. But then my eyes fell upon the
unmistakable face of our father. I flipped frantically to the
next *Schutz-Pass*. It was our mother's. Her name was there in
plain sight: Lili Beck. And then Attila's! "*Son*: Attila Beck," it
said, along with his birth date.

"There's no picture of you," I said.

Attila shook his head. "I was just *son of* then, before I
became a Titan."

I turned back to my father's picture, stamped with a
royal seal, and looked again at the three crowns and the word
Schweden below. There were two other such documents with
photos of Klari and Robert. Our grandmother looked a little
younger and even thinner, more like Hermina now, and my

grandfather was older than in the photos I'd seen. His hair, here, was white.

Attila said, "Now look at the signatures below. Can you read them?"

Above the signatures were three words printed in another language, then translated into Hungarian:

Königlich Schwedische Gesandtschaft
Svéd Királyi Követség.

"It's signed on behalf of the Swedish king," Attila said solemnly.

Two other passes had belonged to Hermina and Ede, whose name we saw now was short for Edward. The signature on both of their passes was difficult to make out, but my brother worked through it. "C.I. Danielsson," he said.

I tried to make out another signature, the one on my grandfather's pass. "R. Wallen—"

"Raoul Wallenberg!" Attila said, slapping at the *Schutz-Passes* in my hand. "Now look at these," he said. He handed me the passes of our parents.

"How did Aunt Hermina get hold of our parents' and grandparents' passes?"

"They must have sent them to her. Maybe Mom did or Mamu. For safekeeping, I guess. Just a keepsake, probably."

I stared at the signature on them. This was even more difficult to decipher. I could make out a *P* in the first name of the signature and a *B* in the second, but what a hurried scrawl it was.

"Paul Beck!" Attila shouted, angry, slapping my shoulder

from behind. "Look at it." And when I did, I saw that he was right. I wondered how Paul Beck hadn't been taught to write with better penmanship. He would not have gotten away with it in Mrs. Molnar's class.

"The mystery man," I said.

"Do you know what these are?" Attila said. "They're national documents. It makes our parents and grandparents and me *Swedish*!"

"We're not Swedish," I said lamely.

"Of course we're not Swedish, my little monkey boot." My brother jammed the passes at me and started rummaging through the other bundles of papers and photographs. He got right down on his knees with his head inside the trunk.

So these were our confidence men, Raoul Wallenberg and Paul Beck, our family's own secret men.

"Look," Attila said. He handed me a photo of Hermina with our grandmother and maybe Agi, their sister, and four other women, all of them in their teens. "Look at *this*," he said, a moment later. It was a grainy photo of a boy bound to a man back to back with heavy rope. They were standing on a bridge with some guards attending to them. I couldn't tell which bridge it was, but I could tell from the parliament buildings in the background that it was the Danube and Budapest.

"What was going on?" I asked.

"I don't know," my brother said.

Another photo showed a long lineup of well-dressed people. The street looked familiar, Terez Boulevard, possibly. And there was another picture of a man seated at a card table, the table set among people on the sidewalk, it looked like. The man was signing a document.

"Now look at *this*," my brother said. He had moved on to the next exhibit. It was a belt with a bold silver buckle embossed with a powerful-looking eagle standing on a bicycle wheel with the spokes bent. A swastika. Three words I could not understand were inscribed below the bird: *Gott mit Uns.*

"What does it mean?" I asked.

"I don't know; it's German," Attila said. He was still foraging. He handed me a postcard. On the front was a colorful picture of an army truck and on its side the swastika. It was not being driven but pulled by a horse with bleeding hooves. A soldier walked alongside the vehicle. He wore a torn and patched uniform with an Iron Cross dangling from his neck but flung to the back instead of the front. At the bottom of the photo was the caption *"L'Allemagne, 1945."* I turned the postcard over. Someone had written on the back:

> *Edward et Hermina,*
> *Vive les Alliés! Merci pour la délivrance!*
> —*Mancus*

Attila handed me a yellow piece of paper. "Look at all the languages the bird-woman speaks."

"Don't call her that," I said. My brother glared at me. "It's not necessary," I added.

I looked at the paper. I tried to sound out the word printed in bold at the head of the document: *"Arbeitsnachweis."* Typed into the space left blank on the paper were names

I recognized: "Dr. Edward and Hermina Izsak." I stared intently at the last word before pronouncing it: "Izsak."

"That's Hermina's surname," my brother said, his voice amplified by the trunk.

Before I knew it, I was holding a yellow cloth badge with a star on it, a six-pointed one, like the one on our temple back home and at the head of the gate of my grandfather's cemetery. The Star of David. As I ran the cloth badge between my fingers, my brother said, "You can pin it on later as a crappy sheriff's badge, and I'll wear the buckle. I'll be the outlaw, and you can try to arrest me, if you can catch me."

Attila thrust another document at me. It was entitled *"Evacuation de Paris—Instructions pour la population."*

An airplane roared over our heads. Then I heard rustling outside. "We have to go now," I said.

"Not just yet." My brother withdrew a packet of letters tied with a blue ribbon. "Look at these," he said. The handwriting was familiar to me, the soft loops, the swooping lines, like embroidery. They were from our mother. I could even tell which pen she'd used, my grandfather Robert's 1924 Waterman fountain pen, which he'd kept in the middle drawer of his mahogany desk. The pen had outlasted him. I hoped somebody had brought it with us from Budapest. The letters were from Lili to Hermina and Ede.

"Sit down," my brother told me. I pulled up a little footstool and sat. He took out the top letter and eyed it feverishly. "Listen," he said. *"Listen."*

1 Jokai Street
Budapest, Hungary
July 18, 1945

Dear Aunt Hermina and Uncle Ede,

Our Paul did something that, now the war is over, looms over these days like some kind of monument, the way Paul himself does over each of us.

I don't know how much information made it out to you, so you might or might not know that he was helping the Swedish diplomat Raoul Wallenberg to issue false papers to us Hungarian Jews. They were agents of heaven, the two of them, and they were fearless. Jews and Gypsies would be rounded up and marched to train stations, sometimes, for deportation to Auschwitz, where my own poor brothers and sisters and parents died.

Mr. Wallenberg would set up a small folding table at the station and from a briefcase he'd brought with him pull out files and set them out neatly, like a notary, 60 or 70 or 75 newly minted Swedish passports each time, in alphabetical order, complete with photographs. Our Paul was his sidekick, a deputized Swedish diplomat himself, with his own false papers, like ours.

There was disorder at the station, as you can imagine. I say "disorder" rather than "chaos" because our captors managed it all with the butts of their rifles. Sometimes, though, there was a din on the platform, and Mr. Wallenberg would have trouble delaying the proceedings, so Paul would climb to the top of the train itself and blow a whistle. Imagine it. He'd blow his shrill whistle and, when he got people's attention, captors and captives alike, he'd announce that there were 70 (or however many) Swedish nationals on board and that the Swedish officials (Paul and Mr. Wallenberg) demanded their release. The Germans would cooperate, since it was they who had proclaimed that they were deporting certain groups, and certain groups only, but certainly not Swedes.

One day Simon, our little Attila, Dr. and Mrs. Beck and I were rounded up and marched away. That day, strangely, we saw no sign of Paul or Mr. Wallenberg. We were crammed into a windowless car with far too many others. It was this time last year, a hot July day. I felt especially sorry for Dr. and Mrs. Beck, who had never experienced anything but the most respectful treatment. Yet they didn't cry or complain. Surprisingly, even our usually restless boy was subdued that day. I suppose it was all such a shock, maybe for him a dark adventure. I don't know what he was thinking.

To head us off, our Paul borrowed a Swedish embassy car, an Alfa Romeo, no less, from Mr. Wallenberg. He drove a good distance outside of Budapest, parked the car across the train tracks, got out and waited for our train to approach and come to a stop.

Aunt Hermina and Uncle Ede, try to imagine:

the train stopped, the commander got off, along with
a few officers, and Paul told the Einsatzkommando
that they had four Swedish nationals, plus a boy, on
board and he demanded their release. He presented
our papers to the commander. The officer looked
Paul over, had heard his perfect German, without
even a trace of a Hungarian accent, or for that matter
a Swedish one, and walked down the row of cars,
sliding open one door after another. The German
called out, "Beck! Robert, Klari, Simon, Lili, Attila!"
People on board, we imagine, didn't know if it was a
good thing or bad to be a Beck. It was generally not
a good thing to be singled out. Usually it was not to
receive a reward that your name was being called.

Well, imagine our surprise when our door was
thrown open and the sun fell on us. As our eyes
adjusted, there stood Paul, wearing his camel hair
cape and Panama hat. He was dressed too warmly,
but with his cornflower eyes and the tipsy red curls
beneath the brim of his hat, he looked every bit the
Swede he was playing.

We wanted to shout "Hallelujah!" but of course
couldn't and didn't. We couldn't give any sign that we
knew the man in the cape, and I signaled to Attila to
be quiet. He looked scared. The four of us knew right
away what role we were to play, and Attila knew too.
He sensed it, I suppose.

"Get down," the officer said. "Aussteigen."

The five of us worked our way to the door. Simon
helped Klari down to the gravel. The officer studied

our faces and compared them to the photographs on the papers Paul had given him. Since I am blond and blue-eyed, my papers were placed strategically on top. And there was my blond boy with me. Swedes, to be sure.

Finally, the commander said in German, "You may go."

"Wait," Paul said in German. "Halt. Did you take their valuables?"

"Yes, we did," the commander said.

"May we have them back?" Paul said.

We couldn't believe what we were hearing. The officer looked at Paul and then his eyes ranged over our faces. "Get it," he finally said to a junior officer.

The man ran to get a burlap sack. Paul said to us in German, and in a voice as cool as the commander's, "Get your things. Get your jewelry."

Dr. Beck looked in the sack, reached in and pulled out a pocket watch. He read the inscription on the back and slipped the watch into his vest pocket. Klari combed through the bag and took out an emerald pin, which she held up to the light, closing one eye to focus before fastening the brooch to her jacket. It went with her rose jacket perfectly, though it was not her pin. Simon shook his head, and then the sack came to me. He took Attila from my arms.

They had taken my wedding ring, so I reached into the bag and tried on several rings before finding one that fit. When I did, I slipped it on and smiled.

I still have that ring, and wear it as my wedding ring, though it is inscribed "Ivan. 13 Aprilis 1935." I wonder if the poor man and his wife ever made it back.

Paul helped each of us into the Alfa Romeo, and he did so in the most patient and civil manner imaginable, considering we were holding up the train run by the Germans. The car was cream-colored. It matched Paul's outfit.

He drove us to a building annexed by the Swedes, and as you may know we lived out the remaining months of the war in an office.

Uncle Ede and Aunt Hermina, even as I recall those days and relive them, it's hard for me to believe that we were once so trapped. It was worthy of another chapter of the Bible, so big was the shape and feeling of it. I know your own personal chapter was even bigger, considerably darker. Yet here we are, all of us. We made it. Aunt Hermina, I often hear about your mellifluous singing. Uncle Ede, I hear about your brave work on the frontiers of medicine.

Paul doesn't say much about you, I'm afraid, but he doesn't say much about anything. While most people are trying to get on with their lives, he spends his time in his uncle's study with the lights switched off and the curtains drawn, most often, and he hardly stirs, even when we call him for a meal. He must be wondering about his hero and ours, Mr. Wallenberg, who was taken somewhere by the Russians in January, taken from Debrecen and has not been seen since. But more than Paul's hero, Mr. Wallenberg was his mentor, his inspiration. There was no going back to the simple practice of law after what Paul accomplished under Mr. Wallenberg's tutelage. I sometimes think that for someone who bore so much, Paul is unable now to bear the weight of his thoughts. Still, I will tell him I have reported to you about him and his circumstances.

His sister Rozsi is here with us too. Poor thing is waiting for Zoli, her fiancé, to return from the war. He was taken as well but slipped out of reach of the Swedes and their helpers. With each passing day, we become less hopeful.

Paul did give me permission to write to you both, the aunt and uncle he most admires, I believe. I would say he might even have been pleased that I was willing to do so.

Aunt Hermina, I do hear that you are singing again. It makes me happy to think that someone is, that people are singing again, I mean.

I send fondest regards and love from all of us to you and to Uncle Ede.

Lili Beck

Attila looked up at me. He'd read the letter like a trained actor, consumed by it. His eyes were red and bursting.

"Do you remember?" I asked.

"Not a thing," Attila said, his voice cracked now. "I wonder what happened to Aunt Hermina and Uncle Ede. Why was their chapter worse?"

I shrugged my shoulders. I felt unable to tell Attila. I didn't know what he would do.

Attila folded the letter methodically and tucked it back into its envelope. He tied the blue ribbon around the little bundle, placed it all back in the trunk, closed the lid, and then, without saying a word, shot out of the shed like a bird. I had to run after him, rushing to close the door of the shed behind me, slipping, almost, on a patch of mud.

Inside, he was searching for our father. Our mother, grandmother and Babette were in the expansive kitchen with its sunny windows. When my brother joined us, Lili asked where we'd been. "Don't disappear like that," she said, "please, my darlings." She took each of us in her arms, but Attila broke away.

Babette was standing by to make my brother and me an omelet. The two of them were beaming out smiles like rapiers back and forth across the kitchen.

Everyone noticed Attila now. He was shifting his weight from one foot to the other. If cartoon speech balloons had been shooting out of his head, they'd have contained only exclamation points and question marks.

"Where's Dad?" Attila asked. "Where is he?"

"He's out," our grandmother said. "What is the matter with you? Why don't you sit down?"

"I'd rather stand on my own legs," he said. He actually snorted and stamped his foot. "Don't you think it ironic that chairs are always standing?" No one answered him. "And what about Aunt Hermina? Why did she have it worse than we did?

How could you have it worse than being placed on a death
train and then hiding out in an office building?"

My mother got to her feet. Her smile was gone. "How do
you know that?"

Attila stamped his foot again. "What really did become of
Paul Beck?" he asked. "We were in Hungary for eleven years
after Paul left. We were under Russian rule. The Russians *came*
to our house. They kicked us out. They let us slip out of the
country altogether, though they themselves had issues with
our men, Raoul Wallenberg and Paul. What is it about this
story that doesn't add up? Help me, oh Lord, to see the logic
of your ways. Help me, oh humans."

"Your father will be back any minute," our mother
said. "He's been out with Aunt Hermina, making some
arrangements for our departure. He's under a great deal of
strain. Please don't add to it by asking your questions. There
will be time enough for everything."

"What did Hermina mean about Dad's cousin?" Attila
said, snorting again as he did. He clenched a fist. "Where did
Paul go? Where is he? Did Father ever see him again? Did any
of you, any of *us*, see him again or talk to him? What is going
on, exactly? Did Paul go off in search of Raoul Wallenberg
after the Russians took him?"

"Why are you cross-examining us?" Lili said.

"Because I want to know."

"You already know too much. Don't you think we want to
know more too?"

Babette approached my brother, not knowing what was
being said but understanding the tone. She took my brother's
chin in her hand and smiled at him until he took a deep breath.

Then she set to work making our eggs, aiming her décolletage toward the stove, where it could serve little purpose.

"We want to know as much as you do, dear," Klari said. "We've been looking for Paul for years. We don't know what became of him. We've looked everywhere. We've looked for years, and we're still hoping. He was strong-headed enough to go hunting for Raoul Wallenberg in Siberia, for all we know."

"But he was with us in our house. Wasn't Paul with us in our house? What happened? Where did he go? *Why* did he go?"

"Please, Attila," our grandmother said. "Let's take this into the other room."

We left Babette and moved down the hall to the solarium. Lili, Klari and I sat on a low flowered divan while my brother paced back and forth in front of us.

"I need to know everything that happened. What happened to Paul and to his sister Rozsi?"

"Why do you have to know this now?" said Lili. "I'm trying my best to keep you and your brother from harm, but you won't let me. You fight me and your father."

My brother stopped, took our mother by the shoulders and said, "You're not protecting us from harm by keeping this from us. Our history belongs to us as much as it does to you."

Lili glanced at Klari, who looked down. Lili got to her feet. "I'll tell you if you sit down."

"I want to stand."

She looked Attila dead in the eye. "I will tell you if you sit down." He plopped himself down beside me, where she'd been sitting, and she stayed on her feet. "You're not going to like this story," she said.

"Then why do you insist on telling it?" Klari said. "They have plenty of time to find out."

"They've earned it, Mother," Lili said. "They've come such a long way. The boys have come such a long way on this journey with us."

Klari sighed and leaned back, but the soft divan had no back to rest against and she sat forward again.

"It was after the war," Lili began.

"Right after?" Attila asked.

"Not right after, but soon after, 1946. Robert— Dr. Beck—your grandfather, came home from his clinic one day to find Paul in his—your grandfather's—study. Paul spent a great deal of time in there. His sister Rozsi was prancing around the living room, saying she'd finally found herself a pair of nylon stockings. She had drawn seams up the back of her legs with an eyebrow pencil, and I must say, the lines were drawn with some skill, because they looked quite straight, and in dim light you might have thought she was wearing stockings. I had arranged at the druggist for Rozsi to have sedatives, because every time we went looking for her fiancé, Zoli, at the train station and didn't find him, she fell deeper into despair. Her Zoli had been taken away and never came back."

"Who took him away?" I asked.

"The Germans took him. He was deported. The deal back then, *after* the war, I mean—the law, actually—was that two able-bodied people from each family, if the family had two able-bodied people left in it, would have to go out to rebuild the city. We each had our assignments. I was helping clean up the National Gallery, which was damaged, and your father was helping to rebuild the Chain Bridge across the Danube. The Germans had bombed all the bridges. You were already with us, my darling," she said to my brother. "But we hadn't started on you yet," she said to me, and smiled. I blushed. "So your father and I went on this work detail each day, and Paul and Rozsi did not." Klari was shaking her head, wishing Lili would stop, could stop.

"Who looked after me?" Attila asked.

"Your grandmother."

Klari smiled.

A cloud passed from above the solarium and the room lit up spectacularly. My brother shut his right eye. "Why didn't Paul and Rozsi go?" he asked.

"I don't know. To this day, I don't know for sure. But I didn't care why they didn't go or couldn't go. Rozsi was depressed. Her man was gone and would not return. Paul was depressed. His hero—and ours—was gone. I don't know. I didn't care. Paul had saved us. I didn't care." The room clouded over again. It felt cooler, all of a sudden. The white radiator was ticking. "But Paul and Rozsi didn't go, so your father and I went. We were happy to do it, and we had your dear grandmother to look after you, Attila, as I said. You were growing like a weed, a pretty weed, a dandelion. It didn't seem a problem for us. We'd made it, whoever was left of us. We were alive. We could make it work.

"But the arrangement was not sitting right with your grandfather. And one night at dinner, after months together, he said to his nephew, 'Paul, are you and your sister ever going to go out on the work detail in place of Lili and Simon? They have a child now. They want to have another one.'

"'I don't think so,' Paul told him.

"We went on eating quietly for what felt like several minutes, several awful minutes, until your grandfather put down his fork, wiped his mouth and said, 'Paul, I think you and your sister should go out on work detail tomorrow.'

"Paul wiped his mouth too and finished chewing. He replied, 'And what if we refuse?'

"Your grandfather said, 'Then I think you and your sister should leave.'"

The radiator seemed all of a sudden to be working extra hard. I felt flushed, put a cool hand up to my cheek. Klari put her arm around me.

"What?" Attila asked. "Then what?" He was getting to his feet. The room brightened again. His eyes were blazing blue.

Lili put a hard hand on his shoulder. "Stay there," she said. "I'm telling you the story."

My brother stayed where he was.

"In the middle of that night ..." She paused. My grandmother removed her arm from around me and covered her face with her hands. "In the middle of the night, Paul left. We found Rozsi dead in her bed. She'd taken all her pills but one. She'd left me a note urging me to take that last pill to help me sleep."

I could feel my grandmother's body convulsing. She was still covering her face.

"And Paul was gone," our mother said. She clapped her hands together, held them up to her chin, as if she were praying. Her eyes were welling up too. "There was no trace of him, not anywhere near his own house, which had taken a direct hit, not in his old law office, not in his usual haunts, like the New York Café and Gerbeaud. We caught up with his brother Istvan in Szeged, and he told your grandparents that Paul did not wish to be found. Istvan said his brother had left 'for the Americas.' We thought, actually, he might have come here to Paris. He adored his aunt Hermina. We thought he might stop here on his way to something."

"To *what*?" Attila shouted. Now my brother did stand up.

"How do I know?" Lili went to reach for Attila, but he wouldn't let her touch him.

My brother pulled Klari's hands from her sodden face. He asked her too. "On his way to *what*?"

"We don't know, my dear," our grandmother said. "We can only guess, like you."

"Your husband banished the man who saved our lives, and a decade later we're sitting around guessing where he might have gotten to? Was he looking for something?"

"I'm sure he was looking for something. He would have been trouble to the Russians the way Wallenberg was. Wallenberg was a subversive where the authorities were concerned—whatever authorities. That's all the Russians cared about. Make order. Clear out the rabble-rousers. Clear out subversives, troublemakers. Paul would be on the warpath. There was no proof Wallenberg died. There still isn't. We don't know what happened. Paul would still be agitating. He would still be a menace, if he could be."

"And that's *it*?" Attila slapped at the air. I thought he might connect with one of us and I ducked.

"You have some of Paul's qualities," our mother said to Attila.

"Is that so?" he said. He was fuming.

"What about me?" I asked.

"Actually—" my mother began to say, when Attila interrupted.

"*Actually*, you were named after our grandfather, the man who evicted Paul from our house, the man who banished our savior."

"Attila!" Lili snapped. "Why would you say that to your brother? You don't know who to be angry at."

"He is Robert, is he not? I'm angry at all of you—all of *us*!"

I took off to our bedroom in the library and slammed the door. I looked at the books huddled together on my side of the room. You had to wonder what they were thinking. I threw myself down on the daybed beneath them, hoping they'd collapse and bury me in their considerations.

Of course I knew I'd been named after our grandfather, but now it seemed I had not been named Robert so much as branded. In how many ways could a single soul be branded? It was hard enough being an earthling, receiving the light of expired stars, but to be a branded earthling, a marked earthling. To be 9.8 and relegated to childhood and childish ways and questions was one thing, but to be a Hungarian—or maybe not even a Hungarian—a Jew, a child on the run, to have seen a redheaded relative die at the foot of a lamppost, a man with combed hair—also red—hanged, another with his hat blown away, complete with his head, to have pictured a dear aunt hung out on a frozen line in Munich, to have suffered the ignominy of longing for a pretty nun with a soft white neck in a convent in Austria, or even a girl with banana string hair and succulent lips who would end up in another section of heaven—a loftier section, no doubt—to have watched our father beat a propeller judge, these were brands aplenty. But to have been made a Robert, too, not a Paul, not a Raoul, not even an Attila, but a Robert, the man who banished our savior—this was a branding meant to burn deep.

Do I not take in the air like other earthlings? Do I not have opposable thumbs, enjoy a PEZ or two when I can, have organs cleverly assembled to perform multiple functions, eat marzipan and relish the company of monkeys and opera singers and smellers of every arcane and secret scent ever emitted by the beings, large and small, of this planet? Can I not at least be a Meek among earthlings, stand to inherit a small tract of land, as well as a few earthlings, even meeker, to work upon it? I was joking with myself in this way while fountains of tears issued forth from mine eyes.

I had my back to the door, my arm folded over my face, when my mother and grandmother slipped into the room. My mother kissed me on my temple and smiled her starry smile at me. Klari gently waved Lili away, and my mother kissed me again in the same spot before departing. "It will all be good, I promise," Lili said.

My grandmother said, "You were named after a good and noble man."

"Yes, the man who threw out the man who'd saved him, and you."

"That was not your grandfather's intention. He made a mistake."

"So why didn't you name me Mistake?"

"My first Robert was a kind, brilliant, imaginative, loving man, the way my second Robert is. Yes, he made a mistake. It only made your grandfather human. He would have cherished you if he'd met you."

"Why not Paul? Why didn't I get his name?"

"Because he may be alive. We are hoping he is alive."

"And what about Raoul?"

"Raoul too. We pray he is alive. He would be a saint to us, if we had saints." She sighed. "You have the chance to redeem the name Robert. Your grandfather would have given anything to have Paul back, and he would have given anything to have met you. You look like him. You have much of his character. We must have divined something when we named you."

I heard music coming from the other room, Medea singing. My father and great-aunt were back. Hermina had brought bags filled with clothing for Attila and me. She'd even bought us proper suitcases to carry our new things in.

We all met in the kitchen, but my brother was missing. My mother searched the house for him. I found him in the shed. When I opened the door, I saw that he'd been crying. He was sitting on top of the black trunk. "Hello, my fine Hungarian boy," he said. I knew this was the best he could do just now.

The late morning sun beamed in the window, gilding his face, turning him into a glowhead. His face was shiny with tears. I wanted to hug him, but that would have been going too far. I'd never seen my brother this way. Granted, I had shared only 9.8 of his 13.7 years, really just 71.5 percent of his life, but I had never seen him so moved. In fact, I'd never seen him moved at all. I was not present when our aunt sang "Pur ti miro" and he was moved to imagine real love.

"Do you know what?" he asked. "I found a diary."

"In the trunk?"

He didn't answer me, but he pulled the leather-bound notebook out from under himself. "I found it before."

"Before what?"

"Before you were in here."

"And you kept it from me?"

Attila didn't answer. We were even now, even if he didn't know it. He opened the diary to a page he'd marked, and he read out loud again.

November 7, 1951

I didn't think there could be much surprise left for me in the world, and yet there is. — Our tormentor, Colonel Josef Dortmund, showed up at Ede's office today! He was complaining of a stomach ailment and asked my Ede to help him, the only doctor he trusted. The Dortmunds are living in Paris now! They were originally Volksdeutsche from Alsace, living on the French side. Now they have moved to Paris! He spent three years in prison for his crimes. We have been invited to visit with them when Colonel Dortmund gets better. They live over on Rue du Maupassant, number 21. He gave the address to my Ede freely. Imagine it! — We could now be friends. Take a gâteau to their house, sit and smile and have tea and cake. I would, of course, wear my elegant gloves.

My Ede will do his duty and help the man if he can. They are both men of duty. — Ede will do his duty, just as Dortmund was doing his.

My brother looked up from his book. "This man hurt our family," he said. "I don't know how. I searched earlier in the diary, but there's no hint."

I was about to tell Attila how but was worried about how he'd react, and in any case, he didn't give me time. "It's the Second Coming," my brother said. "Do you see it?"

I took a step back. "Yes, I do. No, I don't. I'm very young."

"I want you to listen now," he said. "I want to show you Statue Graveyard in living Technicolor."

My brother reached behind him and pulled out an army helmet. With a grunt, he plopped it onto his head. "Heavy," he said. He turned his head one way and the other, modeling it for me. It had a golden eagle on its side, standing on the same wheel with the bent spokes, the swastika. "The helmet was in the trunk," Attila said to me. "The question is how Uncle Ede and Aunt Hermina came to have it."

"Maybe they saved the man's life," I offered. "The helmet wearer's life."

"Yes, the helmet wearer's life—what a bright little seedling you are. Do you think they spent more time with Colonel Dortmund than we know? Do you think their tormentor would show up at Uncle Ede's office if he didn't feel safe?"

The helmet was too big for my brother's head. He kept adjusting some straps inside, and finally it sat just right, if a little heavily, on his head. He began his speech again. "Everyone is searching for the meaning of life. We belong to certain categories, like Rock, Bird, Human, but it is only humans who choose categories to subdivide themselves into. Pigeons and carp don't do that. Adam and Eve lived in a very good place, very, very good. But part of the original plan of creation was that they would choose to fall. Oh, yes." My brother held up his index finger. "Oh, yes. The Lord saw it coming. He is omniscient. If everything is good, how can God's special creatures choose him? They don't know any better. So he sent along the serpent and said unto it, 'You make sure they eat the fruit of the tree of good and evil.' And on that day, we became choosers. Eve chose the fruit. Adam chose Eve. Sometimes we're good at it, sometimes not. Sometimes we choose well; sometimes we don't." My brother wiped his wet cheek suddenly and violently, as if a fly had landed on it. I wondered if these were fresh tears or the original ones. It was hard to tell in the shadow cast by the helmet. "Later on, when we had scattered, some of us had wandered too far from the Garden. We might feel listless one day or, worse, we might feel downtrodden, and then we begin to say, 'We are great— we are the greatest.'" My brother reached behind him and then raised his *Gott mit Uns* belt buckle to his eye. "'God with us,' it means. Mamu told me."

"You showed her the buckle."

"No, I just asked her what it meant. God with us. So you see, you've found God after all. " He slapped the side of his helmet. "You have found him again, far from the Garden, and now you're able to say, 'I am the greatest.' We all want to say it, but to be the greatest implies that someone else is not so great. To this person I award a shitty cloth star." My brother held up the cloth Star of David and spoke to it. He had a number of objects behind him on the lid of the trunk. "You are base," he said to the star, "you are vermin, and we must get a special pesticide to eradicate you." He flung the star across the room.

I went to retrieve it. I wondered about the star, who had designed it, which one it was modeled on, whether its light was still on.

My brother said to me, "Finding too much difference in others is a problem. Those people are not in fact worse than you. They are not better than you either, by the way, though it is harder to see how anyone being gassed to death can be seen as wrong simply for being born what they were. They didn't start anything. They didn't do anything to you, actually. They are better than you insofar as they didn't start anything and you did. They are not vermin, though the actual vermin would argue they could use a little respect too. They are merely going about their business."

I took a seat on the footstool. "So everyone is exactly the same?" I asked.

"Yes, the same, but prepared differently, cooked differently. People find themselves in different circumstances, sometimes good, sometimes bad, sometimes of their own making, sometimes not. So eventually the ones in bad circumstances rise up, especially when they see others in better circumstances, but first they have to believe they can. They have to talk themselves into it. They have to say, 'I am Gargantua and you are a pea—no, a flea, an insect.'" Attila pointed down at me, sitting on my footstool. "So where does that leave us?" I shrugged my shoulders. "It brings us to the heart of the matter," he said, "that's where. Give me your sleeve. I want to wipe my nose."

"I'll give you the back of my underpants."

He ran the palm of his hand under his nose and up his cheek. A cloud passed over the sun, graying the room, giving it drama. "You see," my brother said. He was pointing to the window. "The eye of heaven blinked. It is here, my slovenly boy, that things fall apart. Bear with me."

"Who else am I going to bear with?"

"Someone says, 'I am the greatest,' and mows down what is in his path, since everything and everyone else must be less than the greatest. It is the only thing that makes sense, based on the formula. Then a second group comes along and says, 'No, you are not the greatest,' and this second group pushes back. Some from this second group secretly want to be the greatest too, and want to prove it by beating the first group. There is a third group, sensible and orderly, and they just want to go on with their lives, make the best of what they have, do whatever good they can for themselves and others, carry on, carry on, carry on, until they inherit the earth. This group contains our grandfather Robert."

I was pleased to hear him say *our* grandfather. "He meant no harm," I put in.

"No, he meant no harm. Usually. But this once he lost his head. He wanted to be the bigger man, or as big, just once. People in this group mean no harm, even if they cause some. Many of the people we know are in this group, maybe we are too. Right?"

"Right. But maybe you're not. Maybe you're slightly disturbed."

He ignored me. He said, "Then there is a fourth group, a few people who say no to the ones who think they are the greatest." My brother reached behind him to pull out the packet of letters and *Schutz-Passes*. "Risking their own lives, and finding the only meaning they can in doing so, they fight to help their

peers, help them and save them, put themselves in harm's way
to do so. Our own Paul Beck is a member of this group. Hitler's
resisters even in his own country are in this group. They lost
their heads in resisting; then they lost their actual heads."

"What about Raoul Wallenberg?"

"And then there's Raoul Wallenberg. Raoul belongs to his
own group. Sometimes it's not even a group, just a solitary
soul. This is the fifth group, the apex. They don't even belong
to the heroic fourth group, which contains Paul. They come
out of nowhere, or somewhere, the Garden of Eden—they
can still smell the Garden of Eden—and they know what it
takes to get us back there. They have no other reason to help
or even save people other than that scent, that sense of the
possibility of things. Raoul is the Second Coming. Or Raoul is
the First Coming, depending on whom you're talking to, and
he is the one foreseen by Isaiah. How else is he going to show
up? Dressed in a toga? On a beam of light? No, he is a random,
a thin, balding young Swede, who shows up in Budapest
wanting to do good and ingenious enough to figure out how to
do it, charming enough to persuade a small group of helpers
to work with him, including our father's cousin, determined
enough to persuade even the enemy, using the enemy's own
rules, and charismatic enough to gently slow the killer's big
machine. And then someone takes him away, the Russians in
this case, and martyrs him. It's a pattern, part of the plan. No
Via Dolorosa this time. Not even Andrassy Avenue this time.
A shitty street in Debrecen. Take him away. Poof. He's gone. "

Attila was crying again, quietly sniffling under the shadow
of the helmet. The sun pushed through the window once
more. He closed a single wet eye against it.

"When do you have these thoughts?" I asked him. "Can you think things while you're swinging through the trees?"

My brother cleared his throat and wiped his cheeks and nose on his sleeve, a bold move, since he liked to keep his shirts neat and clean. His rainy eyes had turned stormy now. There was no stopping them up.

"Maybe it was the tree and the flowers," I said.

"What was, my dim-witted boy?" He sniffled. He stopped crying.

"What if it wasn't the Lord at all who expelled Adam and Eve from the Garden? Maybe it wasn't enough for them to slosh around among the flowers. You can have too many flowers," I said.

"Yes." My brother pointed at me. "Yes, you can have too many flowers. Where is Noseboy when we need him?"

"So maybe it was the flowers," I said.

"Yes," my brother said. He was still pointing at me, pointing at the air. He started shouting. "The flowers saw a chance in Adam and Eve, and yes, you have it—you can have too many flowers, too much perfume. They saw a chance with the humans, like the wall coming down, like the border opening between Hungary and Austria. They saw their chance. The humans could spread the flowers outside the Garden. They could spread the flowers all over the world. The flowers rose up against them to cast them out of paradise. They thrust up their pink lady dicks with the seeds standing out of them like expectant fireworks. 'Take us,' they said. 'Let us rub up against you and leave our essence on you, so you can scatter us, so your wicked children can plant garden after garden all over the world. We'll color your planet. We'll sweeten your planet, and if you don't like color or sweetness, we have no use for you.' And so they went forth, Adam and Eve and their wicked children, and their wicked children after them—or after the one, to be precise—and the joke was on them because of the cycle of things, my fawn-eyed boy. You spend the rest of eternity trying to get back to the Garden. You have a live electrical wire that drives you on, drives you toward that golden land, in whatever feeble or misguided or half-witted way you think you can make it. Yes, a spark, a live wire."

My brother was standing now, quite straight and tall. I said, "I think yours is more live than other people's wires, until it's switched off."

"We have a job to do," he said, ignoring me. "If we don't do something while Paul might still be alive, we'll be banning him a second time from our lives."

"What if he doesn't want us to find him? What if he's had enough of us? It's more than ten years."

"We have to find him, maybe even Raoul after him, *with* him, with Paul's help. This is history we're talking about, the making of history. History isn't finished. We have a job to do, and if I go, you must carry the torch."

"Where are you going?"

He ignored me. "We have to find these people, these saviors. It's the very least we can do. We wouldn't be here, still roaming among the grasses and rocks, if they hadn't come along."

He took off his helmet, turned toward the trunk and then, with a flourish, turned to face me again. A gun had appeared in his hand, an impressive one.

I leapt to my feet. "Where did you get that?"

"We have to avenge the men who hurt us," he said. "And we have to save the men who saved us. We have to find them. The Russians took Raoul, and Paul probably followed. I don't know. Who knows? I would have followed."

"I know you would have."

The door of the shed opened. My brother dropped the gun into his pocket. Our mother and grandmother were standing there. "What are you two doing in here?" said Lili. The she noticed the items on the lid of the trunk. "Oh, no."

"We have to find Paul and Raoul and Colonel Dortmund," Attila announced.

Our mother gasped. "What are you saying?"

Klari was calmer. "Come and eat breakfast," she said. "You still haven't had breakfast."

"We can't delay." My brother looked at me. I could feel the fury fumes beating their wings around me, beating their wings until I rose with them or rose against them. There was no middle ground.

"We'll have breakfast," our grandmother said. "That long we can delay."

Babette was whipping up a fresh batch of omelets flecked with mushrooms. Lili and Klari sat with us. Our father was in our parents' room, and Hermina was playing Handel in the solarium, but I could hardly hear it now. I could hear her voice, though, singing along with the record. My father had probably asked her to keep it down.

"My sister's replacing all my records," our grandmother said, "the ones that were lost and even ones I left behind at home. She'll be shipping them to us, wherever we end up." She sighed. I pictured the night some of her records were lost, and

Judit was lost. It seemed far away and long ago. Our mother put her hand over our grandmother's.

Babette smiled at each of us as she brought us our eggs. My brother was brooding. He didn't even take notice of Babette's amplitude, or breathe in the cream of her skin. Nor did he ask a single question of anyone. He didn't roll out his thesis concerning mushrooms, even though we were eating some. He didn't ask, "How many people, through trial and error, do you suppose, consumed mushrooms and then died before we realized which ones we could eat and which ones we couldn't?" He didn't say, "Since word traveled poorly in the first mushroom-eating days, in how many tribes, hamlets or labyrinths of caves did bad-mushroom eating occur before the news spread and a conclusion could be drawn and then relayed back throughout the land? How many would it take, and how many deaths, roughly?" Also, "Did the mushroom call out to people? Did everything call out to people until people decided to steer clear of the wrong things? Can you imagine how many red roses people ate before they thought better of it? Was the mushroom an attractive item to consume, compared to an orange or an apple, let alone a peach, even though biting into the first peach must have been a little like biting into a juicy cardigan?" Finally, "What about the types of mushrooms that altered mental states and brought on spiritual journeys such that the eater ambled about precariously embracing and even kissing a member of a species he or she should probably not have? Still worse, conversely, how many mushrooms have laid down their lives for us on this day?"

Babette poured each of us a glass of milk. She swooped

around my brother's shoulder to pour, resting there too long, I thought. I had never been so aroused, and I was more than a little jealous. This was the first time in a long time that I had an inkling of a new category to be added to Fluttering Things and Glowheads and to be called Creamy Goodness. It harkened back to the days 7.8 to 9.8 years before, when I'd lain with Lili, her warm blond milk fortifying me against the winds of the world.

Yet my brother was unmoved. A butterfly of light fluttered on his face as he drank. I expected something. We were all waiting for something out of him. He didn't ask, "Are dairy cows really just wet nurses of the bovine world, their milk diverted to the wrong species? And what if a great cow one day, an Einstein cow, say, figured out this scheme? How would the cow world react? Imagine." All my brother did was stare down at his plate, picking with his fork at the lacy edge of his egg.

Our father came into the kitchen just as my brother and I were finishing. The music stopped and Hermina joined us too. For the first time, her pink, curved hands were naked in the daylight, taking in the air. She had bought my brother and me matching sailor outfits, complete with caps, and presented them to us. My brother looked grimly at the outfit and wouldn't take it from our aunt.

"Attila!" our mother said. I put on my sailor's cap to make Hermina feel better.

Babette cleared away our plates and glasses as she smiled broadly at us all and said something sweet-sounding in French. She was as pink and white and fragrant as a blossom.

Simon said, "Boys, just because we're refugees doesn't mean we can't be tourists too. We are privileged, thanks to our generous relative. She has agreed to take us into the city to see some of Paris's legendary sights."

Aunt Hermina clapped her hands together, but they clopped instead of clapped on account of their hollowed-out shape.

Attila stood up, faced our aunt and said, "We have to find Paul. Robert and I know what happened. We know everything. We can't wait. We have work to do."

A storm brewed behind my father's eyes. It was a look he shared with Attila. But he spoke calmly. "It's been over a decade," he said. "We have tried, believe me. We don't know what happened to the dear man, but if ever he reappeared I'd give him anything he asked for, anything I could give him, not that we have much anymore."

Attila slapped at his side. "Well, that's not going to happen. He's not just going to show up after all this time, especially after what happened. We have to search for him."

Simon took Attila's shoulders in his grip. "You have to forget Paul Beck," he said. "Paul is trouble. Wallenberg was arrested for standing in the way of trouble, and Paul might have followed him."

Attila shrugged free. He was shaking. He said, "So you agree with that man on the bus. Is that what you're saying, Father? That Paul was a menace? Raoul Wallenberg was a menace?"

"Of course I'm not saying that."

"Paul's not trouble," Attila said. "He stood in the way of trouble too."

Hermina clopped her hands together again. "Paul *was* trouble. Thank God for his trouble, that darling man. Everyone needs a savior of some kind."

"Yes," our father said, "but the savior doesn't always come along in time. This is not a world of superheroes. You're better off saving yourself, believe me—if you can—*if* you can."

"Why are you so angry, Simon?" Klari asked her son.

"You're right. I am angry. Aren't you?"

"Of course I am," Klari said, "but my antidote is to do what I can to clear up the past."

"You can't clear it up. It's the past. You're deluding yourself. There is too much darkness there. The best you can do is search now for the light, that's all. Don't delude yourselves, *all* of you." He was looking at Attila. "Yes, Paul stood in the way of trouble," he said more calmly. "But when countervailing winds blow up against each other their fury touches off a tornado." Attila snorted like a bull. "Paul needed to assert himself. He needed to be who he was. And my father, your grandfather, needed to be who he was, to assert himself, to be the head of his household and assert what he thought was right. That's all. We were past considerations of saviors— who was one and who wasn't. Saviors often go unappreciated. It's the nature of the calling. They don't go into that business to be appreciated. It would diminish them, ironically, to be appreciated." Everyone stared at our father, but no one spoke. "Now here's what we are going to do today," he said, taking hold of my brother again. "We are going into Paris to see one of the great European wonders. There is no other city like it. I don't know when we'll be back here. Certainly, I will not be back."

Looking straight into our father's eyes, Attila said, "Do you think it's all right just to drop your cousin from your thoughts?" He swatted Simon's hands away. "I'm not talking

about Raoul Wallenberg or Jesus Christ. I'm talking about
Paul. He saved us. He made it possible for all of us to be here
to have this conversation. The least we can do is find out what
happened to him. We can't be cowards now."

"Attila!" our mother said.

"I'm sorry to have disappointed you," our father said,
with a steely evenness in his voice. "No one questions your
suitability as a child. Why do you question mine as a parent?"

"What?" Attila asked, and Simon was about to answer, but
our mother stepped between them. My brother turned and
marched off to our room.

Klari said to Simon, "Gratitude is not supposed to be
exhausting, dear."

"Mother, please." My father had a murderous look. I
thought of Medea and quickly followed my brother.

Lili brought our sailors' suits to us. She did this right away,
too soon. She said gently, "Attila."

"Please!" he snapped, and she withdrew.

I got into my suit, including the cap, as my brother stared
out the library window. He wouldn't look at me or answer me,
and when I put my hand on his shoulder, he brushed my hand
away. I waited quite some time, and then I heard music again,
singing, not a record this time, but our aunt, singing softly
down the hall in the solarium.

I wanted to please her with my outfit, so I made my way
down to her. She was swaying there as before, hugging her
shoulders with the claws of her hands, dancing with herself.

I wanted her to see me in my outfit, so I walked boldly
in. She noticed me and smiled and took me in her arms to

join her in her swaying. My cap fell off. The music was as sad as it was pretty. "What is it?" I asked, but she kept singing, smoothing the hair at the back of my head. I was very hot. The song was quiet and seemed, at moments, to stand still, the notes hanging there in the quiet.

"It is by Rameau. *Castor et Pollux*," my aunt said. "'Tristes apprêts, pâles flambeaux.'" She said it to the same tune, singing out the story to me as we danced. "Sad finish, pale flames. They're brothers."

"Who are?"

"Castor and Pollux. They're brothers from ancient Greece," she sang. "But they're different in one important way." I waited. "One will live forever and one will die."

"One will die? Why?"

"They have the same mother. Her name is Leda. But Castor's father is a person, a human, while Pollux's father is Zeus."

"The god," I said.

"Yes, the god of gods." Hermina stopped singing. She was speaking now, too close to my ear, I felt, as we continued to dance, and she held me with her bird hands. "Zeus appears to Leda in the form of a swan and seduces her, forces himself upon her."

"The *swan* does?" I tried to pull back, but my aunt resumed her singing, the same haunting tune. "Why was it a swan? Why wasn't it a serpent or a lion or a wolf, possibly?"

"No, he is a swan, but a swan infused with the power and sorcery of Zeus. After a time, Leda lays an egg from which the brothers hatch."

"After how long?"

"I'm not sure."

"After nine months, like babies?"

"I think so, yes, after nine months, most likely, but both Castor and Pollux are hatched from an egg." I pulled away and Hermina sang the rest, her eyes half closed, humming and singing as if she herself had known a swan who was too good to be a bird. "And so one brother is mortal, the other immortal," she said. "The brothers fall in love with Phoebe and Hilaeira, but the girls are promised to two other boys, so Castor and Pollux spirit them away to Sparta. The rival boys catch up to Castor and Pollux and they battle to the death for love. Castor does die. He dies of a fatal wound. His brother is the only one left standing. Pollux lifts up his lifeless brother, holds him up to heaven, shakes the body, loose as a skeleton already. Pollux begs his father to let him share his immortality with his brother, let them both go to the underworld together or both to Olympus. And do you know what Zeus does for his son?" I shook my head. "Zeus raises the two brothers to the heavens in the form of the constellation Gemini."

"Gemini! I know the brothers. I *know* the constellation Gemini. And Castor and Pollux are the brightest stars in that constellation!"

"I thank you," my aunt said, "for putting on the sailor suit."

I blushed as if I had been exposed, and she sang the soothing notes of the song again. I was moved even more by the song this second time. "I love this song, those notes, how they go together, as if they've always been together," I said.

My aunt was delighted with my remark but paused before answering me. She was still humming, singing some words.

Then she said, "Those notes, those holy notes." She put both hands on her heart. "Music is our answer to flowers, the green world—life!" She was singing again, then humming.

"Aunt Hermina," I said, after another moment, and I did so as warmly as I could, "then why do you sing so many songs about dead children?"

She stopped singing. My great-aunt sat right down on a chair and covered her mouth with the bowls of her hands. "Oh," she whispered. And then she said, "The hope is in the beauty of the song." I could hardly hear her. She was nodding at me but didn't say anything more. She looked distracted. I didn't know what else to say either. I got to my feet to hug Hermina but didn't manage it. She was slumped over a bit, not in hugging mode, so I slowly backed out of the solarium instead.

I returned to the library and waited on my bed for a whole hour. My brother was still there. He had his back to me. He was busy with things on the desk. But it was Attila, surprisingly, who finally broke the terrible silence. He'd been studying maps he'd found in the desk drawers. He turned around and asked me if I wanted to go into the city, as our father had promised.

"Yes," I said, very happy about the change in his mood.

He went out to the salon to ask our mother to ask our father if he was still willing to take us. Our father said he was not.

"But you have to," she told him.

"I do not."

"Yes, my darling," Klari said. "You have to. These are your boys and they have a chance to see Paris, and we cannot leave until they do."

Just as he relented, someone banged at the front door quite hard and then banged again. It sounded like a fist. Aunt Hermina came out of the solarium but Babette was ahead of her. We all followed. Babette opened the door with a smile.

Two burly men dressed in suits and trench coats stood there, blocking out the light. They asked for my parents by name: "Simon Beck, Lili Beck." But when Hermina asked in French what they wanted, we realized the men were not French. They were Russian. They said something in Russian, and each took one of my parents by the arm. Attila threw himself at them, but one of them swatted him away. My brother went flying against the wall and crumpled to the floor. Our mother screamed, but they pulled a burlap hood over her head and another one over our father's head. They hustled our parents out to a waiting car and sped away.

FIFTEEN

"WHERE ARE THEY TAKING THEM?" I asked. I was sobbing, gasping for air as if someone had punched it out of me.

My brother was out cold on the floor. We didn't notice his state at first. He had a cut over his eye, and Babette ran to get something for him. Klari and Hermina, the calm and calming sisters with their comforting caramel eyes, looked ready to pull at each other, pluck out feathers if they had any.

For a moment, only Babette seemed to know what to do. She arrived with a linen towel to hold over my brother's eye while she cradled his head in her lap. Hermina seemed to want to rake her own face with her hands. "I'll call a doctor," she said. She said something else to Babette, and Babette agreed. Hermina said, "I know the chief of police. I'll call him. We'll go to the police. I feel completely responsible. We'll get your parents back. But first the doctor."

Klari, Babette and I moved Attila into the library and laid him down on his bed. He groaned but didn't open his eyes. His eyelid was swelling up. Babette switched on the lamp above his head and kissed him on the forehead. She kissed me too, and she had me hold the cloth while she went to get other things. She smiled now, but only in that sorrowful way.

I stared at my brother and whispered his name, but he didn't answer. I barked his name, but he didn't flinch. I saw on the desk that Attila had got out a French-Hungarian dictionary as well as maps of France and Paris. I pulled the chair back from the desk; underneath he had stashed the German helmet from the shed, the war helmet with the eagle and the swastika. Inside it were the flashlight and the pistol.

I remembered our parents were gone. It came over me in a wave, which had mistaken me for a rock. What if they were gone for good? What if Attila was going? I had to suck back a new round of sobbing, but in its place I uncorked a flood of hiccupping. I'd be an orphan. I'd be parentless, brotherless. Yes, I'd still be grandmotherful and auntful, but it was too much to contemplate all at once. Things were happening too quickly, and to my young mind not one of them seemed right or earned or natural. I was hoping we had eluded history for now by taking this detour into France, but I guess I was wrong. It would not have suited my brother, in any case, to elude history. If he had seen it looking the other way, he would have redirected its focus back on us in a hurry.

I turned again to my brother. There he lay, still in the lamplight, shiny, pink and appled up for the New World— he made no sense this way. I watched him breathe in thinly, breathe out through the reeds of his throat, the books around us huddling in a conference over him, the secret society. I gently pried open his unharmed eyelid—he had the dead glass look of the hanging man. I let the lid fall. I felt myself salting up again. There were bad omens floating in the air, soap bubbles of them, and I wanted to dispel them. I wished my aunt would sing. I wished she would put on music, something to distract us, to rouse my brother, to lure an angel to slip in through the window all set to inspire the composer.

That was exactly what we needed. In what creature other than an angel did fluttering things, glowheads and creamy goodness intersect? She'd be a wonder. My brother would spring straight up in bed if he saw her. He'd feed off her. She'd be humming a melody for all the ages to the waiting composer, but my brother would want to know first why she looked like us. Why was she an extra-beautiful version of ourselves? Why did she have hair? Did she have hair in the other places too? In other words, was she almost entirely like us? Did she have internal organs, or just airy ones, celestial ones? Did she have a scent, or was it something only Noseboy could detect? Never mind the wings. My brother would be handling them like mad. He'd ask if they were designed only to make her shuttle up and down, or fly to and fro as well, the way a bird does. She wouldn't need to cruise like a gull, surely, or swoop like a hawk after spying the movement of a field mouse in the grasses. What would be the point of it? Attila would be inspecting her closely, wanting to know how the wings attached to the back, wanting to pluck out a feather, keep one for later study, then finding that he couldn't, that these were not bird feathers but more durable—these were dateless feathers, feathers without end, wings without equal, something crystalline rather than feathery. He'd be touching the angel as she hummed, handling her overly, admiring her angelic boobs. What would an angel's boobs be for, except to admire? He would want to know if she was part of the cycle of things. Was she the afterlife of sheep or something more, a dead soldier in a field, the brass buttons on his coat, a toppled statue, a star, the light of old stars, an aurochs, shattered glass. What about numerals, the parts of speech—adjectives, adverbs, pronouns? And what about events? Could you throw a whole event into the constitution of an angel—the storming of the Bastille, the coronation of the Emperor Franz Josef, the first flight of the *Hindenburg*, the discovery of penicillin? How about events that had not yet happened to go with the timeless wings and airy organs— relocating Eden, having a picnic on Mars? Could you not— *should* you not—blend these all together in an angel so that she could carry down a melody from heaven for you to play?

My grandmother looked in on us. She kissed my brother and inspected his swelling eye. It was his right eye, the eye he most often closed to the sun. And then she sat with me on my bed to stare at him. For a giddy moment I wondered if my brother had just gone to sleep in an instant, the way he always did.

My grandmother held my hand. I felt a chill come over me. "I'm scared," I told her. Klari was silent. She was having trouble looking at me. I realized she wanted to say it as well. She wanted to say, "I'm scared too," but she couldn't. She wasn't supposed to. What a bind she was in. I could wallow and wail in my sorrow and fear if I wanted to—but she couldn't, not usually.

The doctor came to examine my brother. He was a Hungarian expatriate, a friend of the family. All of us were in the room when another call came from the police to say that Hermina and Klari could meet with the authorities downtown. The doctor knew the situation and said he knew a member of the French National Assembly, if we needed him. He bandaged up my brother's cut. He then lifted Attila's eyelids, and his blue eyes still had the dead glass look in them. I felt I might get sick. I covered my mouth. The doctor said we'd have to keep an eye on him, but he didn't say what we might or might not see. He also told us Attila might wake up or he might stay down, depending—but he didn't say on what. He said he'd be back first thing the next morning and was gone. Babette covered Attila's forehead next to the bandage with a wet cloth and kissed him repeatedly just where the cloth met the forehead. She kissed him and breathed in and out, taking in his essence, wanting to suck out the harm, it looked like.

Hermina's hands were trembling. She asked her sister to accompany her downtown—she'd feel better if the two of them could go together, that Babette was very capable of looking after the boys.

Babette smiled and said something to my brother in French as she resolutely held her place beside him and went on administering wet dabs to his forehead, careful to avoid the dressing beside the eye.

A few minutes after my grandmother and aunt were gone, Babette stretched out beside my brother on his bed and cradled his head in her arm. I stood and watched, enthralled. She signaled for me to join them. Attila had the bigger of the two daybeds in the room, but with three people in it I guessed we'd be cramped. She beckoned to me, though, and beckoned some more, smiling all the while, so I squeezed in on the opposite side and wedged my head in the other warm cradle.

A blue vapor rose in the room, blue being the color of creamy goodness in its gaseous state. I might have dozed

off, or swooned more likely, so I don't know how or when it
happened—a minute or an hour or a week later—but I was
wakened by a slurping sound and turned to find my brother
sucking like a vampire mollusk on Babette's white neck. His
eyes were still closed—had they opened at all?—and now he
rubbed her abdomen lightly before rising, taking the shape of
her breast in his hand. His hand was trembling. I didn't dare
move, didn't dare let on that I was conscious. Was my brother
conscious? Was Babette? Everyone's eyes seemed closed in the
lamplight, even mine, some of the time. Babette had a love
bite on her white neck as deep and sharp as a tattoo, a purple
carnation, possibly, the petals etched out by Attila's teeth.

"Have some, my little wolf cub," my brother suddenly said.

"*Some?*" I said.

He was looking at me through the warm cut of his eye.
"Yes," he said. "Yes, yes, yes." Babette's plump breast was out,
the one nearest my brother. It was out, taking in the light like
a plump sunflower. My brother latched on to the thick nipple.
Babette unleashed her second breast and offered it to me. She
was a human pudding. I was glad my brother's plan to have
a single one in the middle, a bruiser, had not come to pass.
I took the warm bud in my mouth. Babette made a French
sound. I knew from the current running through me to the
base of my spine that this moment would enter the boiler
room of my memory, that even if there were ten of me, there
was enough fuel to last each of us a thousand years. I glanced
over the soft pink terrain at my brother. The flesh seemed to
give off light, empurpled only by the shadows of our heads. I
was sucking so hard, I thought I would bring forth milk.

We were Romulus and Remus, set to remake the world.

My brother could found Rome, and I could found Reme, a city not yet born, a city to be built on a soft pink rock.

If ever there was a time to renegotiate the tenets of creation, this was it. We could retrace our steps to Eden. We could start again with darkness and light, certainly, and the water, and the land and air and fire, the sun and the moon, yellow and silver. But after all that? Ban the serpent. Let there be fruit but not fruit hanging from the branches of the tree of the knowledge of good and evil. What good is it? What's wrong with staying stupid? Stupid is better than smart—stupid is better than smart power, smart killing, might is right. We love you, Lord, but let us be stupid people who love you without thinking. What's wrong with having stupid people love you? So there it is—there we are—we can smell the sweetness of the flowers, the green flesh of them, the many-colored petals, though we cannot name the colors, not even the green.

Was that paradise up ahead, or was it Rome?

Babette unlatched each of us and sat up. She kissed my brother on the forehead and smiled, seeing that she had cured him. And then she hovered over me too, missing my muscled lips with her soft ones as she slid up to my forehead to kiss me. She got up, rearranged herself, covered herself, switched off the lamp and walked lightly out, pulling all the warmth with her, floated on air and was gone.

"We have to go now," my brother said to me in the darkness.

I switched on the lamp. "Where?"

It was then that the wave rolled over me again. My mother was gone. My father too. But I have to be honest in these times: the wave brought Lili first. Lili was humanity's answer to bright light. How could you throw a burlap sack over light that bright? I could understand gold and jewels, but light? She would smile, surely, and, seeing the light, they would let her go.

"Come, my boy," he said. "We have much to do."

"Much?"

"Yes."

"Why are you talking like this?" I felt feverish, and at 9.8 I was far too young to be feverish without an illness.

Attila was already getting up and fidgeting, checking his bandage, looking under the desk for the helmet. "Didn't you hear, or was I speaking to myself? Colonel Dortmund lives in Paris now."

"So what?"

"So *what*? So something. So *everything*. Just stick with me."

"What are you talking about?" I looked at my brother's bandaged head.

"And they have them," he said. "Or weren't you paying attention to that either?"

"Who does? What are you saying?"

"The Russians. They took away Raoul Wallenberg and now they want Paul too. They've taken our parents because they think they can lead them to Paul."

"But they can't."

"I know they can't, but they won't believe them. They'll question them. They may even hurt them."

"*What*? What can they do to them? What can we do? Where would they have taken them?"

"Where would you have taken them?"

"I don't know," I said. "I've never taken people."

My brother took hold of my shoulders. "They've taken

them somewhere secret. Paris has a vast underworld. It has a sewer system underneath the whole of the city."

"A sewer *system?*"

"Yes," he said. "Les Égouts de Paris." He was up on his feet and getting out the map he'd been studying, together with the dictionary. "We have to find them. We have to try. We'll find them. I know of an entrance near a bridge, the Pont de l'Alma."

"How can you know that? How did you find out?"

"Les Misérables."

"What?"

"It's a novel, by Victor Hugo." He was pacing again, all the while adjusting his bandage. He started proclaiming. "He called the sewers 'the conscience of the city,' Hugo did."

"Is Tarzan in the novel?"

"No," he barked.

"Whisper to me," I told him, *"Whisper."* My brother took a deep breath. I whispered, myself. "How are we going to get there? How are we getting *out of here?*"

"We'll sneak out the back, where the shed is. We can't let Babette see us. We'll get there, trust me, to the Pont de l'Alma. We'll get back our parents. And we'll get Colonel Dortmund."

"We will? You and I?"

"Yes. As I said, we have much to do, places to go. The Rue du Maupassant. The Pont de l'Alma." There was all this French coming out of my brother's mouth, as if it was the Angel of Tongues who'd come to visit him rather than the Angel of Music. He clapped his hands. "We won't be seeing beautiful Paris. We won't be seeing the Eiffel Tower and the *Mona Lisa* and the Arc de Triomphe. We'll be seeing ugly Paris.

We're not seeing the beauty; we're seeing the beast. Hugo said it was the 'slime, minus the human form.'"

I felt a chill come over me. "I don't want to go there," I said. "Why would we have to go there?"

"I told you. To find our parents. It's where they've taken our parents. I'm certain of it. But first Dortmund."

"Dortmund," I repeated. My heart was pounding. I said, "And then what will happen? So we'll find our parents, and then what? Are we bringing them together with Dortmund? Are we going to beat up those men who came here?"

My brother retrieved the gun from underneath the desk and put on the helmet. He shone the flashlight in my face. "I'll do the dirty work. Please, leave it to me. I can go alone, but I'll need you to hold the flashlight for questioning."

"Questioning," I repeated aloud. "Will I need something? A helmet or a sword or anything?"

"You will have the flashlight. You'll light up things."

He took out notepaper from the desk as well as an impressive black fountain pen. He wrote something on the paper, 6 Rue Père Goriot. He said, "This is Aunt Hermina's address. Have it with you, in case."

"In case of what?"

"In case we get separated."

"I'll memorize it."

"They won't understand you when you say it, no matter how hard you try. Just keep the note." I shoved the paper into my pocket. He took off the helmet and put it back on, adjusting it around the bandage, tucking the bandage under the strap. The helmet was much too big for him, but he did something more with the strap to make it fit. Though he looked ridiculous, the helmet seemed to give him courage. A determined look came over him. "We have to be very quiet now, my cloven-hoofed boy," he said. "We'll find money somewhere and go. We'll find French money. Come, my gaseous essence of love. Come."

Before making our way to the back, my brother pulled me in the opposite direction, toward our aunt's bedroom. When we were inside, he closed the door behind us and switched on the light, a pink chandelier with floral stems, like leaves, and petals holding the bulbs. The theme was repeated on the bedposts. They seemed alive, seemed to move when you half looked away from them.

The cream dressing table, though, had on it blond wooden arms, the hands held up, like greeting hands, waving hands, each wearing a glove, each pair a different color—pale green, pale yellow, pale blue—the gloved hands casting dramatic shadows on the wall.

Who made those wooden hands for Hermina? Did she look at them in the night or the half-light before waking and imagine her own hands whole? Pink lady hands rather than bird hands?

I kept picturing her out there in the cold, hanging. How can you hang out a singer in the cold by her fingertips, like hanging a nightingale? How about hanging someone by the fingertips who's not a singer, who's tone deaf? Or someone who merely likes music? Or someone who doesn't like music at all? It was hard to think of a person suitable for hanging by the fingertips.

My brother was looking at the same table. "There," Attila said.

"The hands?" I said.

"Yes, it's an old trick of the ladies."

"The *hands* are?"

We approached the table and he felt each of the fingers. "Wait," he said. He opened the only drawer, where other gloves lay dormant and handless. He took out several, pulled on one pair after another, and then: "Damn." He clanged his helmet with a fist.

"What are you doing?" I asked.

"I'm looking for money. Mamu keeps money in the fingers of her gloves, or she did back home. Mother too. Where do you think I got extra cash when I needed it?"

"But Hermina doesn't."

"Damn."

"Why don't we ask Babette?"

"Because she can't know we're leaving, my baby assailant. I thought that part was clear."

"Very little of this is clear."

My brother threw the gloves back in the drawer. What I wanted in the worst way was to steal a pair of the waving wooden hands themselves. I don't know why. I would not have bragged about them or shown them to friends. I just wanted them to look at when no one else was around. I wanted to measure them to see if they would fit into my bag, or maybe the small new suitcase Hermina had bought me.

Attila said it was time to go. He adjusted his helmet. I had the flashlight. He had the gun. The Baby Diviner already growing inside my crowded boy's womb saw trouble up ahead, saw now that there was no real way to avert the trouble.

We got outside as quietly as we could and waited for a sound from inside before we moved on. We could see the shed in the moonlight, but ragged clouds curtained over the moon.

We made our way toward the streetlights of Père Goriot and began our walk toward the concentrated lights of Paris. Each time a car passed, we turned to see if it was a taxi. One did approach, but it zoomed by, possibly when the driver caught sight of my brother's helmet. When another slowed and then sped up again, my brother developed a new plan. He leapt into the road in front of the next taxi that turned the corner in our direction. He aimed his gun at the windshield. The car screeched to a halt. Its engine even cut out.

"Twenty-one Rue du Maupassant," my brother said to the closed window. He even knew how to say it in French. The man was trying to restart the engine.

My brother's hand was on the door handle.

"What are you doing?" I asked. I gripped his arm, the one holding the gun.

"Just watch me," he said.

The driver was as terrified as I was.

We got in. "Twenty-one Rue du Maupassant," Attila said more fiercely. He pointed the gun at the back of the man's head. The driver screeched away even before we were settled in our seats.

The Baby Psychologist inside of me rose up to remind me that determined people, if they didn't die trying, generally got their way. And for a single, eye-of-the-tornado moment, I felt unaccountably safe in the company of someone so determined.

Paris looked as beautiful as everyone said, with its river and its elegant buildings, each like an overgrown sculpture, its lights, many soft and amber like Hermina's, like night embers. But we tore by them all, smearing the light.

When we arrived, the driver said something incomprehensible to us. But Attila, being Attila, now wanted advice from the man. He handed me the gun, unfolded his map and seemed to be asking how we get from the Rue du Maupassant to the Pont de l'Alma. It turned out it was right around the corner.

"Just as I thought," Attila said to me.

I looked at my brother. "Who *are* you?" I said.

He snatched the gun back and we got out. The car screeched away even before I'd closed the door behind me.

We walked for only a couple of minutes before we arrived at a squat brownstone building right on the corner. We had to climb over a low wrought iron fence and edge along a flowerbed to get to the front. The townhouse was guarded by an impressive elm tree. It had tall windows, and lights were on inside. Attila and I crept toward a lighted window, crunching over some fallen leaves.

Inside, a man sat in a leather chair reading a book. "Colonel Josef Dortmund," my brother whispered. A trim middle-aged woman came in and set a cup of tea by his side. Then a boy with hair as blond as Attila's but a couple of years older looked into the room and said something to his parents, which caused them both to answer and shake their heads. The boy slapped at the doorframe and marched away. He could have passed for Attila's brother (more easily than I could).

I looked over at my brother, who was aiming the gun at the window. "What are you doing?" I whispered.

"Exacting revenge."

"You don't even know what he did."

"He hurt us."

"So you're executing him now?"

"No, just scaring him," he said and fired the gun through the window, shattering the man's lamp and, of course, the window itself. We heard shouting and scrambling inside.

"Let's go!" my brother said, and he pinched my upper arm hard before we leapt over the fence and flew away from there. "This way," he said, yanking me down an alley and over into another avenue.

My legs had noodled over. I could barely stand. I braced myself against a building, but the sound of a door closing inside caused us to rush off again.

"There it is!" Attila said, pointing with his gun. "The Pont de l'Alma!" And he laughed! He actually had the presence of mind to laugh.

We crossed another street, and then the stench hit us.

If ever you are searching for the a-hole of the world, search no further. My brother and I found it in Paris, by the Pont de l'Alma. There were houses all around it, and a romantic bridge. What sort of romance was possible as lovers sauntered over this bridge holding hands, or went to their beds in the homes nearby? I would love to know the number of babies made in this neighborhood.

"These are the 'intestines of the city,'" Attila told me. I was still gasping, trying to breathe right. The gate to the sewers was unlocked but had an impressive clang and squeal to it as we pulled it open. Iron spiral stairs led to the sewers. We clumped our way down, expecting to encounter rats and criminals and the abductors of our parents. Nothing and no one would have surprised me.

But the stench, the intensity of it. The Baby Irishman already growing inside me declared that we had found Shite River. For a moment, even my brother was stupefied as we paused to watch the dark river glubbing by. We had to stop. We had to pause to admire this wonder of the world. Lights down below illuminated a network carrying everything we wished to expel darkly or hurriedly or carelessly or unexpectedly from the land above: leftover cabbage soup, *digested* cabbage soup, fingernails, an earring, toenails, the nightly bath water, a razor blade with a bit of face still stuck to it, prophylactics, cigar butts, the flow of a bad stomach, the flow of a good one, a gold wedding band, bones, parts cut up, knives, guns, blunt instruments, a fluttering thing, the vomit of remorse, dead goldfish, live molly fish, hairs—blond, brunette, silver, auburn, true black, dyed black, dyed blond, dyed red—hairs by the million and trillion, short hairs, long ones, eyelashes, underarm hairs, leg hairs, pubic, nose, butt, a mother-of-pearl button—*the Baby Noseboy was rioting inside of me—feel it kicking, feel it thrashing*—marzipan monkeys, real monkeys, a guitar pick, brown milk, a tooth folded into a handkerchief and dropped by the Tooth Fairy, a clarinet reed, a clarinet, creamy goodness, twenty thousand francs rolled up in the fingers of a long glove once white, possibly, the yellowing-over of fluid— red wine, white wine, clear water, juicy plums, red beets—the browning-over of everything—succulent salmon, pretty pink petits fours, tepid turnips, the pus from a pimple just before a date, the pus from a lanced boil, toothpaste, the bleeding from gums, the tip of the finger of a glowhead, a gold watch chain, blood from a nose, amniotic fluid, the last two pages of *Madame Bovary*, thoughts of you washed off a face, a stillborn

Baby Psychologist, a lapis lazuli to bring out your eyes, a Baby English Grad Student, the testicle sweat of a Greco-Roman wrestler, the testicles of a bloodhound, the spray of opinions, the foul underarm zest of deceit, tens of thousands of trillions of X's and Y's wiggling their way to defeat. It took all the Babies growing inside of me to compose this list.

"We have found the river of Hades, the river of the underworld," my brother said. "It's the River Lethe, the river of forgetfulness."

A bat flew through, and then, as if on cue, a rat scurried by, creatures traveling the sky and ground of this underworld in search of things they could use to sustain them. Was everything down here in the sewers expelled from somewhere else? Was it possible there were also splendid beings resident here, or were even the splendid beings lapsed versions of themselves, splendid beings cast out of the Garden by the flowers?

You felt as if you wanted a mighty wind to blow through, a hurtling rain. My brother stopped suddenly and held his head, held his helmet, actually. He had a strange look in his eyes. I didn't need my flashlight to see that his eyes were bloodshot, but I shined the light in his face anyway to give my findings a more diagnostic effect. All around us, rivulets of refuse flowed through pipes into Shite River, the River Lethe, trickling, gurgling, flowing out to the Seine to tint the round ocean.

All at once out of the far darkness, we heard a yelp. A girl no older than I was, dressed only in a drab nightgown, flew at us. She grabbed on to Attila for a second. Her black hair was wild and her face crazed, evident even in the dim light. She couldn't speak or catch her breath. Sirens sounded in her all the way down to her bare little feet.

We quickly knew the cause. An even wilder man, who could have passed for Rasputin, was upon us, clutching the girl by the neck just as she let go of my brother. I thought we were finished, all of us. I was paralyzed.

But Attila was not. He flashed his gun and the girl flew to me, clinging, the way a cat might, all nails and needles and panting heart. It hurt quite a lot, but not as much as she must have been hurting, fearing for her life. Attila aimed the gun straight at the bearded man's face, barked at him (in Hungarian) to let the girl go, watched the wildness shift in the man's eyes as he did. I joined the assault with the light of my flashlight, the girl took off and, with a single brute shove, my brother toppled the man into Shite River.

"Let's go," Attila said to me. "Now!"

I couldn't move. I was in love with the girl. Following Babette my love-falls would always be this immediate. Everything in my life would be measured against it: pre-Babette and post-Babette, her fruits the fruit of the knowledge of good and evil.

Rasputin thrashed brownly to the edge, left a wet handprint on the brick. "Let's go!" my brother yelled again. I checked to see that the girl was gone—she was—and I ran off after my brother, panting in the stench, becoming strangely used to it, forgetting its palpable presence. We ran and ran, down one alley, turning sharply into another, all of the alleys joining, flowing together in dark harmony.

As we slowed to a walk, we could hear the pipes whooshing, trickling and flushing, refuse from above emptying. We could hear a shower being turned on. I tried to imagine the naked, balmed and perfumed showerer, looking like Babette, possibly, the glad water flowing over her arcs and nooks and curves. It was like the march of water, good water, bad water. Water musicians, water clowns, water acrobats, water slaves, water killers, a symphony of water, an industry of water, the childhood of water and the death of it, the kamikaze drop of it.

But there were no Russians here, no Lili, no Simon, no Paul. We walked for hours, but I was not hungry, only thirsty. Yet I would not have trusted any kind of drink offered in this subterranean world.

We came to a wall with a hole in it barely big enough for each of us to crawl through. "Let's go," my brother said. He looked more tired than I was. "I'll help you through first."

It was dark in this new chamber, and the sound of water was less pronounced—even the raging scent was quiet. As I helped my brother crawl through, my flashlight was aimed high at a sign: Avenue du Colonel Rol-Tanguy.

"Are we on a street?" I asked.

"*Below* the street," my brother said. "Everything here is below everything else, below the living world." And then he said, "But it's where the living world ends up."

"What?"

"Look behind you."

I beamed my flashlight on the walls around us and beyond us, down this new corridor, and I dropped the light. I screamed like a girl.

"The catacombs," my brother said. He clanged his helmet with his hand. "It's an ossuary. I read about these." I picked up the light again. "They're bones. The bones of the dead. Millions of dead. Moved here over the centuries from overloaded cemeteries. But also the dead of wars and street riots — the riots in the Place de Grève and the Rue Meslée. Many who fell during the French Revolution. People who died of the Black Plague. And just people. Dead people. The dead of Paris."

I gazed at the rows of bones, the wall of them going on far into the darkness, except the bones had been arranged in a decorative way, not the way the Lord had arranged them. On the top and bottom were femurs and fibulas and scapulas, ribs and phalanges and tarsals, laid out neatly in rows, like bone bricks. But in the middle were the skulls, facing out in their own row, as if they were sentinels watching us.

My brother said quietly, "Do you know about the royal cemetery in the ancient city of Ur?"

I shined my flashlight into his face but Attila didn't blink. His look gave me a chill, here among the bones. "How ancient?" I asked.

"Two thousand six hundred BC. Archaeologists have found the ancient tomb of Queen Puabi. She was buried in her finest raiment, still wearing her crown and gold necklaces and bracelets, as if her throne had simply been laid on its side with her still sitting in it. But best of all, in the outer chambers was a vast tomb surrounding the queen's. In it, lying in neat rows, wearing all *their* jewelry made of gold leaf and lapis lazuli, were her attendants and servants, dozens of them — her guards, her dressers, her cats, her hairdressers, her advisors, her musicians, complete with their instruments."

The chill now juddered down my spine. "What happened to them all?" I asked.

My brother's voice took on a weighty sound. "When

Queen Puabi died, they took poison so that they could attend to her in the afterlife."

"Poison," I repeated, clutching my neck. "I didn't know." I headed back to where Attila waited. I followed a swath of red paint, which rolled over a group of bones, but the bones nearest my brother featured a heart painted over the surface of the bones, with an *L* and a *G* in its middle. L and G had come down here among the dead to be in love. Did they know that the heart they had painted was offered up to us by bones, its shape given to it by the dead? Did they forget that these were once other people, with flesh on their bones and eyes in the sockets, who might also have been in love?

To the right of the heart, in fact exactly up against the heart's red swollen right curve, an extra-small skull looked back at my brother and me. I thought of the little girl in the cowere tonight. I took a step closer. I had an impulse to touch the small face, but it was not a face, only the bone behind it. I thought I might be taking a liberty, so I held back.

I said, "Attila, let's go. Our parents aren't here in the catacombs. No one is here right now."

We climbed back out through the hole to the sewers. Their odors reminded us of their force. "Can we go home?"

"Not just yet. We can't give up just yet. It's our only chance." He put his hand on my shoulder, and I went with Attila to the left, where the sewers continued.

I didn't know how far we were going, where, underneath Europe, we were heading. I would not have found my way back, even on the streets above, and would not have known how to ask. Was it possible our parents were in this place, that we would find them, free them and beat a path out of here?

The deeper in we wandered, the less I believed we would ever come up for air. But my brother was undeterred and, once we forgot about Rasputin, not even scared. He said we could stop again, wanted to sit down on some stone steps leading up to a black steel door, but I stayed on my feet. Water flushed into Shite River from the building above. Attila was holding his head again, rubbing the place near the bandage, which had shifted to the back, underneath the helmet. I wished he would take off the helmet.

And then we heard some voices. The sound of them echoed, crept over us like creatures. They were coming this way. My brother said they might be Russians. "Finally," he said. He got to his feet and took his gun out, but the voices sounded French. I was filled nevertheless with a deep and sudden dread. The Baby Diviner growing inside of me said unto me that, if we sallied forth, I would not reach 9.9 years of age, nor my brother 13.8, that we'd have trouble rescuing ourselves, let alone our parents. I was hoping it was the Baby Odds Maker masquerading as the Baby Diviner who was sounding the alarm, but I couldn't be sure.

Four boys—young men—French men—why wouldn't they be?—turned a corner and walked right up to us as if they'd expected us to be waiting for them. Two of them were wearing leather jackets. One of them was smiling. He lit a smoke with a lighter, and the flame flared wildly. I wondered if the sewers were flammable. What were these boys doing down here?

A tall, thin one, one of the ones who was not wearing a leather jacket, slapped my brother on the helmet from behind and started guffawing. He was slightly walleyed, so I thought he was staring down Attila and me both at the same time. He pointed to the swastika, and then he and the other one not wearing a leather jacket each thrust an arm straight out above them. They chanted, *"Sieg heil! Sieg heil! Sieg heil!"* and goose-stepped in a circle around my brother and me. The smoker released an impressive cloud of smoke and then flicked his cigarette into Shite River. We could hear it sizzle. He joined the goose-steppers, and the four of them circled Attila and me. Attila stood in front of me, blocking me, trying to shield me from harm. I clutched the flashlight in my pocket. My brother raised his gun to the smoker's face but took a terrible shove to the back from above my head and fell over. He sprang to his feet and someone slapped him—on the face this time—and said something to us in French.

In that time between languages, the only French words I knew were the words to "Habanera," the song from *Carmen*, so I tried one out feebly. *"L'amour."* I took quite a slap too for my efforts, a slap that echoed. I said, *"L'amour! L'amour! L'amour! L'amour!"* I sounded like a bird.

A cloth-coated French boy—not the walleyed one—shoved me with his foot to shut me up, and I fell to one knee. My brother went mad. He rushed to my side. I wished I could have stayed upright, but the surprise of the shove had toppled me. I was an invertebrate.

Attila sprang with his gun at the smoking boy, grinding the muzzle into his cheek, screaming Hungarian swear words at him. Two of the thugs jumped back, but one was behind him. My brother was walloped from behind again and fell forward, his gun cascading along the stone floor. Attila started coughing, and when I went to embrace him, I heard a wet thudding sound at the back of my head, and was out.

SIXTEEN

I FELT MYSELF SINK SOMEWHERE, possibly down into the earth. I could taste grains of earth in my mouth, like poppy seeds, but then I saw grains of light mixed in, and heard grains of sound. A woman's voice. My name. I heard my name.

It was my grandmother. "Robert. Oh, my Robert."

"Where's Attila?" I asked, looking around me. I was in his bed, my brother's bed, with a wet cloth on my forehead. I guess this was the bed for head injury cases.

"Your parents are looking for him with your aunt Hermina. They're down at the police station again."

"My *parents?*"

"Yes, they're all right. They're fine. A little shaken up, but they were released. They were very lucky. We are very lucky. They had little information the Russians could use. We were afraid we'd be sent back."

"What kind of information did they want?" I asked my grandmother. "What are you talking about?"

Klari was not looking at me directly. "Your father did know something but didn't say."

"What did he know?"

"He knew something about Paul. And Paul knew something about Raoul Wallenberg."

"My father was in touch with Paul?" I tried to sit up but my head hurt.

"He was in touch with Paul once, and Paul was here once, at Hermina's. But years ago. When we got to Paris this time, something happened. We were followed here. From the bus station. Agents. They knew we were here. They were tipped off by someone. Your parents got off lightly. We're all very lucky." My grandmother looked grim, anxious. "And you, my dear—you were brought back here by a guard in the city sewers. What on earth were you doing there? And please tell me where your brother is."

"Oh, no," I said, closing my eyes. Klari took my hand. "Attila wasn't there too?" I asked. "He was with me. Was he not there? Oh, no."

"No, he was nowhere to be found."

I could feel myself salting up again, the familiar waves of dread. "There were four boys," I told my grandmother. "Attila stood up to them."

It was her turn to say it. "Oh, no." She covered her face with her hands. She knew him, knew what I knew right away. "He's like your father. Your father came home with a black eye and fat lip."

I was sobbing uncontrollably now, and my grandmother took me in her arms but could not comfort me. There was an absoluteness to my brother's bravery, a stupid absoluteness.

Babette looked in on us. She smiled broadly at me. She was glad to see me awake. She came over to stroke my cheek. I could see the love bite on her neck, the Mark of Attila.

Memories of the next six days came to me over the years in flashes, always unwelcome but insistent, even urgent. My parents and the kind Hungarian doctor were often down with the police, down in the sewers, searching underneath Europe.

My grandmother and aunt took me all over Paris to distract me: the Eiffel Tower, the Champs-Élysées, out to Versailles, the Cathedral of Notre Dame with its fierce gargoyles, and café after café—Le Petit Château d'Eau, Les Deux Magots over on Saint-Germain-des-Prés, and the Café de la Paix. I could have as much cake as I wanted as often as I wanted, and I did. I began to learn the names of the ones I decided I'd ask for again: *éclairs, Jésuites* with frangipane cream, *madeleines,* gâteaux St. Honoré and, a very favorite, *bugnes,* angel wings, ribbons of pastry sprinkled with sugar. In each place, I hoped to find a monkey, but not a single café thought to employ one.

I fell in love with the *Venus de Milo*, every bit as much as I had with the girl in the sewers and the girl with the lips at the convent, maybe more. Even Babette, though possibly not Babette. I visited Venus three times. She stood there, in her lighted hall in the Louvre, and I loved the armlessness of her, the softness of her stone flesh, the mad folds of her dress. She gave you the impression that a sculptor had suggested a shape for her and then given her over to the wind and the rain and the moon to finish her, over time, over many years, though never aging her, never daring to. I wanted badly to bundle her up with me, offer her a pair of the wooden arms of my aunt and steal her far away from here.

And each day when we got home, I raced in, hoping to find my brother. Each day, he was not there. I said to my family one evening over dinner, "I couldn't stop him." No one answered, so I said it again. "I couldn't stop Attila."

"Why not?" my father asked.

"Simon!" my mother said.

"Why couldn't he?" he said. He set down his fork.

"Could you have stopped him?" Klari asked my father. "Can I stop *you*? Can you stop yourself, once you get started?"

My father got to his feet, squeezed my shoulder and walked out.

Then on the seventh day word did come. It came in the morning by phone. I was having breakfast, the last one to do so, eating eggs again, poking the dark lace at their edge with my fork the way Attila always did.

The Baby Creative Writer in me could barely tell, let alone show, what happened next. My brother had been found, washed up in the sewers somewhere, hardly identifiable, covered in sludge but still wearing his helmet.

My brother was buried right next to our uncle Ede in Père Lachaise Cemetery over in the 20th arrondissement. The cemetery was a slapdash gallery of sculptures, some of them angels, some other figures, waiting patiently for the wind and rain to take away their extended arms or even, possibly, their heads. On the way out, my aunt took us to see the grave of Georges Bizet, who'd composed "Habanera." She wanted to steer us next toward the grave of Marcel Proust, but Lili wanted to leave. My mother had lost her voice and her smile. She looked like someone sleepwalking. Klari shook her head no to Hermina, and she took my mother by the hand and led her away.

I remembered the catacombs. I looked back over my shoulder to where we'd laid my brother, and I shuddered.

My aunt said quietly to her sister, "Attila must have thought that youth would shelter him from anything, from death even. The war should have taught him it didn't—the *wars*."

I hoped the going down of my brother was just a switch— switch on, switch off—not gradual. The Baby Diviner rose up in me again, but I shoved it back down. I didn't want to know more just then.

SEVENTEEN

WE'D GOTTEN MY BROTHER to the edge of Europe but not past it. And "not yet fourteen" was the way that we were always going to describe it, forgoing preciseness for the larger sense of the loss.

We boarded a ship, called the *Jean-Jacques Rousseau*, in Nantes, the old slaving port. My grandmother held my mother's hand quite a bit of the time. The two sat staring at a radio in our cabin, though the radio was not on. Sometimes they started bobbing, like someone rocking a baby. My father spent hours in the ship's bar, but thirst was not the issue, so the one-eyed drink stared up at him, neglected, the whole day through.

I heard my grandmother whisper to my mother in the dark one night that my brother's death was senseless, like the deaths of my mother's parents and brothers and sisters in the Hitler war. But what death is sensible? In my 9.8 years on earth, almost 9.9, I had yet to encounter a sensible death. It was hard to understand the mechanism that Adam and Eve had set in motion. Despite their newly acquired knowledge of good and evil, even they must have had trouble understanding once Cain and Abel went at each other.

Now and again, I pictured my golden brother lying there in that box in the ground, the worms nibbling away at his thoughts and questions, and not even silkworms.

Maybe Attila had got himself a pair of wings and was flying too near the sun, daring it to melt them.

Maybe my brother had been wrong about the sun. Maybe the sun's aim was to set fire to the sky but it wasn't strong enough. It was very strong, but not strong enough to do that.

The sun could have been a fluttering thing just as easily as a ball, fanning out waves of light and gusts of warmth.

It was so unreal to me, that time, those days, that for a giddy moment I thought I had met the Messiah, possibly, that Attila had spawned Attilanity, and it was my job to spread the gospel. For a start, Attilans would have to wear pendants featuring a wiggly Shite River, topped by a helmet. The image would apply to wall mounts too, and to icons in houses of worship.

At the very least, I'd added my brother to my Afterlife Portfolio, elevated him to the head of it, above the sheep and the dead men and Judit, not to mention Medea's children, Mermeros and Pheres, as well as Castor and Pollux, Romulus and Remus, the Brothers Goose, the Brothers Grimm, the Brothers Karamazov, and even the stars.

Attila and I didn't mean for the fish to take wing or the stars to tell us old stories. We meant only to ask questions.

A porter had helped with our new suitcases. My parents let me take my brother's satchel with us along with my own. My father carried both of them for me as we boarded the *Jean Jacques Rousseau*. He also carried a cloth bag holding the two Mark Twain books together in their leather housing. It wasn't until we were installed in our cabin that I opened my brother's bag for the first time. In it, he had several items, including his Scarecrow PEZ, his cowboy gun, belt and spurs, of course, plus a hunting knife. But I was surprised to find that he had also stashed away my crayon drawing of the sunflowers, the one I thought I'd lost.

The very first night at sea, my father asked if I wanted to get some air. He still had his black eye, but it was fading to purple and violet now, like smeared makeup. He and I stood out on deck, not saying very much, and afterward I stood by myself. My mother had taken to not speaking to my father at all, so I was concerned about both of them.

I wondered where my brother was at the moment, whether he got to stop off on the moon for a break from his long journey. But there was hardly any moon that night. It was black out, a deep black, as black up and down and ahead and behind us as it must have been the day God had decided to switch on the light. I thought of all that unmade light, where the Lord must have bundled it, and all the unmade eyes waiting to receive it.

I don't know what's next after humans, but I was hoping Attila could ask the Powers That Be and send me a signal.

I heard a cooing sound behind me and turned to see a young woman sitting on a bench under the glow of a deck light, feeding her nipple to her excited infant, who could have passed, with its black fuzzy hair, for a monkey. When the little thing had latched on finally, the woman began babbling joyously at her baby, and I thought, at first, she must have been Hungarian. But only the sounds were familiar, not the words. I later learned from my parents that the woman was Turkish.

Her baby was as content as could be—and what a clever size it was! You've got to wonder: What came first—the design of the womb or the size of the baby? Should it be just big enough to take up residence inside its mother? What an interesting challenge it must have been. Should I make the baby small, the size of a guppy, make many of them, a thousand at a time? Should I make it bigger but still small enough to grow inside an egg until it can break free? (And, incidentally, what color egg—white, spotted blue like a robin's, or brown and gold, or beige, like a snake egg?) How about the full-size newborn—have it grow until it's as big as the mother, turning her inside out to break free, or tearing off from her, finally, tearing the gummy tissue like some Siamese creature? Or unfurling from her mouth, like a magician's mouth, like a long ribbon reconstituting itself before her eyes? Or sprouting from her head, the way Athena did from Zeus's?

It was odd. I'd just given up hope of seeing anyone I knew when, walking on deck the second evening, I ran into the tall boy who'd been on the rival swim team from St. Hilda's School in Budapest, the boy whose name my brother had forgotten and who had forgotten my brother's name. It turns out the boy's name was Attila. Ha!

"Where's your brother?" the boy asked me.

"He didn't make it," I said. I told him the story, and the new Attila shrugged and looked down quite a distance at his feet. "Do you want to see something?" he asked me.

I said, "Sure."

He took me to his cabin and pulled out a radio from under his bed. "It's a shortwave radio," he told me. He plugged it in and fiddled quite a bit with it and then said, "Listen." There was static, but I could hear a man's voice, a radio announcer.

"What is it?" I asked.

"It's a radio station from Canada," Attila said. "Ontario. He's saying the weather."

"How do you know?"

"I know some English. My mother is English."

"What's the man saying?" I asked.

"The man is saying snow—there's a lot of snow falling. It's a weather forecast, and he's naming the Ontario counties and towns. An early blast of winter—in mid-November!"

"Snow," I repeated in English, my first word.

We listened. The radio man's voice sounded soft and calm. I did not know the names then but know them now: *"Essex, Kent, Lambton, Elgin, Middlesex: snow, high of twelve. Huron, Perth, Grey, Bruce, Waterloo, Wellington, Oxford, Brant: snow, heavy at times, high of eight. York, Durham, Belleville, Quinte, Northumberland: snow, mixed with freezing rain. Peterborough and the Kawarthas, Parry Sound, Muskoka: heavy snow, whiteout conditions through the night and bitterly cold, high of minus two. Algonquin, Renfrew, Pembroke, Barry's Bay: periods of snow, clearing in the morning, high of eight. Ottawa, Prescott, Russell, Cornwall, Morrisburg: light snow, but very cold, high of minus seven. Wawa, the Sault, Cochrane, Timmins, Lake of the Woods: whiteout conditions, high of minus twenty."*

It sounded as if the gentle radio announcer was calling each of his children to bed, by name, one by one.

I went out on deck after that to watch the great beast of a ship sloshing along, clearing a path through all those fluttering, quivering and slithering things in the deep waters below us, a path through all that striving. The sky was a clear black but flecked with stars, like notes flung over the hood of the Atlantic, glowheads each and every one. I swear I could hear them twinkle. Twinkle is too childish a word, but look at them. How else can you say it? It's what they want you to say.

ACKNOWLEDGMENTS

It would be difficult to overstate the excitement I felt when I first got the letter from Nicole Winstanley at Penguin saying she loved this novel. And she assigned the book and me to the wonderful and inimitable editor Adrienne Kerr, who has acted as a godmother to *The Afterlife of Stars*. I also thank Alex Schultz for his keen eye during the line and copy editing phase, as well as Sandra Tooze, David Whiteside, Jessica Cooney and their teams at Penguin for getting the book out there.

I thank the good people who gave me valuable advice on the manuscript: foremost among them Ken Ballen, but also Richard Bausch, Barbara Berson, David Bezmozgis, Andrew Clark, Trevor Cole, Margaret Hart, Peter Kertes and Antanas Sileika.

I thank Cynthia Good and Jackie Kaiser for guiding and advising me.

I thank the kind writers who took a chance when they agreed to endorse this novel: Richard Bausch, Trevor Cole, Anne Michaels, Tim O'Brien and Nino Ricci.

I thank a special lady, my late mother-in-law, Athena Papageorge, who was as excited as I was about each of my books.

And I thank the Canada Council, the Ontario Arts Council and the Toronto Arts Council for buying me valuable research, travel and writing time.